Milli Finds Her Bench

a novel

Ruth E. Weiner

We spend our life trying to bring together in the same instant a ray of sunshine and a free bench.

—SAMUEL BECKETT

PART ONE

Chapter One

Milli was tickled to realize she had slept on the oak bench beneath the lilac tree, the exact place where her family had sat, oh so many years ago. She rotated her shoulders and pulsed out her fingers. Surrounded by lilacs, daffodils, and the earthy smell of spring, Milli knew her dream had come true, the one where she, Leo and Lionel were still alive together.

Milli's daffodil days were long gone, but what was wrong with recreating the moments, even if New Dawn Retirement Village was hell-bent on canceling them. Thoughts of that dead-end place swirled: how she had been banished to the basement room, how she had snuck out on false pretenses and made her way to the Seaside Arboretum, and how the staff of New Dawn was probably canvassing the area for her body. *Damn them all, especially that know-it-all Ms. Fagan, pretending to care.*

Milli had confronted the woman months ago. "Why do I need permission to leave Downtown Crossing? I just want to take a stroll."

"We're responsible for you, Dear."

"But in my high rise apartment, I was free to come and go."

"The rules are different here, my Dear. Not everyone is capable of being on her own, you know."

"But I am."

"So you say, Dear. But it's a precaution for those who have. . ." Ms. Fagan took a breath, "limitations."

Milli wanted to shout; instead, she reached into her purse, found two green pills that soothed her, and swallowed them along with her pride.

"So will you give me a pass or something?" Milli asked.

"I'll contact the nurse at the front desk. She'll determine if your well-being is in jeopardy."

Milli cleaned herself up and dressed in slacks and a button-down shirt. She brushed her hair and pulled it back with a velvet headband. Then she applied a hint of rouge and a dab of lipstick. *I look pretty chipper for eighty-four years old if I do say so myself.* She signed her name to the ledger, writing down that she would be strolling nearby and would be back within the hour. She expected the nurse to put one of those leg monitors on her or watch out the window as she left, but no one interfered.

That first time, she crossed the Commons to a triangle of straggly trees and overgrown shrubs. No lilacs. No daffodils. Barely any grass. But there was a wooden bench where, at the very least, she could imagine she was sitting in the Seaside Arboretum where flowers sprouted like children. An hour passed, and she signed back in, smiling at the nurse. On her next outing, she wrote she'd be walking to the Gardens on the far side of New Dawn. Once there, she looked up at her former balcony, but she was painfully reminded of her nephew Bernard's betrayal and her eviction from where she had lived for five carefree years. She limped back to her basement room like a wounded animal. A few hours passed before she remembered to sign back in, but no one seemed to be looking for her and the nurse on duty didn't seem concerned.

Milli set herself a goal: to see the lilacs in the Arboretum before she turned eighty-five in June. But an excursion like that required accompaniment, as if she were infirmed and needed a caretaker for the day. A plan whirred and took shape. She waited until late May when the lilacs and daffodils were in full bloom. Then she signed out with the acceptable excuse that she had her yearly dentist check up on Main Street in Oldham and had arranged for The Friendly Ride Transportation service to pick her up. Milli strode out of New Dawn alone, got into the car, and stated her destination. When they arrived, she asked the driver to help her to the front door. "Thank you. I can take it from here," she told him. Then she waited for him to leave, slipped outside and walked to the Arboretum, just a half-mile down the road.

What she hadn't counted on once she had fulfilled her dream of sitting on her bench and reliving her moments with her husband Leo and her son Lionel was falling asleep and staying the night.

As she woke, Milli was so self-absorbed in her thoughts that she barely heard the muffled cries. She looked around until she spotted a woman sitting under a nearby tree surrounded by balled up tissues. The morning light cast a shadowy glow around her.

"Missy, what could possibly be the matter on such a promising day?"

The woman craned around to see Milli. "Damn it all, you scared me."

"I didn't mean to," said Milli.

Stretching her bottom lip, the woman stammered, "I thought I was alone. You look like you slept here."

"Yup. Right here on this comfy bench, under the stars," . . . *even if all of New Dawn Retirement Village is out looking for me!* Milli unzipped her puffy jacket and removed her hat and gloves. "Lucky for me, I was dressed warm and the night was mild."

"It's soothing being up so high, like I'm sitting on a cloud."

Milli patted the bench. "Why don't you tell me why you're so sad. Maybe talking it out will help." It had been years since Milli had shared confidences with her friend Anne Marie or her sister Linda Mae, may they both rest in peace.

Milli was taken aback as the woman approached, noticing that her head was an odd shape, but it was her hair. One side was closely shaven, the other was curly black with blond streaks. *I'm so out of sync with youth today. What happened to good old symmetry? Styles change and nothing stays the same. I might as well accept that as truth.* "Tell me your name," Milli said, trying not to stare at the girl's hairdo, "so we won't feel like strangers."

"I'm Keysi. My mom says it means trouble. That's me, trouble, all the time trouble." Her lips trembled and her dark eyes deepened and then a lightbulb seemed to go off. "But in Chinese, my name means cut silk. You know when you see a tapestry and it's woven with soft thin threads? That Keysi is classy."

Milli noticed how Keysi sat straighter with her feet anchored firmly in front of her when she said the word classy. "Seems to me, Keysi, you're cut from fine silk." Even if that weren't true, Milli knew that compliments could make someone's entire day.

"Do you think so?" asked Keysi, forcing a smile. After a while, she asked, "How about you? What's your name?"

"Millicent. But everyone calls me Milli. My father said it's an Irish name for a lower class working girl who's loud and boorish. But I prefer the French definition. A woman of brave strength."

As the girl nodded, her shoulders sank. Milli wanted to put an arm around her, to be grandmotherly, to tell her everything would be all right. Leo used to call her *The Quilt* because she liked to wrap others in her warmth. But that hadn't happened in so long, Milli was afraid she'd scare the girl away. "Keysi, my young bench-mate, I'm here to listen."

"I'm not so young. I'll be twenty-three next week," said Keysi, rubbing her eyes with the palms of her hands. "You make me feel foolish for crying and waking you up, even though I didn't see you sitting there."

"Crying cleanses the soul," said Milli. *My soul must be lily white by now.*

Keysi's chin twitched. "I'm really sad," she sighed. "My boyfriend's texting other girls." She lowered her chin and picked at her cuticles. "I read his posts after he fell asleep. He doesn't know I snooped. I'm so ashamed."

Milli thought about Keysi's admission. "Are you ashamed that you snooped or that you think you're not good enough for your boyfriend?"

"Both." Keysi brought her knees into her body and hugged them.

"Is it possible to tell your boyfriend you saw the texts by mistake and wanted to let him know?"

"I get blotchy when I lie. He's seen it happen. Besides, his phone is like his best friend. He keeps it close, except last night when it fell out of his pocket."

"Does he have access to your phone?" asked Milli.

"I leave it lying out all the time. I have nothing to hide."

"Apparently, he does." Milli removed her jacket and set it on the bench. "Tell me about your guy. Do you love him?"

"I'm crazy about him, at least I used to be."

"Until you saw the texts?"

"No, before that I was having second thoughts." Keysi blinked away tears.

"What's his voice like?" Milli had loved the sound of her husband Leo's voice, velvet like a radio announcer. Her son Lionel's voice had that crackly tone that accompanied puberty.

"At first it was soft and dreamy, like a harp," she said, her lips lifting into a smile.

"What changed?"

"He started to sound like a trumpet. You know, 'Why are you always late? Do you have to wear such low-cut tops? Stop telling your girlfriends where we're going and what we're doing?' Harping on me, and not in a good way," she grimaced.

"What does your boyfriend sound like lately?" asked Milli.

"Like drums. Beating on me over and over again."

Milli's eyebrows arched. "Are you saying he hits you?"

"No. No, it's his voice, always drumming at me. You asked about his voice, right? I'm telling you," she snapped.

Milli felt the pinch. "I'm just trying to help."

"I'm beyond help."

If the girl were my daughter, what would I say? What was my mother's advice when my first crush cheated on me? 'There are other fish in the sea,' as if that would make my pain go away.

Milli wanted the girl to think about her self-worth. "I'm curious, Keysi, what kind of instrument are you?"

Keysi thought for a while and pulled tighter into herself. "I have no music in me."

"Is this something new or have you never had music?" asked Milli, who had gone through music-less phases, but always emerged as a flugelhorn—jazzy but mellow, thoughtful yet forthright. *What would it take to be that again? Are my days of jive and boogie gone forever?* At eighty-four, Milli was more harp and waltz.

"Okay. Well, if I had to be anything, I'd be a violin," said Keysi.

"Why?"

"Violins make me teary, all emotional." Keysi heaved a sigh and stretched out her legs. "I don't know why I'm telling you all this. You're a homeless old lady sleeping on a park bench. What do you know about boyfriends or violins or planning for tomorrow?"

"You're right about my being old. It gives me perspective about my fears and worries. I'm still learning how to deal with them, but I have a few thoughts about how to move forward."

"I'm all ears, but you gotta admit, it's pretty weird for you to be here and not in a cozy bed sipping your morning tea."

Fat chance in that basement prison. Milli put her own troubles aside and forged on. "Keysi, what scares you the most about your boyfriend's secret texting?"

"That he doesn't want me anymore." Keysi's bottom lip quivered. "He'll leave me and I'll have nothing and no one. All my dreams will come crashing down."

"What are your dreams?" asked Milli as the lilacs nodded to her and the daffodils swayed and the bench held her like a fitted sheet.

Keysi pulled at a strand of hair and tilted her head. "I want to be loved."

"We all want that, Keysi. Love, security, acknowledgment. Tell me, what kind of companion is your boyfriend? Does he compliment you? Does he make you smile?" The best part about her late husband Leo had been how he made her laugh. It broke tension and worry, and created shared joy.

Keysi chewed her bottom lip. "At first he was so perfect I couldn't believe he was real."

"How long have you been together?"

"Four months, two weeks, and one day."

"Where did you meet?"

"At a pub. I was kicking back with some girlfriends and he was playing pool. I watched his moves for an hour before I got the courage to speak to him. And that was that. Love at first sight. We haven't been apart since."

"So you live together?"

"He sleeps at my place most of the time. I have a two bedroom that I share with a friend."

"Does he have his own apartment?"

"No. He lives with his parents."

Milli's spine twinged. "Keysi. Look at me." Milli squared her body and framed Keysi in front of her. "Shoulders back. Chin up. Be the silk Keysi!"

Keysi pursed her lips, but she complied.

"Now go like this." Milli let her jaw fall like a puppet's and flapped it open and shut.

Keysi did the same.

"Now make some noise," said Milli, making um-um-um sounds.

Keysi pumped out ums.

"That's you making yourself heard. So far your guy's been making all the noise: harp, trumpet, drums. It's time for you to face this man. No hiding, no snooping, no worrying if he's going to out-power you. Be a tuba."

"What if he tells me we've been a mistake, that he's not sure if he loves me and he wants to move on."

"Then you have to decide if you want to fight for him or let him go."

The girl bit her lip again. "So it's up to me?"

"It's always been up to you. You can cry, or you can find out what's going on. Speak up, Keysi. Then listen to what he has to say. Figure out what YOU want to do." Milli folded her arms. "That's the best I can tell you." Milli sat back and exhaled; the depth of the conversation exhausted her. "Would you like a power bar? That's about all I have left to offer."

Keysi stood and paced the lush grass in front of Milli's bench. Milli watched as the girl's body unwound, her chest expanded and her breath took on a steady rhythm. "I never thought of myself as wimpy, but I've been acting that way, letting him get control over me." Her eyes sparkled, not with tears this time, but with resolve. "You're right. I'm in charge of me." Keysi gave Milli a hug. "You know, I have a friend who has a problem that's getting her down. You really helped me, maybe you can help her too. Can she come and talk with you?"

Milli gazed at the lavender buds on the lilac bushes and caressed the soft wood on her bench. "My door is always open."

Chapter Two

Milli stretched out on her bench and thought about Keysi. How could that child get herself caught up with a man who disrespected her? Leo might have been difficult, especially when it came to finances, but he put Milli and their son Lionel first. *Oh Lionel. How different today would be if you were alive.*

If Keysi had children with that cheater of hers, she'd be alone. Milli knew the type: me, me, me. But Keysi had to find that out for herself. She needed to ask the questions and get the answers, not the ones she wanted to hear, but the ones that might hurt. Then she could throw the bum out, or not.

Milli closed her mind to Keysi, figuring she'd never see her again. When a woman was approaching her eighty-fifth birthday, she didn't need someone new in her life to muddy up her thoughts. Milli preferred to imbibe the heady smell of lilacs and daffodils, and dream about her husband and their son instead.

But thoughts about New Dawn kept cropping up and try as she may, she failed to tamp them down. She should be heading back, claiming confusion, but where would that get her? In the memory ward? Oh how clearly she remembered the day when Ms. Fagan demoted her to that hell-hole basement.

"This is your new home," Ms. Fagan had said, beaming like she built the place herself. She opened the door and ushered Milli in. "Didn't I tell you I found a charming room with two windows. Now isn't it lovely, Dear."

Sure, two high narrow windows. I'll be looking out at feet all day. What a joy. Milli crossed to the cot-sized bed and sank into it. "I just need some time alone to adjust." She closed her eyes as Ms. Fagan shut the door behind her.

At her age, Milli envisioned sitting on her balcony in the high rise, watching spring emerge with its riot of colors. She'd sip a glass of Cabernet. Read a good book. Chat with a neighbor. She and her nephew Bernard would walk the gardens together and he'd be attentive and outgoing. Maybe they'd drive to the nearby cemetery and reminisce about their family.

Milli needed to stay in her lilac dream a little longer. She refused to think about Bernard, his squandering of her money and his sudden death leaving her to the mercy of Ms. Fagan. Instead, she stared at the Atlantic Ocean in the near distance, spreading its blue blanket just for her. She longed to walk in the soft sand, to hear the waves crash and smell the briny sea.

Might I stay just a little longer? The morning was balmy and she didn't want to be saddled with the weight of her coat, knit cap, and gloves. She surveyed the area figuring out the least visible point, and decided to stow them in the nearby thicket. She spread her clothing on the ground and rolled the bundle tight into a long sausage. Then she doubled it over and sat on it until all the air seeped out. She tucked it under a cluster of brambles and rocks near the bench, sure that it was well hidden.

Before leaving her slice of paradise, Milli bowed to the lilac bushes and daffodils and thanked them. *You are my slice of heaven, right here. I claim you as mine. I'll come here again because I can.* She repeated the words until she believed them.

She made her way down the concentric circle of road slinging her heavy purse over her shoulder. *I am in charge of myself.* Milli's legs were steady and strong, but the descent wasn't easy. *When had going downhill gotten so difficult?*

A white golf cart with an orange-striped hood pulled by her side. "Hey, Darlin'. Can we give you a lift? You look like you could use some help," said a man with bushy eyebrows, hairy ears and a friendly smile who sat in the front passenger seat.

He looked innocent enough. "Sure, if you're going to the beach."

The driver and Hairy Ears nodded to each other. "We're headed to the golf park, but we can take a detour. Hop on."

Why the heck not? I might as well take advantage of a free ride.

The sun was shining, the buds blooming, and flowers lined the side of the road. The park sprouted with joggers, dog-walkers, and baby carriages. She felt safe sitting on the back bench of the cart, tucked between two leather golf bags, with her body facing the bald patches on the men's slick skulls. "Do you pick up little old ladies often?"

"Only if they're cute," said the driver with the soft wispy comb-over.

"Whaddaya mean?" said Hairy Ears. "We only pick up youth-ful women with old experiences." He turned sideways and flashed a broad smile. His teeth were perfectly aligned and bright white, clearly not his own. "We're poets, you know."

"What do you write about?"

"Life's blessings. Flowers and moonbeams, kittens . . . and tequila."

Comb Over said, "He's just fooling with you. We're not poets. We're just two adventurous dudes looking for action."

Milli went along with the joke. "And you think I'm available?"

"We're equal opportunity guys." They elbowed each other and chuckled.

"You're just messing with me, right? And here I thought you were sweet old guys."

"Did you hear that?" whined Comb Over. "She thinks we're old."

"But sweet," said Hairy Ears.

"Whattaya say we treat you to a little aged meat? You look spry enough to handle the two of us. You still have your own teeth, yes? We don't want you gumming us to death," chuckled Comb Over.

The men shook so hard with laughter that the golf cart wobbled. From under the seat, Hairy Ears withdrew a silver flask. He swigged with gusto.

Milli's face drained of color. "Stop the cart now and let me out," she demanded. "I don't trust you."

Comb Over kept driving and Hairy Ears' voice grew gruff. "Let's have a little sport with the young woman first. If you can answer my next question, we'll take you directly to the ocean."

Milli's eyes welled. She felt like Pinocchio, tricked by the fox and the cat. "So you're going to ask me a question that seals some sort of fate for me? I thought you were decent men. Now all of a sudden, you're going to humiliate me unless I play your little game?" Milli hadn't raised her voice in so long that the words came out in fits and starts, like a child trying to catch her breath.

She blubbered on and the tears fell. Finally, Comb Over pulled the golf cart to the side of the road near the entrance to the Seaside Arboretum. The men snickered and passed the flask between them. "You're a cranky old crone!" shouted Comb Over.

Milli staggered off the cart, pointing an accusing finger at the men. "You are sick perverts," she cried.

Swaggering by, two boys stopped to help Milli steady herself. They looked at her with soft eyes and open faces. "Hey, you two!" said the young man whose hat was on backwards and his pants slung low. "We heard you treating this lovely lady with disrespect. You need to be nice to Granny. She's da bomb!"

The other boy moved in on Hairy Ears. "It ain't right that you got granny crying. You need a lesson in how to treat a woman. Geezers like you should know better."

Milli dabbed her face with a tissue. "That's all right, Boys. These men were just about to apologize. Right?"

Hairy Ears shook his head. Comb Over puffed out his cheeks.

"We're waiting," said low pants, bearing down on the men.

"Yeah, sorry. We were just having a little fun," said Hairy Ears. "Can't you take a joke?"

"A joke is for sharing. Something tells me you're the only ones laughing," said Milli.

"You tell them, Granny," said the boy as he high-fived his friend. "You men run along now and leave her be." The boys went on their way as the club car accelerated down the street.

Milli had a vision of her friend Anne Marie hopping onto their front seat, sitting on Hairy Ears' lap and nestling in like a bird. She would have used a come-hither voice as a tease: "She'd say, 'Listen, ballsy men. It's never too late to learn a thing or two about women. We're not fragile honey buns. We're powerful and in control of our own bodies.'" Milli giggled thinking about Anne Marie pressing down on his lap and squirming around a bit. "Do you like my moves? You see, you're not the only one who loves a good laugh at someone else's expense. It's all in the delivery. Now you good little boys, go along. Go pick up another little old lady just for hee-haws. But be careful she's not carrying scissors in her mysterious purse."

But Milli was not Anne Marie and realized it was a waste of breath talking with people who would never value her. Even so, she yelled as loud as she could to the fleeing golf cart, "You can't fix yourself by breaking others."

Chapter Three

Walking toward the ocean clutching her overstuffed pocket-book, Milli replayed the scene with the two repulsive men. At first they seemed so harmless. They transformed into cruel as they descended the hill. *How did that happen so fast? And did it happen often?* Leo could get angry, but it was usually over rational issues. "Watch where you're going! Don't talk to that vagrant. Stop accruing finance charges and pay the whole bill!" But he was never intentionally mean for the fun of it. Now that she was up there in age, she thought foul-minded men no longer existed in her sphere, that somehow they were on the fringes of society, not in a place as beautiful as the Seaside Arboretum. She thought she was way past the #MeToo movement, but women were always the endangered species. Men powered their way into their lives as if they had a right. Look at Keysi. She was too cowered to speak up. And if she did, would the boyfriend respond with kindness or vitriol, like Comb Over and Hairy Ears?

Being old was no guarantee for gentlemanly behavior. She had been warned. But what had surged up Milli's skin was a spark of energy; it made its way to a tingle at the crown of her head, like in her youth when something unusual was about to happen and she would anticipate it with a tic and a twitch. She looked around and couldn't believe she was outside, in the real air, with no one to thank but herself.

Milli thought about the advice she had given Keysi: take control and move forward. *Those men will not invade my day. I'm Milli brave and Milli strong!*

The encounter with the skanky men receded as the roar of the tide greeted her. The ocean rose up to say her name: MILLI. She never liked her given name, Millicent. It sounded like someone was holding her nose and whining. Being called Milli was fun and happy, like she was worthy and loved. Leo called her his Silly Milli, his Dilly of a Filly. She missed him, especially the way he hugged her. "Milli," he'd say, "We're the lucky ones."

Not so lucky, Leo. Her vibrant husband had become distracted and distant after their son Lionel died, like his lights had gone out. Leo's body knew it and allowed his despair to fester. Their last hugs were fragile and skeletal and he smelled like sulfur. Milli chose to remember the bear hugs when he smelled like honey.

Leo hadn't loved the beach like Milli did, but he indulged her. He read a book as Milli walked. The beach that lay before her now was flat and hard-packed. She could almost feel the sea foam tickling her toes.

When Milli neared the ramp to the sand, she realized that the incline was too steep for her arthritic hip and weak knees and there was no railing for support. Just because she envisioned herself walking along the beach didn't mean she could, even with the boost of adrenalin after railing at those two lowlifes. When Milli noticed the boardwalk bench, she sat to take off her socks and shoes and roll up her sweatpants. She settled her purse behind her back and lounged into the sun.

But the bench wasn't comfortable like the wooden body-molding one in the Arboretum. It was metal and cold and had holes in it disguised as art. She rose, but dizziness overcame her so she sat right back down. She wiggled her toes to get the circulation moving. *Ugly toes*, she thought. Yellow and crooked with brittle nails. She needed to soak them in the sea. Salt water cured everything. Again she stood, but this time her body refused to behave. Her heart pounded. Her forehead erupted with sweat. Then her legs gave way and she fell back onto the bench, that steel, unyielding bench that caught her without complaint.

She realized she hadn't eaten all morning. That would cause hot flashes and dizziness. She was used to going to the dining room or having her meals delivered. She reached into her purse for a granola bar and a bottle of water. *Ah, much better.* She had to remember to eat or she'd never have the strength to even think about walking the beach, never mind making her way back to the Arboretum, retrieving her clothes, and then somehow getting back to New Dawn.

As she let her snack digest, she made up stories about the people who sauntered by. The sweet hand-holding couple. *Newlyweds. So in love.* The power-walking woman buying into a culture that said keep moving if she wanted to live to be one hundred. The middle-aged man with the biggest roundest belly she never wanted to see. *Definitely a couch potato.* And the twelve year-old gangly skate-boarding boy who resembled Lionel, all sunshine and hope without a care in the world.

No one nodded hello or acknowledged Milli's presence until a young woman who had been pushing a baby carriage sat down beside her.

"Nice day," smiled Milli.

"For you, maybe," said the woman.

"And why not for you?"

"Too damn tired to appreciate it."

The woman's eyes told her story. They drooped like a basset hound's.

"I feel like I need six arms. I never get enough sleep. No one appreciates how hard I work every day. Laundry and shopping and cooking and cleaning. Ugh. I wonder why I even bother."

It was almost like the woman was talking to herself, venting to the air. Milli just happened to be within earshot. The carriage was positioned so she could see the baby's face. Milli loved babies and this one stole her heart immediately. It sucked on a pacifier in its sleep, like it was having milk dreams.

"The worst part is going home and seeing what I haven't done. Will it never end?" the woman looked directly at Milli as she said this.

Milli knew the answer. Time passed all too quickly. But what good would it do to tell this harried woman that before she snapped her fingers, that baby would be full grown or worse, that her baby would never grow old.

"Babies are a lot of work," said Milli. "Even one child is overwhelming."

"One? I'd be thrilled if I only had one. I've got four. A nine-year-old daughter from my first marriage and twin seven-year-old stepsons. Then the hubby and I had this little cherub."

"Might I ask your age?"

"Twenty-nine going on forty."

"There are advantages to being forty, but I see why you're so tired." Milli was late to motherhood—forty-one when she gave birth to twins, two bouncing screaming darlings. If she only had a crystal ball, she would have hugged them longer and kissed them fiercer during those first few days. Who knew that the littler one wouldn't survive his first week? And who knew that the bigger one, her Lionel, would never get beyond puberty.

The younger woman tilted her face toward Milli. "You remind me of my grandmother. She was the highlight of my childhood. Baking cookies. Staying up late with her and watching TV. Telling her my secrets. And she never judged. She only listened."

"Listening is often the only thing needed to help someone," agreed Milli.

The woman nodded and stared out to the ocean, as if it too had ears.

A dozen questions rattled through Milli's mind, but she chose the one that focused on the problem at hand. "Do you have any help? How about the twins' mom? Is she in the picture?"

The woman's lips turned down. "My husband's wife died in an automobile accident. When I met him, he was so lonely. He told me if it weren't for his boys, he'd have done himself in."

"When our loved ones leave us, there's a gaping hole that's hard to fill," said Milli, thinking about Leo and Lionel, Linda Mae and Anne Marie.

"My husband says when he met me, his whole world turned sunny. I bring him joy, he says. I think he just wanted a wife, you know someone to cook and clean and care for his kids. I'm alone much of the time, swamped by household drudgery."

"Is there nothing you enjoy about being a mom?"

The woman looked at Milli as if she had slapped her. "Of course I enjoy my kids," she rolled her eyes, "especially when they're sleeping. No, really, they're sweet. I'm the rotten one. I don't deserve to be a mother."

Milli sympathized. "Do you ever get time to yourself?"

"Are you kidding? Time to myself is at midnight or four in the morning. And sometimes not even then."

"Perhaps women are supposed to feel overburdened and under-appreciated when our children are young, so we'll work harder to make their lives easier."

"Well wouldn't that be an ass-kicker. Like everything is backwards."

"Think about it. If we spent our time concerned with ourselves, our children wouldn't have any security. They'd founder on their own. We're supposed to sacrifice when our children are young so they won't need us later on. Then they'll be responsible enough to take care of us."

"I never thought about child-raising that way. To me, so far it's been take take take."

"I don't know a lot, but there's one thing I can guarantee. Giving yourself to your kids without reservation is the best way to ensure healthy adults. If you can put your needs aside for their growing years, it will be worth it in the end."

"So do your children dote on you now?"

Milli's face slackened and her eyes closed. *Dote on me? I thought Bernard had cared.* But her nephew was a drug-addicted turn-coat who betrayed her and forced her out of her high-rise and into that black hole. Was her sister at fault for his failures? Had she paid more attention to herself than to Bernard in his growing years? And what was Milli's responsibility as his aunt during that time? Sure, she spoke to her sister regularly and she asked about Bernard all the time. But had she gone out of her way to talk to him? To see him as a person, not just her sister's son? But the woman didn't need to know about any of that. "My son Lionel, well, he was a dream child. He didn't live long enough to be a burden."

"I'm sorry. I didn't mean to pry." The woman bit the inside of her mouth as her lip twisted to the left. She ran her finger below her nose, like it itched from neglect.

"Don't be sorry. Asking questions is part of living. I'm always suspicious of people who aren't curious. They're too concerned with themselves."

"What happened to your son?"

"Lionel caught a cold. We kept him home from school for a few days, gave him aspirin and tea, and he seemed to improve. But when he suddenly ran a high fever, my husband and I took him to the emergency room. He never came home. Reye's syndrome, we were told. A rare condition that made his brain swell and his liver lose function. There was nothing we could have done to prevent it. My husband never recovered from his grief."

"And here I am complaining. I'm a jerk."

"We all have to figure out our own path. You're overwhelmed right now. That's natural. It would be great if your husband weighed in to help, and it sounds to me like he believes in you."

The woman repeated the words. "Do you know he says that to me every night? Rashida, he says, you always do right by these kids. I believe in you."

Milli felt more comfortable offering advice now that she knew her name. "But you don't believe him, do you, Rashida?"

"How can I? I feel used. Like he just says it to take away his guilt."

"How is he guilty?"

"For marrying me. For making me feel shabby and tired."

Milli wanted to relieve this woman of her pain, but she had no idea how. She thought back to when Lionel was little. Her mother-in-law lived far away and her own mother had died before Lionel was born. Leo was a baker and worked long hours—up early in the morning and bushed when he got home. Most days she felt so alone. She knew she needed help, but she had no money to pay anyone. So she got creative. Milli was a good seamstress. If she could barter her skill, she might get someone in to give her a hand.

"Rashida, do you have a job?"

"I waitress some nights, but that makes everything worse. I feel like a zombie the next day."

"Do you have a skill that makes you happy, that is if you had enough time to pursue it?"

"I can fix a flat tire in three minutes and jump a car in four. My dad taught me how to tune up an engine and change the oil. I keep our car humming. That's another reason why my husband married me."

"I wonder how you could build on that skill and use it to your advantage. Maybe other moms could watch your kids while you fix their cars? You could even do this in your own driveway. You could build up the business and make some money too." What Milli would have given to have a reliable mechanic. Her car had constantly needed attention.

Rashida rocked the carriage as the baby stirred. "I have a neighbor whose car is always in the shop. She has an infant too. Maybe she and I could work something out?"

"You're either part of the solution or part of the problem. Which would you rather be?"

"You know, I've been blaming my husband for so long about sticking me with the daily drudge that I never thought clearly about solving it myself. I've resented him for never being home for me and the kids. And when he is home, he's tired too. Seems like we're never on the same page."

"Then it's time to re-examine your relationship. But first, you have to believe in yourself."

"Whoever you are, you make a lot of sense."

"Just call me Milli."

"Well, Milli, I'm listening. I'm a damn good mechanic. Maybe I can make that work for me."

"What do you have to lose?"

The baby fussed as she awoke from her nap and began to cry. "Movement keeps her happy. Time for me to go. So nice to meet you, Milli. I hope to see you again. Maybe I can fix your car!"

To live is to keep moving, thought Milli. She waved to Rashida as she and her baby rushed away. *What do I know about moving on? I just talk a good game. Look at me, I'm stuck in that basement with no future.*

Scanning the horizon, she saw the nugget of a black cloud. She knew this cloud would mushroom into rain and she was not prepared. Scanning the boardwalk, she saw a corner coffee shop called Mirage—an appropriate name for a woman who was living on the edge of make-believe, thought Milli. She put on her shoes and socks, grabbed her bag, and crossed Beach Avenue.

Chapter Four

The coffee shop was cozy with benches and high tables, making the room feel communal and friendly. Centerpieces were pink flamingo caddies containing napkins, condiments, and swizzle sticks. The powder room beckoned first, a happy haven for a windswept woman. She delighted in the hot water and soft lighting. Cleanliness, she decided, was indeed godliness. She emerged into the café feeling refreshed.

She ordered black coffee and a blueberry muffin and brought them to a corner table. Close by sat a well-dressed woman and a younger man who appeared to be her son. He had the same shaped face, nose, and ears and wore an expression of *I'm Perfect*, just like the woman. Milli couldn't help but overhear their conversation.

"I'm telling you. This is a sure thing. A small loan is all I need to get in on the ground floor," said the woman, in a husky smoker's voice. "I'll be set for life. I'm absolutely certain."

"Are you sure this isn't a Nigerian Prince plot?" asked the young man.

The woman pointed a scarlet fingernail at him. "What do you take me for?" The woman groaned. "I've researched this, believe me. It's a sure deal. Ten thousand dollars. That's what it takes to secure my future. Come on. You have it. What's a small loan to your adoring mother? I'm good for it. I'll pay you back, with interest."

"That's not necessary," said the young man, gritting his teeth. "I just want to know this deal is on the up and up. You know lots of people want to dupe old folks."

"Yah, thanks. Now I'm old folks. I'm sixty-three. Not so old."

Milli was surprised at the woman's age. She didn't have a wrinkle on her face, although it was stretched pretty tight.

"You know what I mean," said the young man in a softer tone. "I'm just worried that you're being snookered."

"Snookered? I'm smarter than that."

"Listen, Mother, how about you share the man's emails with me. Let me look them over, take them to my attorney. Let me study this before I write you a check."

"Goddamn it, Alexander. I knew you'd blow me off. You think I'm irresponsible, a frigging idiot when it comes to making good decisions. Didn't I put you through school? Didn't I get you that starter house you wanted?"

"Uh, no, not exactly, Mother."

"What the hell does that mean?"

"That you don't quite live in reality, Mother."

"And you do?"

"I try." The son rose. "Mother, send me the emails and I'll check them out. Until then, we're on hold."

The woman raised her chin and pouted. "Do I have to go to your brother? This is not how I envisioned this ending."

"Marcus is out of the country so you couldn't go to him even if you wanted to."

"A likely story. He's in hiding. He never calls. Such selfish boys who don't give a damn about their poor mother."

The son heaved a heavy sigh. "Listen, I'm on your side. Truly. I want only what's best for you. I'll look into this and get back to you. All right?"

"Do I have a choice?" the woman asked.

The man reached out for a hug, and the woman complied, although the body language said, *Don't get too close. You're on my shit list until you come through with ten thousand dollars.*

When the son left, the mother looked sideways at Milli. "I suppose you heard that whole conversation?"

"There's not much privacy when the tables are so close together."

"Such a son I raised. He doesn't trust me enough to give me a loan. What the hell? Who does he think he is? This generation. You'd think I asked him for the moon."

Milli's lips pursed.

"He was such an agreeable child. Never gave me grief. Now his brother..."

"Marcus?" asked Milli.

"So you were listening. Such a nerve." The woman looked around the small café. "Well, I'm glad. Now you know what I'm going through. What would you do if you were handed gold on a silver platter?"

Milli thought the woman's metaphor was all wrong, and she had no reply except to raise her eyebrows and nod.

"Exactly. You'd grab it, right! I gave that man my word that I'd come through with the money. And he promised he'd hold my space for a chance at the million. And now my ungrateful son won't help me. What sort of shit is that?"

Milli held her tongue.

"I'll tell you. You bring them up to be independent and then they take advantage of your love."

Is that how it goes? She never had the chance for Lionel to take care of her. It was her nephew Bernard who sold her home and helped her relocate. At first, he seemed genuinely concerned with her well-being, talking at length with her about aging and responsibility. He and Milli researched senior living communities, under the assumption that she was trading the demands of owning a house for the freedom of care-free living, three solid meals a day, and a chance for new friendships.

Within weeks of securing the high rise apartment at New Dawn, Bernard moved her lock, stock and barrel. Milli still believed that he meant well. Hadn't he doted on his mother before she died? Hadn't he taken care of the sale of her house too? At the time, Milli hadn't known anything about opioids, and she didn't understand that an addict needed money and then more money to feed his habit. That's what happened when older people put their entire faith and power of attorney into their supposedly well-intentioned family, but Milli wasn't about to share that information.

"So Miss Big Ears, cat got your tongue? Don't you think my son owes me? I mean, what's ten thousand dollars to a millionaire? It's like no skin off his back to give me that measly sum. I tell you, I'm pissed."

The woman worked herself into a dither—sweaty and shaky and not in control of her Botox lips, which slid around on her face.

"I hear you," said Milli, who learned to say those words during a grief-sharing class after Lionel died.

"Yeah, sure. Mumbo Jumbo, I-hear-you shit. Those are bogus words meant to distract an overwrought person. I'm not over-wrought. I'm a survivor. Do you hear me! A survivor. Those boys had a father who tried to strangle me, not once, not twice, but five times. And they still talk to the scumbag. Marcus chose to pull up stakes and move to Italy, but Alexander, he's my rock. And now he's doubting me. Such a shit."

Milli decided she had to speak up. "Tell me, do you like Alexander? I mean is he a good man?"

"What sort of a dumb question is that? Of course he's a good man. He's my son."

"But do you like him? Would you choose him to be on your team?"

The woman threw her manicured hands into the air. "You don't know what you're saying, do you? What a stupid question. Of course he'd be on my team. But he wouldn't be my first choice, I can tell you that. I'd pick a strong man. A man with balls. Alexander is ball-less. Always has been. Did you hear his high voice?"

"So you love him, but you don't like him much?"

The woman made a shrew-face. "Love, like? What's the difference when it comes to your flesh and blood?"

All the difference in the world. "I loved my nephew Bernard, but I wouldn't pick him to be on my team because he can be, ah, inconsistent." There was way more she could say about Bernard, but the comparison worked. "He likes to have his own way. You know, my way or the highway type of guy. So no, I wouldn't choose him to be on my team, even though I'd support the team he chose to be on. Does that make sense to you?"

"Not much." The woman's lips dipped and two thin lines appeared, making her look like a sad clown. "So your nephew is a shit like my Alexander?"

"I didn't say that." But she thought it. "I said Bernard doesn't always make good decisions. I don't always agree with him and for that reason, I'd think twice about having him make decisions for me." *Ah, hindsight is wonderful. If only I had a time machine.*

"So I think I know where you're going. My kid wouldn't choose me for his team. I don't make such good decisions, which might be true. But that doesn't mean I'm a bad person, right?"

"Of course not," said Milli. "My nephew usually comes to his senses."

For the most part, that had been true when he was younger, thought Milli, *and if he had lived longer, maybe he would have straightened himself out.* After Lionel died, Milli and Leo were so deep into sadness that she forgot she had an older sister and a nephew who offered comfort. Bernard visited often, buying groceries, taking them out for dinner or a Sunday afternoon drive in the country, but they rarely acknowledged his kindness. What did he know of their pain? After a while, he stopped coming but she and Leo barely noticed. When Bernard was in his early thirties, his path became littered with greasy hair and pills. It took therapy and support for him to kick his habit so that he could help his mother through her final years. Maybe when she died, Bernard couldn't handle it, just like Leo couldn't bear his son's death. *Oh how life throws punches.*

"So you're saying I should thank my selfish son for not lending me what I want when I want it?"

"That's a possibility."

The woman put both feet on the ground. "Old Gal, I don't like you. You have this better-than-thou attitude that makes me feel like dirt."

"No. No. You're reading me all wrong," Milli protested.

"Am I?" The woman huffed away as if Milli had punched her.

Milli lowered her chin, looking into herself for answers. *Who the hell am I to make that woman feel less than whole? Look what happened to me, putting all my trust in my nephew. If only Bernard had come to me, I could have helped him and maybe he'd still be alive and I'd still be living in the high rise.*

Chapter Five

Milli finished her coffee and used the facilities again. The rain had passed and it was time to return to reality. She had signed out yesterday for the bogus dentist appointment and had never signed back in. *Had anyone noticed?* Milli had no regrets. She spent an unforgettable twenty-four hours reliving her dream with Leo and Lionel. She would return to Downtown Crossing knowing she could be successful on her own no matter where she lived. *Is that true?* Either way, it was time to get a move on.

But first, she needed to retrieve her clothing from under the bushes. Then, she'd have to figure out how to get back to New Dawn. She gathered up her energy and began to walk toward the Arboretum, but just the thought of climbing that winding hill created irregular thumps in her heart.

She stopped along the boardwalk in front of a real estate office to catch her breath. In the window, she browsed through photos of beach houses for sale. *They're so big and beautiful!* The wide expanse of the ocean flowed out of each picture, the house an afterthought.

One small sign caught her eye: apartment to let. Curious, she opened the door to the realtor's office. A thin-faced, gum-chewing woman looked up.

"Yeah? May I help you?"

"Could you tell me about the apartment for rent?"

"Ain't much to tell. It's on a side street, third floor walk-up. One room. One window. Bed. Bathroom. Microwave and refrigerator. View of the ocean."

"And the price?"

"Two grand for the month."

Milli had cash on her, lots of it. It had been her habit over the years to wad loose bills into balls and toss them into her purse. There must have been two dozen clumps in there by now. But she'd be damned if she'd spend two thousand dollars and walk up three flights of stairs. The ocean view was tempting. Maybe she could install one of those elevator lifts.

"Anything else available?"

"Summer real estate is at a premium. You might find a room in a private home. Maybe barter some babysitting for a bed." The woman hid a grin.

"Thanks for your time," said Milli, always polite, even though her chest was heaving.

Milli hastened along the avenue until the road widened and the beach was almost out of sight. She heard its roar, and it called to her, but she avoided turning around.

What was I thinking anyway? That Leo and Lionel would come alive? I'm as batty as that woman in the coffee shop.

Walking by a high-rise, she saw wicker rocking chairs lining the front lobby. She just wanted to sit for a little bit before going back to that lonely place. Buzzing a random apartment in the building, she was delighted to hear a quick response. She entered and made a beeline for the rocker, collapsing into it. *Just let me relax here for a few minutes. I really need to rest.*

She was rousted awake by an older man with a long pointed beard. He handed her a tissue. "Madam, you're drooling."

"Oh my goodness. How embarrassing." She accepted the tissue and wiped her mouth.

"Are you waiting for someone? I know most of the people who live here. I could speed them along."

Milli thought fast. "My friend is looking at a condo. She's hoping for an ocean view. Me, not so much."

The man tugged at his beard. "Hmm. Must be McNamara's place. It just went up for sale this morning. People have been in and out all day."

"Busy place," said Milli.

"It suits me just fine. I always dreamed of retiring to a condo that has a balcony overlooking both the ocean and the bay. Spectacular."

"Expensive, I bet," said Milli.

The man nodded and beamed, like it was his due to spend his later years in a high rise that met all his earthly needs. *That could have been me living the high life, if only Bernard hadn't died.*

"Tell me, do you know of any rentals that are off the beaten path? Maybe one with a garden?" *I can dream, can't I?*

Tapping his upper lip, the man had an aha moment. "A buddy of mine passed a week back. He had a room on Porter Street downstairs from a flower shop. Maybe the place is for rent. Take a left out of the building, then two more lefts till you see Lila's. Go around back. Tell them Morris sent you."

What do I have to lose? Milli rose to leave.

"Aren't you going to wait for your friend?" he asked.

"I'll call her," said Milli, pretending to search in her purse for her phone. "Thanks for the tip."

As she walked left, left, and left, Milli's feet ached and her knees buckled. *What am I thinking? I should be back in New Dawn having pea soup and crackers.* Then again, she hated pea soup and her only other choice was clam chowder, and she hated that too. Those little oyster crackers that were empty inside, what kind of meal was that? And the square green Jello with a squirt of Dream Whip. You'd think they were serving the moon with cream cheese the way they cooed about the menu. Instead, how about chocolate cake three times a day and a nip of Kahlua? Or a pound of M&M's or Almond Joys bars? A little sugar high was fun, but no, diabetes would claim her if she wasn't careful. *Come on. Who the hell cares? What's a little chocolate parfait or vodka and tonic going to do? So I'll die. Big deal.*

The blocks were short. When she reached Porter Street and Lila's, a small floral shop with a closed sign on its door, she went around back to a weather-beaten patio with two sad trees and a few peeling Adirondack chairs. *Some garden!* She knocked on a screen door.

"Hello," she called. "I'm here to see the apartment. Morris sent me."

No reply. She raised her voice. "Hello. Are you renting an apartment? I'd like to see it. Is anyone home?"

"Keep your panties on, I'm coming," said a smoky voice. "Did you say Morris sent you? How the hell is the old coot? I miss him coming around. Place doesn't smell the same without him."

Milli didn't want to hear about Morris. If he got her in the door, fine. But to find out what he was like after he entered, well, no, no thank you. *Did he smell like beer? Or pot? Or god-forbid, sex? That musky, heavy, smoky swirl of energy? Never my Leo. Even during sex, he didn't smell sexy. More like Popeye, kind of like spinach.* She, on the other hand, thought she carried around a sexual aroma, even now in her eighties. Look at those lecherous old men on the golf cart. They had been attracted to her, right? Even with her hair all in knots. It had to be her scent, like roses. Or lavender. Or three-day old Icy Hot.

An older woman greeted Milli, rubbing her palms on her jeans, and extended a calloused hand. "Hello, I'm Grenadine."

The woman's voice sounded like sandpaper.

"Nice to meet you," Milli managed to say. *Grenadine? Isn't that a thick red syrup? Had the woman's mother been drinking red wine when this child was born? Or worse? Sucking pomegranates?*

"You interested in the apartment?" Grenadine asked.

Milli looked around. The room was the entire first floor, kind of chopped into sections by way of mismatched furniture. A twin bed in a corner with a wicker bureau created one boundary. A synthetic orange leather couch and two beanbag chairs took center stage, and a strip of appliances flanked a long wooden table.

"It's not much, but it's clean. Comes with linens, towels, pots and pans, and utensils. Everything a single woman needs. Cheap too. Especially for a friend of Morris."

"How much is cheap?"

"Speak louder, Woman, my ears ain't what they used to be."

Milli cleared her throat and asked the price again.

"For now, six hundred a month with utilities. Until mid-June. Then the rent triples. A bahgain," she said mocking a Boston accent.

Milli tested the bed and sat on the couch. She caught a look at the small bathroom off to the side: a sink, a toilet, and a stall shower with a handrail! *Ah, made just for me.*

"I'll take it," she said. She turned her back and reached into her purse for several wads of money. She counted out six hundred dollars.

Grenadine eyed Milli's purse. "I should have asked for more," she grumbled. "Listen, I'll mark you paid till June fourteenth, then I'll be back."

To Milli, a month sounded like a year.

"You know, you caught me at the right time," Grenadine smirked. "I'm never here, but I finally got around to cleaning the place. I wanted to check it out once more before it officially went up for rent." The woman tossed back her head, her chins puckering. "The former tenant and I had many a good time rolling around on the floor together like teenagers. Just remembering the old days."

Milli looked more carefully at Grenadine: the thick red lipstick that caked in the corners, the yellow teeth, the wrinkly neck that hung loose like an old chicken. She was a good fifteen years younger than Milli, but time had not been kind.

"So the apartment's been vacant for how long?"

"About a week. So sad."

"Who's upstairs?"

"A florist is directly above us and Madame Seer is on the top floor. She fashions herself a psychic, but she's really a big bosomed fraud, if I do say so myself. I'd watch out for her if I were you. She lies and everyone believes her."

"So you've had your fortune told by her and nothing comes true?"

Grenadine harrumphed. "That's the least of it."

"So she's done you wrong?" asked Milli.

"How the hell would you know that?" asked Grenadine.

"Anger is orange. You give off that color."

"Hmmm." Grenadine shook out her body as if to erase the aura. "What color am I now?"

Milli squinted. "You're red, like grenadine."

"You're a hoot. Do you have a name?"

Milli squinted, like she was pulling her name out of her forehead, thinking it might be best not to tell Grenadine the whole truth. "I'm Minnie Yanover. Pleased to make your acquaintance." Milli extended her hand. "Don't squeeze too hard. I might break."

"You don't seem the type," said Grenadine. "Make yourself at home, Minnie. I'll let the florist know there's a tenant."

"And Madame Seer?"

"She already knows."

"I guess she has special powers?"

"Nope, just pipes that let her eavesdrop. Don't say anything you don't want her to know. She's got big ears." Grenadine raised her eyebrows and wiggled them. She looked like a rubber duck stretching.

Milli listened to thunder outside and the gathering of another storm. She was glad to be sheltered inside but she was even more glad not to be in New Dawn.

Chapter Six

Before she left, Grenadine gave Milli a piece of paper with her name and phone number on it. She tucked the bills into her bra and scooted out of the apartment with a light cackle. "Don't call unless you're at death's door. On second thought, if you're at death's door, bang on the pipes. Madame See-It-All will get here way before I could."

Milli exhaled, then did a little jig. *I'm alone! I did it! Minnie Ha Ha! That's me!* She felt tickled that she had come up with a false name. She didn't think New Dawn would be looking for her yet. Communication was slow in that place, but she didn't want to take the chance.

Milli twirled around the apartment and caught a glimpse of a bookcase against one wall. She perused the shelves and found two books that interested her: *Passages* by Gail Sheehy and *The Feminine Mystique* by Betty Friedan—both oldies but goodies. Milli needed to channel the energy of powerful women.

What should I do first? She emptied her purse and reorganized her belongings, making sure to hide her money rolls deep in an inner pocket that zipped. Then she stripped down and stepped into the shower. She massaged her scalp and kneaded her brain. *Look at me! At eighty-four years old, I'm naked in a walk-in apartment.* She cleansed herself of her recent past. There went New Dawn down the drain taking her nephew along with it. And there went dinners of green Jello and cold soup, slow bingo games and sad sing-alongs. Comb Over and Hairy Ears faded into oblivion, but the encounters with Keysi and Rashida remained, vibrant and energizing.

Milli needed some sleep, so she lay down on the narrow bed and wrapped her tired old body in the blanket. Within minutes she was with Leo, floating in the warm waters of Aruba. She waved to him as he sat cross-legged on the beach squinting into the sun, sporting a smile as broad as the ocean. How she loved his deep dimples. She missed them so. And his soft hair, dark for most of his life, with just a hint of balding on his forehead. She had put away any anger at him after he'd been gone for a few years. What use was there to carry that lump of heat in her chest? They'd had happy days, child-filled days, kite-flying days, and red-hot melding days. At least until Lionel died. Then Leo withered and forgot to make dimples.

Milli woke just before sunset. *I'm hungry. Crazy hungry.* As her stomach rumbled, her brain exploded with negative vibes. *The demons are dancing.* She thought about Bernard and how he had talked her into selling her home.

"Auntie, let me help you," he had said. "I'm an accountant and know the ins and outs of the system. If I'm the executor of your estate, you'll live securely for the rest of your life. Money is the bane of senior citizens. Truly. The more you have, the more the government takes. If you leave the details to me, you'll never want for anything."

Milli should have listened to that constant complaint that her sister repeated when Bernard was young. "My son might mean well, but he's irresponsible." Milli figured he had outgrown his immaturity. Her sister told her over and over again what a wonderful man he had become. Of course, she neglected to tell her about Bernard's drug use. Toward the end of her life, Milli's sister was deep in dementia and denial. But Milli was snowed over by Bernard's sincerity. In hindsight, he was a master of deception, and her last living relative. Now gone. They were all gone.

Milli walked through the studio apartment, glad to be out of the elements, but sad to be away from the lilacs. She loved those purple flowers and those sunshine daffodils, but a shower, a soft bed, and a roof over her head provided comfort. And there was no one around to tell her where she needed to be or what she had to eat. Sure, old people gathered rust, but they also accumulated webs of wisdom. Sure, old people forgot the details, but Milli was creating new file cabinets in her head.

Milli knew life was a snapshot, quick-silver fast, and too sharp-edged for the weak-hearted. She should have told Rashida to get a grasp on what was important. Her children needed her. And Keysi, pay attention. If that man didn't respect her, run. Run fast. Run run run. There was no time for walking. Oh how Milli understood that. And that selfish mother in the coffee shop. She should appreciate her son, not exploit him. Family was precious. But now, today, was all that mattered. Right? Wasn't that what she had learned? It might be twilight, but the day was just dawning on her and the moments were essential. *Why hadn't I realized that sooner? Where have I been?*

Milli pulled on her long-sleeved shirt, sweat pants, and thin socks. She double-tied her sneakers, and from her voluminous purse retrieved Lionel's cap, the one with a blazing sun logo, and Leo's glasses, round like Harry Potter's, more for show than for sight. She needed her family with her. *Come on, Boys. Let's get dinner.* She unwrapped a wad of cash, meted out fifty dollars, and went out to greet the day's golden hour. As she surveyed the boardwalk, she saw a sign for Dino's. *Pizza and beer, now that's living.*

Chapter Seven

Milli hurried along the cracked sidewalk and made steady progress toward the cheesy smells. What gave her pleasure was seeing families strolling together, smiling and licking ice cream cones. That would definitely be dessert.

At Dino's, she ordered at the counter and brought her food to a small table outside facing the bay. The chair was one of those metal mesh high-backed rigid things, designed to discourage lingering, but Milli didn't care. She angled the seat toward the setting sun which fell slowly over the rim of the ocean.

At the next table, a teenage girl sat alone with a fluffy pink-nosed dog curled on her lap. The girl paid little attention to the animal, her fingers flying as she texted, scrolled through screens, then flipped through the pages of a teen magazine, all at the same time, at least it looked that way to Milli. The girl glanced up when a police car wailed by, but quickly returned to her phone.

As the siren screamed on, the dog jumped onto the ground and ran, his leash trailing behind him. It took a few minutes for the girl to realize what had happened. "Mr. Whiskers, come back here, right now." But the dog hadn't listened and ran into the street. The girl screamed as the dog dodged cars and high-tailed it around a corner. The girl gave chase.

Milli wanted to follow them, to save the dog, to stop the traffic. She hadn't heard screeches or loud cries or anything resembling tragedy. That dog could be a mile away by now, hiding under a bush. She knew plenty of dogs even though she only mothered one when her Lionel was young, a great big galumphing golden retriever. Lionel and his friends rode him like a miniature pony, fed him all the food they didn't want, and offered him plenty of bare skin for kisses. Their dog died when her son turned ten; the family huddled together and cried for days. Leo discouraged Milli from getting another dog. He didn't want something else to grieve. Little did he know.

For a few years, Milli fed her animal needs by walking dogs. Favorites came to mind: Rusty the beagle, who gave wet sloppy licks. Miriam, a chihuahua, who tugged so fiercely on her leash that she rivaled a dog three times her size. Cisco and Pancho, a pair of afghan show dogs. She had to cover their heads with shower caps when they ate so their ears wouldn't flop into their food. And then the awful ones. Max, who bit Leo in the groin when he went with her to feed him. And Spike, a doberman, whom she refused to watch after he chased her out the door, his teeth bare and his growl on full throttle.

Leo never liked her walking the dogs. It was as if they stole her attention away in the early mornings or weekend nights when she was needed most. One day she, Leo, and Lionel were all set to go to dinner, but she had to walk and feed Sir Anthony first. "We'll stop on our way so you can take care of that foolish dog," said Leo, having met Sir Anthony once when he chased a squirrel up a tree and ran around and around its base until he was so tangled in rope that Milli had to cut the dog free.

When Milli arrived at the house, Leo opened the door too wide and the dog bolted.

They roamed the neighborhood for a half hour calling "Here, Tony, Tony, Tony." Their pockets were loaded with treats, but the dog was nowhere to be found. Leo and Lionel drove around for another half hour while Milli waited at the house.

"Well, we did the best we could," Leo said. "The dog will come home when he's hungry. Let's go."

But Milli couldn't leave.

"Darn it, Millicent. My stomach is growling." Leo's tone took on the I-have-no-patience-for-this and I'm-tired-and-hungry.

Leo left her at Sir Anthony's house with no ride home. About an hour later, Sir Anthony made his appearance and she lured him inside. By then, she was so angry at Leo that the three-mile trek home seemed like speed walking, she was so on fire. Leo apologized, and had even brought home take-out, but he never joined Milli to care for a pet again.

Milli figured that the run-away dog would meet up with the teen-aged girl eventually. Dogs got hungry and they knew where the food was. So when Milli finished her pizza and sat back to enjoy the first stars of the night, she wasn't surprised to see the fluffy pooch at the door of the pizza shop, sniffing around the area.

"Hey Mr. Whiskers," cooed Milli, recalling the name the girl had shouted. Milli took a few pieces of pizza crust that she hadn't eaten and held them out. "Come on, Boy. It's yummy."

The dog lost no time making a beeline for Milli.

"That's a good doggie," she said, and grabbed his leash as he scarfed down the food. She asked the busboy for a small bowl of water, and he obliged. *Now what?* She checked Mr. Whisker's dog collar for a phone number. No such luck. Then she remembered what a lot of the young folk were doing, using identification chips.

"Where's the nearest police station?"

"Up the hill and to the right," the busboy pointed.

That wasn't going to work. Trudging up a hill was out of the question. Her legs hurt. Her feet hurt. Her ankles had swelled. As she puzzled out a plan, a police car cruised the boardwalk. "Now that's what I call service." She jumped up and waved an arm, holding tight to the leash with her other hand, hoping the officer would see her in his rear-view mirror. When he didn't, the busboy ran out to the street and whistled, flailing both his arms; the police car made a quick U-turn.

What if New Dawn sent the police a picture of me? Just in case, Milli pulled Lionel's cap low on her brow so the visor shielded her face and dabbed cherry gloss on her lips. *The new Minnie me!* Then she approached the officer and explained what had happened.

Ten minutes later, Milli, the dog, and the policeman were at the station tracing the dog's identity by scanning the chip embedded behind Mr. Whiskers' shoulder blades. The officer dialed the number on the chip to get the information he needed.

As Milli waited to be sure Mr. Whiskers' owners would be found, she looked around the room. Her eyes gravitated to a board with people's faces on it. Wanted, screamed a few. But then she saw, "Missing: Harold Mussman, Male, age 81, Caucasian, Brown eyes, 5'8", suffers from Alzheimer's. Disappeared from his Oldham home on May 14. If you have any information about his whereabouts, contact the Oldham, MA police." The photo of his face showed a white-haired man with bushy brows and vacant eyes.

When will my photo be plastered on the police station board? She hoped New Dawn would use the picture on her nightstand, the one her nephew photoshopped to rid her of the turkey-wattles wrinkling her neck.

"Bingo," said the officer.

Milli jumped.

"The owner's name is Corazon Wolff, 128 Samoset Avenue, Mayfield. That's the next town over."

The officer called the number on file. After speaking privately on the phone, he hung up with a soft grin. "Her daughter was watching the dog while the mom was at the hair salon. They've been frantically searching and are relieved that you found him. They'll be right along."

Milli offered to wait for the family on the bench outside the police station.

A sleek BMW pulled up and the young girl, with buds permanently growing from her ears, jumped out of the car. "Mr. Whiskers, you bad dog! You nearly gave me a heart attack."

"That's nothing you should be saying around an old lady," snarked Milli.

"Thank you. Thank you," said the girl, who scooped up Mr. Whiskers and buried her face in his soft hair.

"Naughty, naughty," said the girl's mother, a high-cheekboned woman in platform shoes, short-shorts, and a low-cut t-shirt. She wagged a jagged fingernail at the dog. "And would you look at my nails! I didn't get my manicure or my pedicure because of you, you rascal." Her lips pursed like she'd been sucking lemons.

Milli checked her own uneven nails. They were plenty fine for scratching Mr. Whiskers behind the ears.

"How can I thank you?" asked the woman, opening her purse and taking out a mirror. "And look at my hair. I was in the middle of having it brushed out when that careless daughter of mine called. I left the beauty parlor in the middle of my blow-dry." The woman's cadence picked up steam. "I am so out of breath from chasing him down. I didn't even have a chance to eat dinner. I am so disappointed in my daughter. Young people. I can't tell her a thing without her taking offense. I blame her for Mr. Whiskers' escapade. I should never have trusted her, even for a minute."

How many 'I's' could one person spew in ten sentences? Corazon Wolff is seriously self-centered.

"Relax, Mrs. Wolff. Mr. Whiskers is safe and sound. And your hair looks lovely."

Corazon collapsed onto the bench. "I am so worn out. I need to meditate. I'd have less stress if I did."

Milli bristled at the woman's constant use of the pronoun I. "You might have less stress if you used the universal We."

Corazon looked at Milli as if she had three heads. "The universal We. Is it French?"

"Not the French word *oui*. The pronoun We."

The woman pinched her nostrils. "Who are you again?"

"I found Mr. Whiskers and alerted the police."

"Well, for that, I'll say thank you again. But really, implying I say *I* too often is rude." She rose quickly, and whistled for her daughter who had taken Mr. Whiskers for a quick walk.

"I don't mean to be rude," said Milli, "but sometimes the worst place we can be is in our own heads." *Maybe I'm guilty of that too, thinking about myself all the time, not even considering the staff at New Dawn who are probably worried sick.*

The woman tapped her fingers against her body. "I don't need a stranger telling me to get over myself."

"I'm sorry. I didn't mean to offend you."

Corazon's eyes fluttered and her voice pitched higher. "At fifty-two, I have no intention of changing. Oh, *excusez-moi*, there will be no change taking place."

And at eighty-four, I'm ready for change, but is it ready for me?

"You're a cheeky broad. I bet you've heard that before."

"I have actually. Just this morning," said Milli, thinking about the woman in the coffee shop. *Maybe I'm overly obsessed with myself too. What if I called New Dawn to tell them I'm all right, that I'm just taking a break from my real life?*

Cora interrupted Milli's thoughts. "You might have saved Mr. Whiskers, but you're not going to save me."

"I have enough trouble saving myself," Milli chuckled. "But if I may be so bold..."

"No one's stopped you yet."

"Think about asking people about themselves. Be curious. Like you might have asked how I found Mr. Whiskers. I'd love to tell you."

"No need. He's with us now and that's all that matters."

The daughter neared the bench where they had been talking. "You were the pizza woman. The one who sipped the beer. It made me laugh. An older woman drinking beer from a bottle. That was a shocker."

Milli was amazed that the girl had noticed her, what with the iPhone and earbuds and the magazine spread out in front of her.

"Thank you so much for returning Mr. Whiskers to us," the teenager said.

Milli looked at Cora. "Your daughter didn't say I once! Perhaps you've done something right."

"Yes, she has been raised well," said Cora, her lips pursed and pruned. "Now how can we repay you?"

"How about an ice cream?"

Cora rolled her eyes, but the young girl nudged her mother. "That's the least we can do."

Chapter Eight

Milli woke to a literal fog. Through the window of the studio apartment, Milli could only see white, like salt had been poured from a shaker and mixed vigorously by hand through the air. She dressed quickly, rushed outside and felt her way carefully along the side of the flower shop to the avenue. She needed to see the ocean, the waves, the fog rising off the water. She saw only puffs of rolling white. But the sound. The roar. The energy! Vibrations swirled and pulsed around her. She was in the center of a private second. All hers. No one was in her space. She breathed deeply. *This is life. Power and energy and salt and sea air.* As she stood there, a person actually bumped into her.

"I'm so sorry. I can't see an inch in front of me," said a smiling voice in an Irish brogue.

The fog cleared enough for a face to emerge, a sunny full-cheeked redhead with bouncing curls.

"You're a vision," said Milli.

"Right so. Are you okay? Did I hurt you?" The girl led Milli to the barely visible bench in front of the florist's shop. "Please sit before someone else comes along and knocks us both down."

"Aren't we crazy to be out in weather like this?" said Milli.

"We're lucky. Where I was stationed, everyone stayed inside all the time. No telling when a bomb would fall."

"Are you talking literally or figuratively?" asked Milli.

"I couldn't say," the girl replied. "Those words confuse me."

"The word literally means that a bomb will fall and blow your house apart. The word figuratively means that the bomb might be bad news or an unexpected and unwanted visitor."

The girl's curls shook. "The bomb was real enough as well as the unwanted visitors and the bad news. I guess both words apply."

"Where was this unholy place?"

"Syria. My Da was part of the Irish Army deployed to Iraq in the nineties on a peacekeeping mission. I've followed in his footsteps, more or less. Sergeant Aideen Daly, at your service."

"Pleased to meet you, Soldier! Why are you in the States?" asked Milli.

"Boston is dedicating a permanent marker on Deer Island. It's in memory of the thousand Irish emigrants who left Ireland for America during the Great Hunger, but they were too sick to enter the country when they arrived in Boston Harbor. It is my honor to sing the Irish anthem at the ceremony."

"My goodness, a slip of a girl like you. Imagine."

"My father, may he rest in peace, would have been so proud of me."

Milli felt as if they were the only two people on the planet, the fog was still that thick. She wondered how the girl's voice would affect the fog. "Sergeant Daly, might you sing the anthem to me? I've never heard it and I have a feeling your voice is something special."

The girl looked at her watch. "I have a wee bit of time before my ride picks me up and I could use the practice." She cleared her throat and the words flowed.

> We'll sing song, a soldier's song,
> With cheering rousing chorus,
> As round our blazing fires we throng,

The starry heavens o'er us;
Impatient for the coming fight,
And as we wait the morning's light,
Here in the silence of the night,
We'll chant a soldier's song.

When the final note echoed through the air, applause and whis-
tles surrounded them. The fog gave way to bystanders and their faces
beamed with Irish pride.

"Your father heard you. I'm sure of it," said Milli.

"That's why I sing."

"I wish everyone had that attitude," said Milli, thinking back to
her own malaise during sing-alongs at New Dawn, how she mouthed
the words and never allowed her spirit to soar. Maybe the purpose
of sing-alongs was to lift her out of her own dense fog? Milli decided
that if she ever returned, she'd participate with enthusiasm. "Thank
you, Sergeant. It's been a while since I've let music come into my life."

"Music is good for the soul," said the girl, whose whole body came
into focus. From her right knee down, she wore a metal limb with a
shoe attached. "Music has helped me through many a rough patch."

Milli wanted to know Aideen Daly's story, but she knew not to
ask. Wasn't it enough to be in her presence, to feel her strength, to
know she had come through something shattering, yet here she was,
honoring her father and her country?

Milli felt like she had lost a limb when her loved ones died. Why
hadn't she fashioned a prosthesis, something to support her that
allowed her to move forward? For Aideen, music was the answer. For
Milli? Yesterday in the Arboretum brought her peace. At the moment,
it was the sea air and the freedom to enjoy it. If only the sweetness of
Aideen's voice were enough to carry a message of strength and courage
for Milli to keep in her chest pocket, to take out when she needed it.

Aideen's ride arrived and she said her good-byes. Milli lingered
on the bench until her stomach grumbled. She stood, but before she

could take two steps, a woman whooshed by her so quickly, Milli was knocked backwards.

"Whoa, what's your hurry?" asked Milli.

Then she heard a man's voice boom. "Stop! I just need to talk to you. I want to know why? Where did we go wrong?"

The man's words weren't hostile, but his tone blazed. On impulse, Milli stretched forward just as the man ran past her. He tripped onto the sidewalk with Milli flopping down on top of him.

"What the frigging hell?" he shouted.

"Such a racket," said Milli, struggling to rise. "Everyone on the boardwalk can hear you. If you catch up with that woman, you'll wake the whole town. Everyone will know your business. Do you want that?"

The man tried to disentangle himself without hurting Milli. "What the hell is going on?" he asked. "Am I in a frigging alternate universe? And who the hell are you?"

"You make your own hell. Do you know that? If you carry around all that anger all the time, you'll burn from the inside out."

The man managed to roll to his side. "I give up," he said and sat in a heap on the ground. "The world is against me."

"Is that why you were chasing that woman?"

"That woman slept at my uncle's house. God knows what went on. Last night we celebrated my twenty-first birthday and I got crocked. She and my uncle tucked me into my bed like a little boy. And this morning, I went to my uncle's place to thank him for watching out for me, and there she was in his kitchen making breakfast, wearing his shirt. I need to talk with her, to find out what happened. But I have to catch her first."

The man's face peered up at Milli, the tattoos on his neck like knotted ropes. He had piercings in his eyebrows, his nose, and his lower lip. His ears had black disks in them like miniature hockey pucks. Milli felt the heat rise off his body. "Why didn't you ask your uncle?"

"She's the one who's suspect."

"And yet she was in his kitchen wearing his shirt. Isn't he suspect as well?"

"But she's the love of my life!"

"At twenty-one you have a lot of life left to live."

"At twenty-one my life is over."

What happened next made Milli's heart stop. He began to cry; big fat tears rolled down his stubbled cheeks. "I love that girl. I trusted her. Why'd she have to go and ruin it?"

Milli wanted to comfort this strange man who looked like a deranged zombie, at least that's what Milli thought a zombie would look like, all criss-crossed with ink, eyes rimmed in red, and snot running from his nose. She handed him a tissue from her purse.

He blew his nose louder than the foghorn that continued to blow in the distance, the fog having lifted nearby, but not over the ocean.

The man's anger had dissolved, but pain crept across his face like knifed skin, like his body was bleeding out. He raised himself off the ground and offered Milli his arm. They sat on the bench together, his body taking up most of the space. His knee pressed against hers and she felt a current pass between them, the heat of his wounded body spreading through her.

"The pain you feel will pass with time," she said.

"Never. My birthday will never be the same."

"So you'll allow this pain to gnaw at you? Where will that get you? When I met my husband Leo, he was a powerful man, not in stature, but in self-confidence and conviction. When our son Lionel died, he carried around his agony like a millstone."

"And did he ever recover?"

"No, his grief consumed him until he took his own life to stop the pain."

"That's terrible," said the young man. "I'm so sorry. You must be very lonely."

"That's the point I'm trying to make. I carried around my pain for years and it crushed me."

"But here you are."

"Yes, here I am." Milli hugged her arms. "You're young. Tomorrow spreads out for you. Don't squander it on jealousy or anger. It will just eat you up."

The young man tugged at his earlobe; the hockey puck earpiece spun around like a dolly wheel. Milli figured that was his way of thinking.

"I'm so sorry for your loss," said the man.

Milli's eyes teared. "Leo was like a lion, so strong. And my son Lionel was our little lion. Like father, like son."

"I'm sorry they didn't fulfill their names," he said.

Milli had never considered this. Leo wasn't strong in the end and neither was Lionel. Her own name, Millicent, meant brave strength. Would she be able to live up to that? "What's your name?"

"Kedrix."

"A name with power," said Milli.

Kedrix laughed, not at all like Leo's belly laugh that was infectious. Kedrix's was more like a bray, certainly not what Milli expected. She wondered if Kedrix had all those tattoos and piercings to cover up inadequacies. She wondered if he chose women that he knew would hurt him because he felt unworthy.

"And how about you? What's your name?" he asked.

"Milli. Short for Millicent." Her real name had tumbled out and she couldn't retract it. It made her feel vulnerable, but it allowed her to create honesty between her and this disheartened man.

"Tell me, what are you most afraid of?"

"Being alone," he said without hesitation.

"I would have agreed with you when I was twenty-one." *Now being alone is life at New Dawn.*

Kedrix's face pulled to one side. "To me, being alone is hell."

"So you'd rather be with a woman who treats you like a child than be by yourself?"

Kedrix sucked in his teeth. "I always wondered what attracted me to her. She had a habit of slapping me in public and calling me Big Puss. One time she hit me on the rear like I was a kid."

"What about intimacy?"

"I did everything I could to make her happy. I brought her flowers and wrote her poetry. I made sure my mouth tasted sweet when I kissed her."

"What did she do for you?"

He was quiet for a long time. The fog horns faded into the background. Milli didn't prod. She closed her eyes and listened to the wind as it swept away the last mist over the water. She could feel the morning sun warm the air.

"The truth is, she made me feel small. She said I was a premature jerk and I had no control. She said she'd teach me how to be a man. I believed her."

Milli detected an undercurrent of deceit. "So your girlfriend, what is her name?"

"Phoebe."

"I get the feeling that Phoebe is older than you."

"You're right. How did you know that?"

"How long have you dated?"

"About a month."

"And who introduced you?'

"My uncle. He said she waitressed at his restaurant for a few years. He told her to take good care of me."

This boy didn't have a clue about relationships. Milli wondered if Phoebe had been the first woman to come close to him. *Those facial markings are enough to scare away a blind person.*

"I'm going to tell you what I think. Then I need you not to respond until you've counted to fifty. Can you do that?"

Kedrix nodded.

"Okay. Here goes. I think Phoebe is a special friend of your uncle's and he thought it would be sweet if she paid you some attention. Maybe along the line, she enjoyed your company. You certainly enjoyed hers, but she was teaching you the ropes, how to relate to a woman. At some point, your uncle would have suggested she was far too old for you. He might even have pursued her as a mate for himself."

Kedrix's lip trembled, the silver ring clanging against his lower teeth. "But he's my mother's brother. Why would he hurt me?"

"He saw your relationship as something positive, life-changing. He wasn't trying to hurt you."

"That's one hell of a back-fire, don't you think?"

"What I think is that you need to know the truth. You need to meet Phoebe in an open spot like a restaurant and have a conversation."

"And then what?"

"And then you find a girl on your own without anyone's intervention. You can do it. You have compassion and kindness even if you do look like a bull in a china shop."

Kedrix barely blinked. At long last, he nodded to Milli and sighed. "No one sees me anymore. It's like I've disappeared behind my body art. You're telling me square. I feel it." Kedrix's face knotted into a grimace that made him look like one of those wrinkled dogs. Milli reached out to touch his cheek and smooth it out. His face relaxed.

"Can I sit on your bench again and talk with you?"

"Anytime."

"Is there something I can do for you?" he asked.

"Yes. Help me down the beach ramp so I can feel the sand between my toes. Don't leave me there though. I'd never be able to get back on my own."

"You've got it." The man lifted Milli up like a feather.

"Really, I can walk," laughed Milli. "I just need your arm in mine."

"But this is so much more fun," said Kedrix as he crossed the street and descended the incline. He didn't set Milli down until they were on the hard-packed section of the beach where she could walk freely.

"You aren't like my late husband at all, but you remind me of his thoughtfulness. Maybe you could think about one less piece of metal on your face."

"But that's what gives me strength."

"Do you believe that?"

"I used to," he said as they strolled along the hard-packed sand. "Lately I feel weighted down."

"Do you sleep with all that hardware?"

"Yup." He squirmed. "But sometimes when I turn over, something snags on a pillow or a blanket and I wind up twisted."

Milli imagined him screwed into the bed. "It's all your choice, you know."

"But people expect me to look like this. It's called style."

"Sure, it's this year's style, and next year people will cut their toe-nails into spears and paint them black. So you'll do that too?"

Kedrix looked down at his long wide feet. "I'll skip that one." He rubbed his arms vigorously, like he and his tattoos were battling. "I'm going to take you back now. All this talk is making me itchy."

"I'd be honored if you might take me to the beach again. The sand feels so cool and clean, like youth."

"Absolutely. We're buddies now, even if you don't like my piercings."

"I didn't say that. I just wonder if you'll like them ten years from now."

"When I'm thirty-one? Who cares! I like them now and that's all that counts."

"If you say so, Kedrix. When I was twenty-one, I was a beatnik. I went underground to hear Miles Davis. I smoked weed before the hippies did and drank black coffee before Starbucks was at every corner. I was a hip cat." That wasn't exactly true. She was twenty-five during her beatnik stage and thirty during her hippie years. But she got her message across.

Kedrix laughed. "No way."

"Way," said Milli. "Your generation didn't invent cool. But ours was internal, not external, except for berets and greasy hair. Do you dig it?"

"So whattaya saying? That I should remove my metal and have my tattoos erased? That would destroy me."

"No, I'm just saying that styles change with the times so you have to be open to that. Just because someone doesn't have piercings or tattoos doesn't mean that person isn't worth knowing."

"Did I say that?"

"I hope not."

Chapter Nine

It was mid-morning after the fog had lifted completely. Milli had heard a glorious call-to-arms; she felt the sand between her toes; and she might have steered a wayward man-child toward a more positive direction. How would the rest of the day unfold? *With food.*

Dino's was closed, but the Mirage Café was open. She was reminded of the mother and son and wondered if the boy caved and gave her the $10,000. As she entered, she was surprised that almost every seat was taken. Then she saw the woman who wanted a loan from her son sitting at the same table, alone.

"May I join you?" Milli asked.

"You're the rude lady who called me selfish. Why would you join me?"

"I seem to be meeting a lot of selfish people. I'm beginning to suspect that I'm the selfish one," said Milli.

The woman snickered. "I could have told you that."

Milli hated her tone. "Why?"

"Because you have a big mouth. Big mouth people are all selfish."

"I think we got off on the wrong foot. Shall we try again?" asked Milli.

"What's in it for me?" the woman asked.

Milli was about to give up, turn tail, and exit the restaurant. Thai Palace was nearby.

"Forgive me for being mouthy too," said the woman.

"Let's begin again." If there was one thing that Milli understood it was that beginnings took effort. After Lionel died, her Leo never began again. She did, in a way, by working at the bank. Someone had to earn an income as Leo became more and more despondent.

Milli was thirty-nine and Leo was fifty-three when they met and they both wanted a child. Leo encouraged Milli to devote her energies to keeping a warm and wonderful home. Nurturing had been high on her list: both her parents had required her around-the-clock attention. Their demands superseded her own needs, and they absolutely didn't want her sister Linda Mae involved—"she had enough to worry about with that wayward son of hers." When Milli's parents died, she had no life to call her own. . . until she fell in love with Leo and his blueberry muffins.

It had been a cold day in May. That sounded like a bad beginning, but it was heaven inside the earthy oven-scent of the Day Bright Café. There was a bake-off. Amateur cooks throughout the Boston area had submitted their favorite kitchen creations for the chance to win big prizes. The final showdown was at the Boston Convention Center and Millicent Davis just happened to be passing by on the big day. She should go in. She was no longer needed at home. She had no plans. All was said and done. Why not watch someone take home a prize that ensured their future? So she paid her $2.50 and got a front row seat because she was an hour early.

Then two women contestants and one man began prepping their recipes. The ladies commanded the stage, like Julia Childs' clones preparing their ingredients with flourish and flair. It was the man whom Millicent watched, curious to understand how he could possibly be involved in making an award-winning dessert. That was not men's work. Not at all. But this man wasn't whom she had expected. He was small, like a porcelain doll, so fine of features that she felt if she approached him up close and blew a hot breath, he would vanish. And he was hairy, like long hair and side burns and coiling strands at his collar and on his hands and wrists. No man she had ever seen had so much hair. How could such a hirsute person be a baker? It was against everything Millicent understood about cooking and presentation and hygiene. But there he was, this Leo Tarnover, his name emblazoned on his white jacket in bronze and gold letters.

Leo captured Millicent's full attention: the measuring of ingredients, lining them up precisely, adding them to the mixmaster, watching how his head tilted, like his mind whirred and swirled with each rotation of the blades. He baked blueberry muffins, so simple with a crispy crust, and so laden with plump blueberries that he had individually rolled in flour and coated in sugar. The judges swooned at the taste. Buttery, they said. Moist. With a tad of crunch. Balanced. Rich and complex. Leo Tarnover didn't win the bake-off though. He came in second to fifty-layer mocha infused doughnuts, but he did win Millicent Davis' devotion.

When Jordan Marsh Company advertised for a baker to make blueberry muffins, guess who got the job? Leo Tarnover. By then, he was hers. But blueberry muffins didn't translate to happiness forever. Nothing nourished Leo after their son died. No amount of sugar-coating dispelled his grief.

"So what's your story?" the woman asked Milli.

It took a few minutes for Milli to remember where she was. This was not the Day Bright Café. And it was not the common room at New Dawn. She was in a cozy restaurant, with the ocean sparkling across a wide boulevard and a beady-eyed woman staring at her waiting for answers.

"Yoo-hoo. Is anyone home?" asked the woman.

Milli's eyes widened. "I'm so sorry. I was thinking about the day I met my husband."

"Lucky you. The day I met my husband, I was drunk as a skunk and he was being handcuffed for a DUI."

"DUI?"

"Driving under the influence. I met him in a bar in Boston. We hit it off immediately and left the place together. I had an apartment in the North End and he was coming home with me." She winked, her false eyelashes thick and lush. "We never made it there though. His car was parked too tight and trying to ease out of the space, he crashed into the van in front and the truck in back. Cops came along right quickly."

"That's one heck of a first date," said Milli.

The woman pursed her red lips. "I should have known right off that he was a shit, but he charmed me and I bailed him out and that was that."

"So you married him?"

"Sure did, but I'll be damned if I can remember anything else about that day. It was all a fog."

Milli shuddered and imagined her own father, how his black-outs erased all memories of her childhood, adolescence, and probably every other occasion that mattered to her, and a ton of moments that didn't. How had her own quiet, unassuming mother fallen in love with the lush? And this woman sitting across from Milli knew from the git-go she was marrying a drunk. *How stupid.*

"How long were you married?"

"You're a nosy woman, aren't you? I don't know why I'm even telling you this. I haven't talked about that man in years."

"Is he the father of Alexander and Marcus?"

"What are you? A memory machine? How did you remember my sons' names?"

"It's a trick I learned as a child. *Meet and Repeat. Spell out the name. Associate the name with something familiar.* When I saw you with your son and you called him Alexander, I thought of him like a telephone—you know, Alexander Graham Bell—and as his mother, you would call him up and seek his help. And Marcus, I pictured him like Marcus Aurelius, living in Rome, leading his troops."

"So my sons are telephones and soldiers. Interesting. What about me?"

"We haven't been formally introduced," smiled Milli.

"I promise you. Once I tell you my name, you won't need a trick to remember it. It's part of the reason I'm unforgettable."

Milli ran through memorable female names: Mata Hari, Cher, Madonna, Katniss.

"I'm Cleopatra," said the woman. She raised her chin and pursed her lips. If she had been wearing glasses they would have slipped down the bridge of her nose.

"You're right. No trick needed. So do you go by Cleo?"

"Heavens, no. I'm a force to be reckoned with. Didn't you see me with Alexander? How he dotes on me?"

Milli recalled Cleopatra's son chiding her for asking him for $10,000 for what he thought was a Ponzi scheme. *The woman is delusional.*

"I'm curious," said Milli, "do you think your name has influenced relationships that you've had?"

Milli loved her husband and son's names: Leo and Lionel. Lions, both of them. Whenever she thought of them, she felt strength and power. Her own name conjured money and greed. But being called Milli gave her a lift and the hope that tomorrow would be a brighter day. This Cleopatra must have gotten her way throughout her life, but her son Alexander had her number. "What was your husband's name?"

"Reginald. Like a king. I thought we were the perfect match."

Milli's father's name was Bruce, but everyone called him Buster. A perfect name for a man who broke down doors, shattered noses, and destroyed hearts. Her mother's name was Jane, plain and simple, and perhaps a bit backward. To Milli, names loomed large in revealing a person's worth.

"When I was a kid, I felt like a queen. My name defined me. Tell me, have you ever heard of anyone in modern times named Cleopatra?"

Milli expected the Queen to ask what her name was. That was the courteous segue. But this woman put herself first, before her children, before her common sense, and before everyone else. Milli wanted to test her theory.

"You're definitely unique. What about me? Can you guess my name?"

As if on cue, the woman's cell phone rang. She shot a red fingernail in the air, signaling to Milli that the conversation was on hold. But within seconds, the woman turned her back on Milli and left the restaurant. So much for Milli's theory. She wasn't important enough to even warrant a good bye.

Milli ate her blueberry muffin, which wasn't nearly as tasty as her Leo's, and drank her coffee as she watched the patrons in the restaurant. Most sat alone with their laptop or phone.

She didn't mind being alone, with no one but herself to worry about. Her first attempt at independence had ended in failure. She married right out of high school, partly to escape her parents but mostly because she was pregnant. Four months into the marriage, she miscarried. A week later she left the man and had their union annulled.

Milli erased the whole sordid mess from her mind, poof and gone. She neither mourned the baby-seed nor the man. In fact, it was such a catalyst to freedom to be untethered from her mother and father and from an unwanted child and an abusive husband. For a while, she floated in a haze of free-love, bouncing from one light-hearted relationship to another, never tied to a person or a place. But that kind of recklessness backfired when she landed in her parents' house at thirty-one after a near-fatal car accident. By the time she was on her feet again and yearning for independence, her parents' health had spiraled. She stayed in their home as caretaker until they passed.

After Leo died she was alone again, but soon her sister's cancer compelled her to sleep at Linda Mae's until she, too, passed. In the Downtown Crossing basement apartment, aides and cleaning people tramped in and out. There was always someone to answer to, someone who demanded her presence. But the apartment on Porter Street was all hers with absolutely no one telling her what to do or when to do it.

With her time her own, Milli left the restaurant and paused at the bench along the boardwalk. Two bouncy women saw her from a distance and waved frantically.

"I can't believe it's you!" cried a young woman whose head was shaved on one side and streaked black on the other.

Milli recognized her from the Seaside Arboretum, the one whose boyfriend texted in secret.

"We sent up a Milli prayer for us to find you," said Keysi.

The woman with her was the exhausted mom Milli met while sitting on the bench and whose baby captured Milli's heart.

"We were in line in the coffee shop and got to talking about this amazing old woman, sorry to say that, who gave us great advice," said Rashida, whose baby was nowhere in sight.

"Don't apologize for calling me old. I'll be eighty-five in a few weeks and I'm proud of it."

The girls high-fived Milli and crowded around her. "We have a favor to ask," said Keysi, nodding to Rashida.

"Ask away," said Milli. "The worst that can happen is I say no siree Bob."

"Oh, Milli, you're so cute," said Rashida.

"I have a friend who has a problem. Rashida and I convinced her to talk with you because you really listen. We think you can help her too. Would you be all right with that?" bubbled Keysi.

"Tell you what. Walk me back to my place. She can meet us there."

The women took Milli by each arm and caught her up with their lives. Rashida had time to herself today because her neighbor, "bless her soul," offered to watch the baby and she didn't need to pick up her other kids until three. Keysi had a heart-to-heart last night with her boyfriend and they were figuring out their boundaries. When the trio got to Porter Street, Milli set out power bars and glasses of water on the patio. She felt bad that she had little else to offer, but the girls didn't mind. When their friend Bianca arrived, she and Milli went into the apartment to talk privately.

Milli studied the frail girl whose pores oozed fear, streaming down her face, puddling in her neck. Milli worried about this child. "What's the matter, Bianca? Talk to me."

"It's my father," she said in a tiny voice.

Milli hadn't expected that. She thought boyfriend-ooze or hus-band-slime. But father?

"He relies on me, every second of every day. I have my own life, but I feel I have to call him daily or stop by his place, and encourage him to keep going."

"And if you don't, what will happen?"

"He'll kill himself and it'll be my fault."

Milli's stomach somersaulted, remembering her own father's threats, how he said he'd hunt her down and kill her if she left him and Milli's mother in the lurch. "What makes you the one who has this responsibility?"

"Everyone else has abandoned him. It's all on me."

Milli wanted to take a towel and sop up her fear, but she knew it was internal.

"Listen, Sweet Girl. Your father needs more than you can provide. You know that, right?" *I wish someone had said that to me when I was under Buster's thumb.*

"Then what do I do? How do I make him stop leaning on me?"

"Have you reached out to social services?"

"He won't allow anyone else into his home. Just me."

"That's very unreasonable of him."

"Unreasonable isn't the word I'd use. Selfish, mean, territorial, childish, and drunk."

"Ah, drunk. I thought so," said Milli thinking about her own self-ish, mean, territorial, childish drunk father. "So how can you deal with an abusive mean cruel father who won't give you a moment's peace?"

"Yes, yes. How do I do that?"

"Have you tried just not paying attention to him? Not calling? Cutting all communication?"

"Then he stalks me. Follows me around. Gets in his car and comes to me and won't let me be."

"Hmmm. You have a bigger problem than you can solve by yourself."

"Tell me about it."

Milli wanted to stop the ooze from spilling around the woman's body, gluing her into the ground. "People are paid by the state to protect you, to provide you with some safety from this self-serving man." Milli had learned about these avenues way too late.

"I've tried them," said the girl.

"And. . ."

"He points his cane at them like a sword and says he'll take them to court if they don't stop harassing him. They don't stay to argue."

"So there's no helping him?" said Milli.

"Right," sighed Bianca.

"So don't."

"What do you mean?"

"Leave him. Walk away. Not forever, but for a little while. Say to him, 'Father, I need to get away from you for a few weeks. I've booked a trip to Timbuktu or some nether region. I will be incommunicado. Totally. You will not be able to reach me. I will be gone. I will not have my phone. I will not have any way for you to communicate with me.'"

"I can't do that."

"Why not?"

"Because he needs me," sobbed the woman.

"Does he?"

"I'm his only link. He'll die without me."

"Would that be so terrible?"

"I'd be the cause."

"I repeat," said Milli, "would that be so terrible?"

The woman's ooze let up a bit, and some buttery yellow appeared. "So you're saying that if I sever all ties for a specific period of time, he might die and that wouldn't be so bad?"

"What do you think?"

"I think I'd be responsible for his death."

"No, you wouldn't. Besides, if he's as stubborn as you say, he'll wait until you return and the pattern will start all over again."

"So leaving him alone will be for nothing. He'll be twice as bad when I get back." Bianca sank into a heap.

"So you check in on him. Then you go away again."

"You're saying he'll either live or die, but it won't be my fault?"

"Yes. It's all on him."

Bianca stood up and moved one sticky foot. Then another. *Maybe there was hope*, thought Milli. *Maybe?*

Milli and Bianca emerged from the house to join Keysi and Rashida.

"I told you she was wise," said Rashida as she turned to Milli. "You're our talisman."

"Ladies, you know in your hearts how to answer your own questions. Trust in that inner voice. Believe me, I have no magic powers."

"But Milli, you listen, and that's worth so much," said Keysi.

Milli recalled the book *The Talisman* by Stephen King and Peter Straub, how Jack Sawyer held a crystal ball in his hands and knew not only the future, but the present, the past, and all the atoms of forever simultaneously. A power coursed through Jack and he saw all and experienced all. Milli didn't want to be a talisman; in fact, she shuddered with the thought of being omniscient for these young women. Sure she could listen, but who was she to know what was best for them? She could never control her own father. And look what happened when she trusted Bernard. They were wrong to regard her as a vessel of truth. Time discovered truth. That was her only power. She was old. She had lived through elation and depression, loneliness and friendship, scarlet heat and white-knuckle cold. These youngsters believed in her because she exuded age and wisdom. *Bull-shit. Just plain bull-shit.*

The young women hugged Milli. "Can we treat you to lunch?" asked Rashida.

"I never refuse food," said Milli.

"How about Mario's Trattoria on the corner of L Street," said Keysi.

"Will we have to walk from here?" asked Milli.

Keysi answered, "Nope, I have a car."

"Bianca and I will meet you there," said Rashida.

Chapter Ten

Sitting in the restaurant, Milli couldn't believe she was with three young chatty women. She devoured four slices of pizza topped with pineapple, something she had never eaten before and made her feel like she was on holiday in Hawaii. Sated and wistful, she suggested a pastime that she, Leo, and Lionel used to play when they finished their meals but didn't want to leave.

"Do you like to make up stories?" asked Milli.

The three women shrugged.

"How about I say the first line to a story. Then we go around the table, each adding another sentence until the story comes to its natural conclusion."

"I'm in," said Bianca.

Rashida and Keysi agreed.

"Okay. Here goes," said Milli.

Milli: Once upon a time, there was an old woman who settled in a seaside town without knowing anyone, so she was very lonely.

Rashida: Then one day she met three lively ladies who took her out for lunch.

Keysi (squealing): When the meals arrived, each lady screamed with surprise.

Bianca (eyes popping): A live fish flopped around on one of the plates.

Milli (hesitating): On the next plate was something so bizarre that the waiter could hardly set it down without it shaking.

Rashida (with surprise): A miniature frog was hopping around on it.

Keysi (moaning): The third lady was stunned into silence when her plate was put in front of her.

Bianca (emphasizing each word): Because there was a turtle lumbering on her plate, its head shyly peeping out.

It was Milli's turn to further the story along. *Would the fish, the frog and the turtle jump into the center of the table and dance together? Maybe they should sing?* But when Milli imagined the waiter coming toward the table with the fourth plate, all she saw was the woman's lonely heart.

Milli (frowning): When the old woman received her meal there was nothing on the plate, nothing at all.

Rashida (rubbing her eyes): The old woman broke down and sobbed.

Keysi (crying): I have no one. I am so alone.

Bianca (opening her arms to embrace the table): We'll be happy to share what's on our plates.

Milli (glowing, thinking that her Lionel would have used the same story line): You're all too kind.

Rashida (standing, pretending to fill a large canvas sack): The four ladies left the restaurant carrying the fish, the frog, and the turtle in the old woman's handbag.

Keysi (raising the imaginary bag with reverence): They carried the bag to the pond behind the house where the woman lived.

Bianca (removing each treasure one by one): Gently, they released the fish, the frog, and the turtle into the pond.

Milli (shielding her eyes and looking into the distance): Every morning, the old woman looked out her window.

Rashida (batting her eyes): Every morning, the fish jumped out of the water and winked at her.

Keysi (gribbeting): And the frog croaked its greeting at sunrise.

Bianca (extending her neck): And the turtle basked on a log and poked its head in and out of its shell.

Milli (smiling): And the old woman was no longer lonely.

Rashida (beaming): When the three lively ladies visited her and sat together by the edge of the pond, they had a common experience to relive.

Keysi (nodding): The moral to the story: Sharing is what life is all about.

Bianca (standing): So when we experience something that seems all wrong, and we use it to better ourselves, everything turns out all right.

Milli (bowing): The end.

The four women laughed. Milli felt such love from these girls, so new to her life, but so familiar. It was as if Leo and Lionel were sitting on each of her shoulders playing along. *If only life were that simple.*

"I'd like to stay longer," said Rashida, "but I have to get dinner ready, pick up the kids, and put on my sexy for my hubby. It's date night. Let's do this again. Soon!"

Milli saw delight in Rashida's eyes, not the heavy weight that had sagged her down. Something had changed, for the good. Milli wanted to pat herself on the back, but she knew that life threw curves and just because one day went well, it didn't mean that all would follow in the same path.

They waved good bye to Bianca and Rashida as they fastened their seat belts. "I need to stop and do a quick errand. Do you mind waiting? I'll turn on the radio for you," said Keysi.

Milli listened to a rock station, but it jangled her nerves. She switched channels. About a minute into the broadcast, she sat up so straight, her shoulders snapped.

"Millicent Tarnover, age eighty-five, was last seen on Tuesday entering her dentist's office in Oldham," reported the broadcaster.

Milli's face turned scarlet as she leaned into the radio.

"It's presumed that Tarnover became confused when she exited the building and began to wander the neighborhood. Mrs. Tarnover is five feet tall, one hundred pounds, with short gray hair and glasses. She has trouble walking and is easily confused. The director at New Dawn Retirement Village in Monmouth where Tarnover lives, says Millicent keeps to herself and rarely socializes with others. It's been two days and there has been no trace of her. Call Oldham police if you believe you have seen this woman. She may not respond to her own name."

So that's how the world sees me? A doddering disoriented loner with no memory. Bull-feathers! I absolutely have concern for others? Don't I? Is Ms. Fagan responsible for that description? The last time I spoke with the woman, I was fogged up on green pills. Maybe I was distant. Maybe I didn't care about making new friends. Maybe I was just angry at being thrown into the Downtown Dungeon. But that was before I came up with my plan to visit the Arboretum, to make my dream come true.

After hearing the news report, Milli realized that New Dawn was concerned for her safety. *Maybe I should call them? Maybe I should write a letter? Maybe I should tell Keysi my story and have her drive me back to New Dawn to explain.*

As Keysi walked toward the car, Milli panicked and switched radio stations. "How do you listen to that head-banging business? Doesn't it rattle your brain?"

"Believe it or not, I find it soothing. Give it a chance. You might enjoy it. The music gets me away from the everyday drudge and puts me in a foreign place."

Talk about foreign places. I've been away from New Dawn for two full days and look at me. I'm well-fed, clean, and the new best friend of three lovely girls. Look how we sat around together and came up with a story of hope. That last line said it all. Take what seems all wrong and make it right. Isn't that what I'm doing? Getting myself out of a bad situation and creating a new life for myself? I'm setting myself straight. That can't be wrong. New Dawn might be concerned about my safety, but I'm more concerned about my mental state of health.

Milli wondered if her photo was going to be blasted over the television and in the newspaper. Even though she gave Grenadine a false name, these girls knew her as Milli. She tried to recall if she told anyone her surname. There must be more than one elderly Milli in the Oldham area.

Even so, it was time for a make-over. "Would you drop me off at the pharmacy near the corner of Porter Street?"

She went into the store and studied the cosmetics aisle. First she considered hair color. *Dark brown? Too depressing. Pink? Too punk. How about chestnut?* When she caught sight of a temporary hair color spray, she grabbed the one called Fiery Cougar-Red. Then she bought mousse, make-up and jeweled sunglasses. At the Goodwill store next door, she bought capris, a pair of jeans, a few lightweight colorful tops, undergarments, and white sandals.

Returning to her apartment, she read the directions for the hair coloring. "Shake well. Hold twelve inches from your head and spray." An hour later, Milli's gray hair spiked with bright red highlights and her eyebrows were penciled in like asterisks. She had a bounce to her step and a lipstick smile.

Chapter Eleven

Milli was all dolled up with nowhere to go. She tried to decide on her next move. She liked her small apartment on the edge of the ocean. She didn't mind the steady stream of visitors to Madame Seer who clomped up and down the three flights of stairs on the side of the building. She didn't mind the rattle in the pipes or the constant drip-drip of water from the florist shop above her. And she loved the knowledge that upon waking, the day was hers. No claustrophobic tiny room, no nurses or aides coming and going, and no green Jello.

She emerged from her apartment and sat on one of the two rickety chairs on the patio. *If only I had one of those cushy garden benches to stretch out on, then I'd really be living the life.*

But her daydream ended when the landlady, Grenadine, entered the patio area, approached Milli's door, and knocked loudly. No one answered, of course.

Grenadine swung around to see Milli on the edge of her seat. "Tell me, do you know the old lady who's staying here? Have you seen her today?"

"Funny thing about that. Minnie called me this morning and said I should come by and see her new place. But when I got here the door was locked. I thought I'd kick back and wait."Grenadine looked hard at Milli's face. "How well do you know her?"

"We're old friends."

Grenadine leaned in close. To Milli, she smelled like burnt onions.

"Her name's Millicent Tarnover, isn't it?" Grenadine growled.

Milli kept her gaze steady. That woman had heard the news bulletin. "My friend's name is Minnie Yanover. We've been best friends like forever, even before she married Charlie. Who's this Millicent you're looking for?"

"I swear she said her name was Milli Tarnover."

"Maybe you're not hearing too well. My friend's name is Minnie Yanover, not Milli Tarnover. But I see how they sound alike." Milli looked Grenadine in the eye.

Grenadine's lips slid to the side. "Well, if you say so. When she shows up, can you give her a message?"

"Sure thing."

"I've got a tenant who's decided to rent the place for a year, starting on June first. Minnie Yanover has got to vamoose. Let her know, will ya?"

"But Minnie told me she wanted to stay through the summer. So that's not possible?"

"Nope. A bird in the hand is worth two in the bush. Ya know. Unless she wants to give me a full year's rent."

"I can check with her or maybe she can call you?"

Grenadine studied Milli more closely. "What did you say your name was?"

Milli thought fast. "Ruby Tuesday."

"Well, Ruby, tell Minnie Yanover she'd better let me know within five days. Fourteen thousand up front if she wants me to turn down the other offer. She has my phone number."

"I'll be sure to tell her."

Well, if it isn't one thing, it's another. I have one more week of freedom and then it's back to New Dawn unless I find a new place.

Milli was in a pickle. She eased herself back into the chair suddenly aware of her age and her health and felt the weight of her eviction from her high rise happening all over again.

Late last fall, Milli's house phone rang. It never rang, especially at eight in the morning.

"Millicent Tarnover?" asked a quiet voice.

"Yes, may I help you?" Milli asked, bewildered by the early time.

"This is Alexis Fagan, the social worker at the New Dawn Retirement Village. You and I have met several times over the years to talk about your personal needs."

"Yes, I remember you," said Milli, sweat beading her upper lip, familiar with the sound of sadness.

"I'm sorry to tell you this, but your nephew Bernard Monk died suddenly during the night. An emergency phone number for New Dawn was posted on his refrigerator so the hospital contacted my office."

Milli's lips tightened. She shook her head no no no. "How could that be? He was only forty-eight. Was he in a car accident? Was it a heart attack?"

Ms. Fagan swallowed audibly and her voice softened. "As next of kin, you will receive a call from the coroner's office explaining the circumstances, but I wanted to give you prior warning. I know how much he cared about you and how much you depended on him." The woman took a deep breath. "Bernard died from an overdose of opioids."

"That's impossible!" wailed Milli. "Bernard didn't take drugs." *Did he pocket my pills when he refilled my organizer? Were they enough to kill him? Am I to blame?* Milli's eyes rolled back, and her skin grew clammy. She dropped the phone.

"Mrs. Tarnover? Are you there? Are you all right?"

Within minutes, Ms. Fagan entered Milli's apartment with a master key. Milli was semi-conscious on the floor. "Help me," she whimpered as Ms. Fagan called the EMTs.

Milli's pulse was so irregular and her blood pressure so high that it took two days in the hospital for her to regulate. She tried asking questions about Bernard, but the doctors said there was plenty of time for answers. Dr. Boothbury prescribed a sedative three times a day and bedrest. She returned to her New Dawn apartment sad, exhausted, and bewildered.

A handwritten note was tucked under the door with New Dawn's logo.

> *My Dear Mrs. Tarnover,*
>
> *We at New Dawn Retirement Village are so very sorry for your loss. Please accept our sincere condolences on the untimely passing of your beloved nephew Bernard Monk.*
>
> *Per your wishes, his body has been cremated and his ashes will be buried in your family plot.*
>
> *Please contact our office as soon as you are able. We need to plan your future now that your source of income has changed.*
>
> *Sincerely,*
> *Alexis Fagan, MSW*

Milli was too tired to cry. She just lay in her bed and tried not to think about the note from Ms. Fagan. But one line kept inserting itself into her consciousness. Your source of income has changed. *My source of income has changed? How could that be?*

A week passed and Milli still wasn't ready to talk with Ms. Fagan. But a knock came at the door one morning and there stood the woman in her black business suit, her hair swept back, her eyeliner perfect, and her face pasted on.

"Good morning, Millicent. I hope I'm not bothering you too soon. Again, we're so sorry for your loss. Bernard was a. . . a fine young man."

"Thank you," said Milli, hoping that was the only reason the woman had her foot in the door.

Ms. Fagan leaned in. "We need to talk. Is now a good time?"

Milli shook her head, but Ms. Fagan ignored the motion, slipped into the apartment and set her briefcase on the counter.

"Here's the thing," Ms. Fagan said, her lips pursed into little puckers as if she had bitten into sour fruit. She removed a folder and showed Milli a spreadsheet with columns of numbers. "Your balance will not cover another month's fees in the luxury apartments."

Milli's eyes widened. "How is that possible? Bernard made solid investments. He assured me that all was in order and I would never have to worry."

"Yes, well, my Dear, it seems he had a money-flow problem and used your funds to get him through a difficult period." Ms. Fagan's manicured fingernails tapped a series of red circles on the paper. "He let the last few months' fees lapse."

Milli was confused. Bernard had sold her home eight years ago for a substantial sum so she could move to New Dawn. She signed her assets over to him and gave him power of attorney. Bernard was a certified public accountant who knew what he was doing. *Didn't he? There must be some terrible mistake.*

Milli made her way to her recliner. Shaking two green pills out of a bottle, she swallowed them and closed her eyes until her mind stopped spinning and she could sink into the pillowy cushions. She watched through lidded eyes as Ms. Fagan walked through her apartment, nosing into corners.

"I regret to say this," said Ms. Fagan, standing before the picture window, "but your nephew's poor judgment has harmed you in ways he never anticipated."

The words filtered to Milli from a distance. She was vaguely aware that when Bernard visited, he'd mete out her pills and pop a few for himself. Pop. Pop. Pop. Like Rice Krispies. Why hadn't she confronted him? Because he always seemed in control.

But it was all a lie. Maybe he figured that in her old age, Milli wouldn't be around much longer and he could spend her money for his own needs. *But all of it?* She recalled that Bernard abused substances when he was younger, but he swore he had kicked his habit. Why had she trusted her sister's son? Because she had little up-to-date knowledge of finance, and more to the point, she had no one else.

"Isn't there another relative who can help you, my Dear?" asked Ms. Fagan, who was opening random cabinets and closets.

Milli felt weights fall around her—her husband Leo, her son Lionel, her sister Linda Mae, may they all rest in peace. Milli shook her head, dizzying her and leaving her head fuzzy. "I have no one."

Ms. Fagan turned to stare at the older woman, then packed up her briefcase. "You're exhausted, Milli. I'll be back tomorrow and together we'll figure out what to do next. OK?"

Milli didn't have the energy to reply.

At ten AM the next morning, Ms. Fagan arrived with bank statements and files from the controller's office that contained information about Bernard Monk and Millicent Tarnover, as well as an application for federal funding through Medicaid.

"I have Medicare," said Milli, "and I get a monthly social security check. Isn't that enough for me to live here?"

"Ordinarily it would be, but I'm sorry to say that your nephew used up all your saved funds. Your monthly rate in this lovely high rise far exceeds your income." She laid official papers on the table, put on her black rimmed glasses, and took out a gold pen. "Let me explain what will happen. Medicare still takes care of many of your needs but as you age, you'll need more care. We believe in the system here and have your best interests at heart. You have to trust us that we're making the smartest choices for your long-term health."

Milli swallowed hard. "And what about my social security check?"

"Oh, that'll go directly to New Dawn. That's the way it's done, Dear."

"So I can't live here anymore?"

"Of course you can. Just not in the high rise. The monthly fees are way too expensive. We have other accommodations that you can easily afford. In fact, I've arranged a private room in Downtown Crossing, the assisted-living wing of New Dawn," said Ms. Fagan, patting Milli's arm. "The space is perfect. It has a bed with a brand-new mattress, a chifforobe, a nightstand, a desk and a chair. We'll help you pack your clothes and keepsakes and you'll be in your new place by the end of the week. Now doesn't that sound lovely, Dear."

No. No. No, thought Milli. Her stomach threatened to erupt. "But what about my pots and pans and baking tins and bookcases for my jigsaw puzzles and novels?"

"Oh you can donate them to our kitchen and to our library."

"And get a chance to visit them?" Milli snarked.

"Now, Milli, we pride ourselves on all your needs being met. Three meals a day, commons time, concerts, card games, bingo, sing-a-longs. You'll meet lots of wonderful people. Give it a chance, Dear. You'll see."

Milli thought about the money she had hidden throughout her home—wads of bills she accumulated over the years and tucked away for a rainy day. *My secret stash. But it'll never be enough to live on. I'm doomed.*

"I guess I have no other choice," said Milli, her hand shaky as she signed her name to the documents.

Ms. Fagan gathered the papers, smiled widely, and left. After swallowing several green pills, Milli collapsed into her recliner.

Chapter Twelve

Milli had a choice now, she realized. Life was worth living as long as she was in control. To return to the assisted living unit having tasted independence would be self-defeating. Not to return would mean scraping by from year to year with meager funds. On the other hand, New Dawn wasn't a death sentence and there was security and long-range peace of mind.

Milli's late friend Anne Marie sat on her shoulder and poked her in the neck. "Dumb, dumb, dumb moves, Millicent. Turn yourself in! Agree with the newspaper. Tell New Dawn you were confused and disoriented."

Milli balked at the advice. She wasn't in the high rise anymore and never would be again. Downtown Crossing took away her independence and declared her brain-impaired. And what about her new look—a fun hairdo, some foundation, blush and lipstick; chic second-hand clothes; a sun-protecting hat and Jackie O sunglasses. How many residents could boast that accomplishment?

As Milli mulled over her predicament, she watched a variety of people climb the outside staircase to knock on Madame Seer's door. A well-dressed man with a handlebar mustache looked at his watch before approaching the stairs. "Half an hour early. Do you mind if sit here as I wait?"

"Be my guest," said Milli.

"Do you have a session with Madame Sheeya too?" he asked.

At first Milli thought the man had a speech impediment, but he used the woman's name a few times in idle chatter and concluded that her upstairs neighbor was not Madame Seer, but Madame Sheeya. That Grenadine was all wrong when it came to names, giggled Milli.

"What's so funny?" asked the man.

"I was thinking about changing my name," she said.

"Why would you do that?"

"Well, it doesn't fit me anymore. I'm changing, so my name should change too," said Milli.

The man swung his feet back and forth like a child. "When I was a boy, I was called Bobby. During my teens, I was Robbie. For a while, I was Bob, but now I'm Robert. I see what you mean."

"What if your purpose for living shifted? Should your name change too?" asked Milli.

"It's funny that you mention that. I've just opened a shop on the boulevard and I'm calling it Mr. Robert's. It's a men's clothing store. You know, fitness stuff and casual wear. The name sounds responsible and sophisticated. Don't you think?"

"Sounds like a great idea."

"It would be except every time I go into the store to get the place ready to open, I hear voices. And not just happy tunes, but ear-piercing screams and scratching in the walls."

"Maybe there are mice?"

"Screaming mice? I don't think so."

"Is that why you're seeing Madame Sheeya?"

"You betcha," said the man. "She's been working with me to get rid of the ghosts."

"Is it helping?"

"So far, the noises have diminished."

"Is this the only place where you hear strange noises?" asked Milli.

Robert tweaked the tips of his mustache. "Come to think of it, I used to hear sounds in my basement when I was a kid. And under my bed too."

Milli wondered if this man had some unnatural fears and they emanated in weird noises—or worse, a real illness that caused him to hear voices. If the latter were true, Madame Sheeya was not able to help him. No way, no how.

"Do you worry about the success of your new business venture?" asked Milli.

"What a question! Of course I do. I have sunk so much money into merchandise, I can't tell you."

You just did, thought Milli. She studied the man, his short-cropped hair, his meticulous mustache, his polished shoes and starched white shirt. He paid close attention to detail. Milli decided he was overly anxious about his business and needed every aspect to be on point. She was about to offer him advice, knowing owning a store was not for the faint-hearted, but he checked his watch and rose quickly.

"Time to find a solution," he said, hopping up the stairs and entering Madame Sheeya's apartment lickety-split.

"Good luck," said Milli. *That woman must have superpowers.*

Milli lingered in the faux garden, thinking about the imaginative story she and her new young friends had created. She visualized the frog, the fish, and the turtle piping up greetings just for her and she felt surrounded by possibility. After what seemed like minutes, she heard Robert flying down the stairs from his session with Madame Sheeya. "Did you find a cure for your interlopers?"

"I am so confident those ghosts are busted," laughed Robert. He practically jumped around the patio with the news.

She couldn't imagine what Madame Sheeya did to make this man so jubilant. Maybe she was in the pill trade? Maybe she hypnotized him? Milli had only heard the woman's heavy footsteps on the stairs. Maybe she did more for the man than offer advice?

A couple visited Madame Sheeya next. He looked sixtyish and

the woman looked half his age. They were canoodling as they came
through the gate and approached the stairs. They didn't notice Milli.

"What do you think she'll have for us today?" asked the woman.

"I hope it's another love charm," the man chortled.

"Another week like this one and you'll be the death of me!" she
laughed.

"And you thought I didn't have it in me," the man said as they took
the steps two at a time.

That Madame Sheeya was a seer for all seasons: ghosts, love
potions, predictions. Milli wondered if she should seek out her advice
too. But she was way too tired to climb those stairs and she certainly
wasn't going to make an appointment.

When the couple descended an hour later, they glowed. It was as
if a sunbeam followed them and they basked in its light. Milli needed
a dose of that. She reconsidered making an appointment when a thir-
ty-something woman whisked by them, leaving a trail of darkness. A
young boy trudged behind her pushing a baby carriage.

"Listen, Kiddo, you sit in that chair over there and watch your sister until I come for you. Understand?" The woman's voice was sharp,
like the tip of a pencil. Each word seemed to jab at the boy.

"Can't you take her with you?" he whined.

"She's asleep," she said. "Now do as I say."

The mother fled up the stairs as the boy settled into the chair beside
Milli and shuffled his feet. "Hurry, hurry, hurry. She's always in such a
damn hurry." The boy leaned close to Milli and snarled. "My daddy says
that the devil is always in a rush. Are you the devil? My daddy says the
devil is in every woman. If you're old, are you still a woman? I've seen
old ladies with beards. Do you shave?"

Milli stared at the pint-sized toughy. "Why is your mother always
in a hurry?"

"Don't matter if she's the devil. She's going to burn herself up."

The boy stuck a finger up his nose and peeled out crust.

Milli would have been mortified if Lionel behaved like that. "Do your mother and father talk to you about manners?"

"Manners? My daddy says I'm a man. So I have manners. So there." The boy bit his fingernails and spit the pieces on the ground.

Milli's skin began a slow burn. "Okay, little unmannered man. Why is your mother visiting Madame Sheeya?"

"Madame Shitty is what my daddy calls her. Taking his hard-earned money for voodoo. That's a funny word," the boy snicked. "Voodoo. My daddy says voodoo is doodoo and that's why he calls her Madame Shitty." He stood up and paced around Milli's chair. "How old are you anyway? Two hundred?"

"What's the life span of a normal human?" asked Milli.

The boy's lips turned down. "Well, my daddy says people live too long, especially the mean ones. He says anyone over fifty should eat shit and die. And anyone who works for the government should get a bullet through the head and he'd like to be the one to do it."

How dangerous was this father, she wondered. "Do you have guns in your house?"

The boy reached out his fingers and counted. "One in the kitchen. One in the bathroom. One under daddy's pillow and in his sock and in his belt loop. Yeah. I guess so."

"What about your mother? Does she have guns too?"

"My daddy says she's too stupid to carry a gun. She'd shoot her head off."

"And what about you?"

"He says I can learn to shoot when I'm ten."

"And how old are you now?"

"Nine and a half."

Milli was surprised. His size said younger, even if his mouth said older. What could she say to this child? He was so indoctrinated into his father's world. "Where is your dad now?"

The boy raised his head high. "He got shot and now he's in jail."

"Who shot him?"

"The fucking pigs."

"Do you mean the police?"

The boy nodded.

Milli felt bad for this neglected child. Somehow she wanted to help him but had no idea how. *People should not bring life into this world when they're unfit to be parents. That boy and his baby sister have no chance. Ever.* Milli reached into her large purse and took out a bag of Twizzlers she had bought at the coffee shop. She handed a few to the boy.

He took the candy and peered over her to look into her purse. "What else ya got?"

It was time someone set the kid straight. "Not a darn thing for an ungrateful boy, but I've got lots for a courteous young man."

The boy bit off pieces of the licorice. "Thank you, Ma'am."

As he chomped, Milli studied him. His sneakers were too big. His shorts too long. His shirt too small. His hair too ratty. His eyes too filmy and his nose too snotty. What could she offer him to ease his plight? Was he doomed to a life dictated by his father's ill-conceived ideas? And why should she care?

"How old is your sister?"

"Two."

"What's her name?"

"What's it to you?"

Milli bent over the carriage, noticing the baby's eyes fluttering. She hoped the little one would stay asleep. "It's easier to speak with others when I know their name."

"She don't speak."

"Then what's your name?" asked Milli.

"Apollo. It's a dumb-ass name, don't ya think?" said the boy.

"Did you know that Apollo was the protector of the young? He was a mythical god who presided over children's health and education. You have a responsibility to be a responsible young man. Your name demands it."

"How do you know that?" asked the boy.

"I read it in a book," said Milli.

"My Daddy says the Bible is the only book worth reading."

"The Bible is an excellent source of information. Have you read any of it?"

The boy spat on the ground. "Reading's overrated. My Daddy said so."

The mom descended the stairs scowling and swearing under her breath. "Stupid woman. Come on, Brat. Time to get the hell out of here."

"Did Madame Shitty give you what you came for?" the boy asked.

The woman faced her son. "That bitch is a scam, just like the rest of the world. The sooner you learn not to trust anybody the better. If you want something, you have to help yourself."

The woman turned her back to Milli and reached into her pocket. Milli could see the wad of money in her hand. "No one's going to cheat me and get away with it," she laughed.

The boy high-fived her. To Milli, the pair bonded with bad blood. Apollo was a name with potential he would never fulfill.

Milli was over her head. There was nothing she could do to help this mother, her son, or the innocent infant. She could offer no advice that would improve their lot. She wondered why in the world the woman had seen Madame Sheeya and why she had stolen the money. It was none of her business, she decided. She didn't want the kid's Daddy threatening her with his guns.

Milli watched them leave and sat back in the splintery chair. It had been a long day, filled with new faces, new stories, and the alarming news story that New Dawn was searching for her. If she were at the retirement community about now, she'd be playing solitaire and waiting for the dinner chime. Instead, she was all dolled up—with red highlights in her hair, pink cheeks, bright lipstick—and wearing a cute outfit that was youthful and carefree.

Walking along the avenue that morning, she had seen a sign for happy hour at the D-Note, a nightclub on the boulevard featuring live music. She recalled what the Irish sergeant Aideen had said about music, how it was good for the soul. Milli stood up and did a little foot-stompin' jig. She spiked out her hair, gave herself a pep talk, and sang all the way to the club: *Hey Everybody, let's have some fun, You only live but once and when you're dead you're done. So let the good times roll.*

Chapter Thirteen

A black sign with a white skull flashed *Rock Band Boogaloo on stage tonight*. Rock Band? Heavy metal? She thought the place was a jazz club? Adjust, Milli told herself, go with the flow. She sang the last lines to Ray Charles' lyrics: *Get yourself under control and let the good times roll.*

She peeked inside. The room was deep and dark with tables arranged around a dance floor. At a rustic barn wood bar, two men angled toward each other, a couple cuddled, and a woman drank alone. Milli summoned her mojo, entered and hoisted herself onto a high stool.

"What'll it be, Young Lady," said the bartender.

"I'll have a . . . a coke with rum."

"Coke and rum coming right up."

The woman sitting by herself glanced at Milli. "Rum and coke. It's a rum and coke, for pity's sake."

"Does it matter?" asked Milli, admiring the woman's leather jacket, its tassel fringe reminding her of Roy Rogers and Dale Evans.

The woman shrugged. "That's a good question. Is the coke first and then the rum is added, or is the rum first and then the coke added?"

Milli shrugged. "Again I ask, does it matter?"

"I like routine," said the woman. "And I don't like surprises. They throw off my rhythm. A coke and rum just sounds wrong. It's not natural."

"Like if I said cheese and macaroni. Or jelly and peanut butter," said Milli.

"Or tomato, lettuce, and bacon. Or pepper and salt," said the woman.

A man at the bar piped up. "How about saucers and tea cups?"

The other man shouted Eve and Adam, and the bartender added arrow and bow.

Before Milli knew it, people throughout the bar bellowed backwards pairs: paste and cut, chips and fish, Hyde and Jekyll, Bess and Porgy.

The bartender set Milli's drink in front of her. "Coke and rum for the Lady Young."

"To Lady Young," everyone said and lifted a glass.

"To all and one," said the woman who started the whole shebang. And everyone downed their drinks, including Milli.

An hour passed in a minute and two hours passed in five. Music thrummed throughout the club and everyone tapped to the beat. Singers grabbed the microphone, guitarists strummed their tunes. The air, the floor, each strand of hair on Milli's head was alive. She used to think that headbangers were vile and vicious, all out to trip little old ladies or push them down the stairs. Any time there was a story on television about rock stars, it revolved around trashing hotel rooms and dumping people into swimming pools. The last thing she expected was all ages rocking out to hard core music. She liked it. But after sipping her second cocktail, compliments of her new bar friends, she felt her legs quiver. The room spun and her eyes blurred. "Nope, not going anywhere," she said.

The woman helped Milli to a corner booth and told her to stay put.

"I couldn't move if you paid me," said Milli.

When she and Leo had cocktails, it was usually in their home after Lionel was asleep. They'd play strip poker and tease each other as they undressed. Or they pretended to be strangers and seduced each other with made-up names and voices. Milli flashed back on Leo's twinkly eyes, daring her to tell him a bawdy story or wear a flimsy costume. Their alcohol wasn't the poison her father drank; it was fun and fantasy. When Leo first suggested rum to spice up their romancing, Milli resisted, imagining Leo red-faced and rough, but that never happened. He was a happy occasional drinker and she joined him in that capacity.

As Milli rested, the music pulsed through her like gentle ocean waves. Her body relaxed and she dozed.

"I told you she wasn't dead," said a man standing in front of Milli when she opened her eyes. "Hey, Norman, you owe me a drink," he yelled across the room.

A younger man leaned in close. Metal jangled from his nose and his tattoos vibrated. His face came into focus—it was the kid who had carried her to the beach. "Kedrix?"

"Milli? I barely recognized you with the new hairdo," said Kedrix, helping Milli to a sitting position.

"You know Lady Young?" yelled the bartender.

"Sure do. She's my spiritual adviser," said Kedrix.

A skinny man with a long, thin face made his way over to Milli. He wore cowboy boots and a belt buckle that looked way too heavy for his hips.

"Uncle Norm meet Milli."

"She the one who told you Phoebe might be my honey?" he asked.

"The one and only."

"The only and one," yelled the bartender.

The woman who helped Milli to the corner booth an hour ago laughed. "She started the backwards word game."

"To Milli," the patrons cheered.

Milli fluffed her hair and nodded. Her head still felt wobbly.

Uncle Norm and Kedrix took seats across from Milli in the booth. She wondered if he was going to call her a busybody who had no right telling Kedrix what she thought about his birthday present.

But the man held out his hand to her. "You taught this boy a life-lesson, and for that I'm mighty grateful. I thought I was doin' him a service. Ya know, introducing him to an older woman, giving him a taste of adult living. I never thought he'd fall in love."

Kedrix blushed.

"My nephew's forgiven my poor judgment."

"And I did what you said," Kedrix blurted. "Phoebe and I sat down and had a heart-to-heart. She told me she loved me like a brother. That hurt, but we agreed to be friends."

Milli still felt light-headed, but their sincerity seemed real and it clarified her thinking. She was reminded of a Will Rogers' saying. "Good judgment comes from experience, and experience comes from bad judgment." She had said the words aloud.

"See, I told you she was wise," said Kedrix.

"This tired old wise woman needs a helping hand. Might you escort me home?"

"Sure thing," Kedrix whispered. "I need some advice. Are you up for listening?"

When they were out of earshot of Uncle Norm, Kedrix broke into sobs. "I love her, Milli. I can't help it, but I don't want to appear weak and immature. How am I going to survive this?"

Milli reached way up to put her arm around Kedrix as his shoulders heaved. "To heal a heart requires time. For now, you're going to be sad. That's normal."

"I've never been normal!" he cried.

"What is it you loved about Phoebe?" Milli asked.

Kedrix looked down at Milli and their eyes met. "She... she ... she... I liked her laugh."

"That says a lot about you. To like someone's laugh means that you're sensitive and responsive to others."

Kedrix put his arm through Milli's and practically lifted her into the air. "There's something about you, Milli, that makes me feel stronger."

"Could it be your size?" laughed Milli.

"I'm serious. You listen to me. No one ever does. Not even Phoebe. She did all the talking when we met. I barely got a word in."

"Kedrix, please tell me again. What was it about Phoebe that attracted you to her? Was it the sex?"

Kedrix stopped walking and scratched his chest. "The word sex sounds so odd coming from a little old woman like you, even if you do have red hair now. But, Jeez, Phoebe had moves."

"Other women have moves."

"Are you coming on to me, Milli?"

Kedrix lifted her like a feather and gave her a hug.

"I'm trying to get you to say that it wasn't Phoebe you loved, but the idea of Phoebe, and please put me down. Brrrr, it's getting chilly out here. Glad we're almost to my place. It's on the next street."

"I'm sorry, Milli. I've barely paid any attention to you. That's another one of my downfalls. I think too much about myself. I'll tell you what. I'll come by tomorrow morning and take you for a walk along the beach. How does that sound?"

"I'd like that," said Milli. "We can talk some more about Phoebe and how to get past your broken heart."

"It's a deal," said Kedrix as he and Milli entered the patio to her apartment. "I know this is an odd question. I've never heard the name Milli before. Is it, like, old-fashioned or something?"

"My given name is Millicent. Now that's old fashioned. Lately I'm partial to Ruby Tuesday," said Milli, recalling what she told Grenadine. Might as well stick to it, at least for a while.

That night, after Milli got into bed, she thought about the last four days, how on Tuesday she had been a haggard gray-headed washed up old lady who only wanted to walk where Leo and Lionel had walked, to see them again in a setting that was alive and vibrant. And now, on Friday, she drank coke and rum in a bar filled with head-banging rockers, and was escorted to her own studio apartment by a metallic-faced tattooed man-boy who thought of her as his spiritual adviser. Move over Millicent Tarnover. Ruby Tuesday is taking your place.

Chapter Fourteen

Milli's legs cramped during the night. So much activity. So much walking. And those new sandals had no support. If Kedrix was taking her to the beach, he'd better carry her.

When a Harley revved down the street in the morning, she heard him before she saw him. Milli rushed out the door, worried that both Madame Sheeya and the florist on the first floor, whom she had yet to meet, were craning their necks to see what all the noise was about.

Kedrix hopped off his bike. "Hey, Ruby! Are you ready to rumble?"

"I thought you were taking me to the beach?"

Kedrix handed Milli a black leather jacket. "I'd like to take you to an inlet near Pemberton Channel that you'd like, but it's too far to walk. Let's go for a spin on my hog."

"What a sight! An old lady on a motorcycle." But Milli's heart thumped. She'd never been on a motorcycle. Ever. It was always a dream of hers, flying through the wind, free as the breeze. She had just zipped up the jacket and put on the Jackie O sunglasses when a van pulled beside them with the words New Dawn Retirement Village on its side panel. Two people got out, looked at a piece of paper and nodded to each other.

Milli did not recognize the man, but to Milli's horror, the woman was Alexis Fagan, the social worker. It was she who forced Milli into Downtown Crossing and didn't allow her any personal freedom. Sure, Milli was grateful that the woman undertook the Medicaid paperwork that allowed Milli to stay in New Dawn, but there was something too efficient about her. All business, Leo would have said. And Milli hated her condescending attitude, her constantly calling her Dear, and her slowed down speaking voice. She might as well have patted Milli on the head and said 'What a good girl you are!'

Ms. Fagan walked right by Milli and Kedrix and knocked on the apartment door. The man stayed in the street.

"What's going on?" asked Kedrix.

"We're looking for a woman named Millicent Tarnover." The man showed Kedrix the article from the local newspaper with a photo of Milli above the fold. "Have you seen her?"

"Did she do something wrong?" asked Kedrix, eyeing Milli.

Milli's heart beat so loud, she was sure the man could hear it.

"She's in terrible danger," he said.

Milli cleared her throat and gathered her courage. "What kind of danger?"

The man's shoulders hunched. "We're worried that she hasn't eaten properly or taken care of her personal hygiene. She wandered away from the New Dawn Village on Tuesday and hasn't been seen since. We received an anonymous tip that a woman answering that description was spotted in this area."

Milli was convinced that it was Grenadine who called.

"Mrs. Tarnover has not had her medication since Tuesday." The man warned. "That can be lethal for a woman of her age. It's imperative that we find her. Have you seen her?"

Was he making that up? Milli wondered. She had plenty of blood pressure meds with her and the only other pills she took were vitamins. No more little green pills since she decided she was in charge of her own fate. Who was this man who professed to know about her bogus medical needs?

Kedrix ignored the man's question and handed Milli the motor-cycle helmet. "Ruby, you're going to need this."

Milli strapped it on. "Sir, I remember seeing an old woman walking up and down the boulevard yesterday. She was swearing and babbling in a foreign language."

"Have you seen her since then?"

"Can't say I have," said Milli.

Ms. Fagan rejoined the trio on the street scowling like a winter sky. "No answer and the door is locked."

"I know the lady who lives there," said Milli, as she straddled the back seat of the motorcycle. "Her name is Minnie Yanover, not Millicent Tarnover. She's a good friend of mine."

"Are you sure?" asked Ms. Fagan.

Milli arched a painted eyebrow. "What do you take me for? An old demented lady? I've known Minnie Yanover my entire life and she's a force to reckon with, certainly not the woman in that photo."

"Are you ready to roll, Ruby?" asked Kedrix.

"As ready as I'll ever be." Addressing Ms. Fagan, Milli said, "I hope your Millicent is safe and sound. I'll let you know if we see anyone that fits the description of the woman you're after."

On the back of the motorcycle, Milli calmed down as they flew farther and farther away from New Dawn's grip. She had time to think as Kedrix rolled along Beach Avenue. The ocean crested to meet them at every gap in the dunes, roaring its hello as the waves broke. She gave thanks to the sea and to Kedrix for this day. What if he had given away her identity? He knew very well that she was the woman in the photo. It was he who hadn't recognized her in the bar because she had tinted her hair. But the photo was clearly the woman he crashed into on Wednesday morning.

She wasn't surprised that Ms. Fagan hadn't suspected she was Millicent Tarnover. The woman Ms. Fagan knew was worn out and robotic. After Anne Marie died, Milli began taking the pills that left her vacant-eyed. When Bernard passed away, Milli had relied on the pills to keep her from spiraling deeper into depression. Barely able to keep her mind functioning, she allowed the social worker to figure out her future. But Ruby Tuesday exuded energy, pizazz and a good dose of *chutzpah*. *Hah!* thought Milli. They'd be chasing their tails looking for her. Should she be gloating? What if she had lost her mind? What if she were still sleeping in the Arboretum and was prey to men like Comb Over and Hairy Ears? Wouldn't she want to be found? To be sheltered in a reliable home? To be fed three meals a day and entertained with mind-stretching games?

Milli thought about the words to the Rolling Stones' tune Ruby Tuesday: *She would never say where she came from. Yesterday don't matter if it's gone. While the sun is bright or in the darkest night, no one knows, she comes and goes. Goodbye, Ruby Tuesday, who could hang a name on you. When you change with every new day.*

How appropriate, she realized. What was done was done. Each day dawned anew with endless possibilities. She supposed Kedrix would ask her what was going on, but Milli wasn't sure how much of the truth she wanted to tell him.

Kedrix stopped the bike at a sheltered cove at the far end of a beach where the ocean met the bay. He helped Milli off the motorcycle and then reached into a side pannier and took out a blanket and a large paper sack.

Once off the bike, she had a tough time finding her legs, shaking them out and hopping from foot to foot. "Thanks, Kedrix," she stammered, handing him the jacket and helmet. "They fit really well."

"Yeah, I got a kid sister about your size," he laughed. "So Ruby Tuesday, I think you have a secret life. Let's break bread and talk." He cleared away some rocks and set down the blanket. "Somehow, I thought today would end up all about me. You know, Phebes and Uncle Norm. I never considered that you might have problems too. Somehow older people are supposed to have it together. You know what I mean?"

"Hog-wash, Kedrix. The longer we live, the more we don't know. That's a fact of life."

"So I'm going to be just as screwed up at fifty-one as I am at twenty-one?"

Ah, to be fifty-one again. A youngster! To have a second chance with Leo and Lionel. He was a late-in-life baby. When I was fifty-one, Lionel had one more year to live. And Leo had five more years. Oh if I only knew, I would never let them out of my sight. But beside her sat a large metal-faced man whose eyes sparkled and whose future lay in front of him.

"Fifty-one? Any guess as to my age?" she asked Kedrix.

"No hundred-year-old woman would get on a motorcycle. And no ninety-year-old would care about the color of her hair. If you were in your sixties, you might still be hitting on me. Ha! Ha! So I'm guessing seventy something."

"Eighty-four, for a few more weeks." Milli liked this fellow, a lot! "Why didn't you tell the people from New Dawn that I was the woman in the photo?"

"Because you aren't," said Kedrix. "The woman in the photo is old and used up. Ruby Tuesday or Milli or whatever you call yourself is vibrant, alive, eager for adventure. But I have to tell you. The name Ruby Tuesday isn't going to cut it for an alias." He brought out two small white bags. "Close your eyes." He placed them beneath her nose. "Which one do you want?"

Milli smelled sugary-cinnamon in one and peachy-orange in the other. "Can I have a piece of both?"

Kedrix pulled two more bags from the sack. "I thought you might say that." He handed Milli a large paper cup. "I figured two sugars and cream. Was I right?"

"Perfect," said Milli, as she sipped the coffee and nibbled the muffins.

"So spill," said Kedrix. "What's the deal with that creepy man and woman back at the apartment?"

Milli knew if she began a friendship with lies or half-truths, it could never flourish. She decided that Kedrix was an honorable man, a bit naive, but ultimately trustworthy. She might be wrong, but life was full of chance encounters and she decided to be honest with him. "I needed a day away from the monitored home where I lived, so I pretended to have a dentist's appointment. I enjoyed a day alone at the Seaside Arboretum communing with my late husband and son. What I hadn't figured on was overstaying my time and then pursuing my new-found freedom." Milli took a deep breath. "Now I don't want to go back."

"So don't. The place doesn't own you," said Kedrix.

"Ah, but in a way, it does." She didn't want to talk about Bernard and how she was forced to give her social security check to New Dawn each month and rely on Medicaid. She couldn't reveal the money she had hidden that would never be enough to live on if she had the chance. And she couldn't explain the magnetic pull New Dawn had on her because it was close to the cemetery where her family was buried. "I can't just turn into someone new, no matter how much I want to."

"So being Ruby Tuesday isn't the solution," said Kedrix, taking off his shirt, and lying back on the blanket to get some sun. Milli saw raw marks on his chest around the fringes of red tattooed letters: P-H-O-E-B-E. He looked at Milli and grimaced. "I told you I gave her my heart."

"Kedrix, have you heard the story of the Phoenix? It's a mythological bird who dies in a flame of glory only to rise again from its own ashes."

He scratched at his chest. "A Phoenix? Never heard of it."

Milli took off her socks and shoes and stretched out her toes. "Funny thing about the word. It's spelled P-H-O-E-N-I-X. A lot of the same letters as in Phoebe. It wouldn't be difficult to change the B to an N, the E to an I, and add an X."

"But I don't want to. I need her with me. She's mine."

"There will be other ladies in your life, I promise. Everyone has a first love. She just doesn't have to be etched on your chest forever."

"What about you? Who was your first love?"

"No fairytale story there. Met a man, thought he loved me, married him, and nearly lost my eye when he punched me for cutting his sandwiches the wrong way and leaving the crusts on."

"Seriously? What a shit. Did you kill him? Was that the beginning of your life of crime?"

"What makes you think I've led a life of crime?"

"Those people said you were dangerous."

"Is that really what you heard? Kedrix, it's time you learned to listen better."

He laughed. "And you have to lighten up if you can't tell when I'm ribbing you, Milli Tuesday." He laughed again, that high hee-haw that changed him from toughy into lightweight.

"I fell in love when I was a senior in high school. Brian McFerrity, the sexy custodian. Knocked me up in the cafeteria after the graduation party. I married the man, but I miscarried the baby."

"That sucks," said Kedrix.

"Not as much as remaining married to him would."

"So your first love shattered you like Phebes shattered me?"

"It took me fifteen years before I could trust a man again. But then I found the man of my dreams, Leo Tarnover."

"So once you met Leo, you were all better."

To Milli, Kedrix sounded so young, so short-sighted and untried. He'd have to find his own way, but maybe hearing her experience would ease his hurt about Phoebe. "Not quite. A lot happened in those in between years that took a long time to heal, including a head-on collision that left me hospitalized for months."

Kedrix's face blanched; his tattoos paled to gray. "My parents were in a head-on collision when I was a teenager. My sister and I were in the back seat. We made it out of the car without a scratch. But they weren't wearing seat belts and flew through the window smack into a tree. They landed on the ground side by side and died looking at each other. At least, that's what I like to believe."

Milli felt Kedrix shudder. She wanted to capture it, tuck it away, and shield him from the pain. That was the least she could do for him. He understood pain. No wonder he covered up his face and body in metal and tattoos. He hid to keep himself protected.

Kedrix stood abruptly. "Enough about our yesterdays. Let's get out of here and do something wild today."

"I think we have a different understanding of wild," said Milli.

"How about we get you a tattoo?" asked Kedrix.

Hmmm. A tattoo. Why not three? Leo the Lion across my back. Lionel on my heart. Teardrops on my face. What about lilacs on my right shoulder and daffodils on my left? I'd probably get hepatitis by the morning! "Can't I just get those kid stickers, wet them, and pretend I have a tattoo?"

"Okay, then. You think of something."

"Let's have our fortunes told," said Milli, curious about Madame Sheeya. "Maybe we'll both get the answers we're looking for."

"I don't believe in all that mumbo jumbo. Come up with something wild, Milli Tuesday. Something crazy!"

"I want to ride the roller coaster," she said.

"Now you're talking," said Kedrix. "Funland, here we come."

Funland had been the highlight of Lionel's summers. Every year, he looked forward to riding the roller coaster, but he was never tall enough. "Next year," Milli and Leo would tell him. But that last time they went, he stood under the line for height requirement and was a tad short. The tears spilled down his cheeks. "I'll never be tall enough," he pouted. How would Milli and Leo know that Lionel would never grow to have another summer.

Leo put his forehead against Lionel's. "How far off are you for height, my boy?"

Lionel stretched out his body and stood at the line again. Leo measured. "I'd say a shade under an inch. One more year, don't you think, Millicent?"

"There are plenty of other rides. The swings, the train, the caterpillar," said Milli.

"Those are sissy rides," said Lionel. "I'm thirteen and quite able to take care of myself on the roller coaster. What happens to adult little-people? Are they prohibited from going on?"

Milli recalled laughing at the maturity of the question.

"Maybe we can come up with a solution," said Leo. "I'll be right back."

The click-clack of the wooden coaster echoed throughout the park—the screams, the whoops, the whoosh of air as the cars descended the steep hills and clattered up new ones; the rush of kids racing back in line for another breath-stopping ride. Lionel and Milli waited for Leo. And waited. And waited. When he finally returned, Lionel's face lit up.

Leo carried a pair of cowboy boots with good-sized heels. In a bag, he removed a tube of hair gel. Between the two, Lionel exceeded the height and jumped for joy.

"Where did you get those?" asked Milli.

"Shoe store on Shore Avenue. A bargain for my boy."

The three of them rode that coaster five times, whooping and screaming and whooshing together, loving every thrill. Milli glowed thinking about it. And here she was, years and years later, standing beside a giant of a man reminiscing the long-ago treasured adventure.

The day had warmed up nicely as Milli and Kedrix entered the golden gates of Funland. No need for the heavy leather jacket. Just a natural Milli with her big bodyguard.

The park was compact with the coaster undulating around its circumference. From every angle, visitors could hear the frenzied screams as the cars descended and careened.

"Maybe this isn't such a good idea," said Milli.

"Suck it up," said Kedrix.

"I might barf it out," said Milli. But she tingled with excitement remembering Leo and Lionel and their time together on the wooden monster. "Okay. Let's do it."

When they reached the front of the line, Milli was afraid the ticket taker would deny her access because of her age. But he winked at her. "Never too old to have fun," he said as he secured the safety bar.

"And we're off," Kedrix said.

The click-clack began as they ascended the first towering hill. At the peak, there was a moment of silence. Then air whooshed through Milli as the car swooped low. She willed herself to let go until all she felt was the release of gravity. She leaned into turns—weightless, not resisting, not fighting. She was no longer Millicent Tarnover or Milli. She was not Leo's widow or Lionel's mother. She no longer lived on the ground. She belonged to the air. The ride came to a sudden end, but she wasn't ready to stop. She and Kedrix spent the rest of the day in Funland: stuck to walls with centrifugal force and spinning on a pendulum; on swings that reversed her age to childhood; in the fun-house where a mirror contorted her body into a twelve foot Amazon and a two foot midget; and, of course, several more exhilarating rides on the roller coaster.

Wild was not the word for the day. Magical was.

Chapter Fifteen

Kedrix delivered Milli to her apartment late in the afternoon. On her door was a notice:

> *May 19, 2023*
> *To Minni Yanover,*
>   *You have rented the apartment under false pretenses. My buddy Morris didn't know you from a hole in the wall, and those Millicent Tarnover investigators are cramping my style. Also, I have no legal obligation to you, as you never signed a contract. Therefore, I want you out by June 2.*
>   *Grenadine Graziella*

Milli stared at Kedrix. "So she decided that I am Millicent Tarnover after all? That means they'll be coming back to get me."

"It doesn't say that," said Kedrix. "Looks like this is from Grenadine Graziella only. I don't know much about the law, but it doesn't look official."

"Official or not, I have two weeks to figure out what to do next. Kedrix, I want to thank you for the best day I've had in I don't know how long. You've given me something special, my will to live."

"That's a bit of an exaggeration, Milli Ruby Tuesday. Don't you think?"

Milli shook her head, her hairdo limp from a windswept day. "I've wasted so many years. I can't go back and make a brand new start, but I can start today to make a new ending."

"Milli, you're one profoundly wise woman. I'll take you for a walk along the beach next week. OK?"

"You bet." Milli wasn't banking on it though, considering Grenadine's ultimatum.

Kedrix kissed Milli on the top of her head. "Until the next time," he said, as he hopped on his motorcycle and revved away.

Milli didn't go into the apartment right off. She sat on the rickety wicker chair and all the maxims about age flooded through her. *You're as old as you feel. Old age needs so little but it needs that little so much.* Then C.S. Lewis' words loomed up in giant letters: *You're never too old to set another goal or to dream a new dream.*

"By golly," said Milli, "that's what I'll do. But how?"

Back in her apartment, Milli tried to relax, but her bones rattled when the pipes started banging. She thought her heart was jumping out of her chest, knocking down her ribcage, the result of Funland and eviction overwhelming an old lady, but the noise was real.

"Help!" The voice came from the upstairs apartment where Madame Sheeya lived.

Milli got close to the pipes. "What's the matter?"

"I can't get it out," cried the voice.

Milli considered calling the police, but not when New Dawn was hot on her trail. So she put on her cardigan, went to the side stairs, and climbed. At each landing, a vision of Madame Sheeya's clients appeared: the handle-barred mustache-man whose store was haunted, the happy-in-lust couple whose love life got a boost, and the frightening shrew who stole a wad of money and berated her bratty kid. By the time she got to the apartment's door, Milli's lungs were not only on the edge of explosion, but so was her curiosity. She counted to fifty, caught her breath, turned the knob, and wide-eyed her way in.

The front room was dark and smelled like licorice and cotton candy. Trinkets and bells hung from hooks on the walls and dangled from the ceiling—some tinkled, some clacked, some chimed.

"Hello? I'm here to help. Where are you?" called Milli.

"Bathroom," grumbled Madame Sheeya from deep inside the flat.

Darn it all. I have to rescue a fortune teller from her tub. No way can I do this. But when Milli finally found the room, she witnessed a laughable sight. A hulk of a woman towered over a sink yanking at a round styling hairbrush that was caught in her yellow curls.

"It's stuck and it's pulling out all my hair," raged Madame Sheeya.

Milli got closer. "I heard you through the pipes," although truth be told, anyone across the street could have heard her.

"Stop chattering and get this thing out of my head."

Milli was used to hair that was thin and wispy. Madame Sheeya's was poofy, wiry, and wildly bright. "Can you sit down so I can see what I'm doing?"

The woman closed the toilet seat and sat, her thighs rippling over the side. She was triple the size of Milli, but her head was eye-level. Milli rotated the brush counter-clockwise and pulled the hair in the opposite direction.

Madame Sheeya closed her eyes, her fake lashes curling up like centipede legs. She sucked air in and out through pouty lips as her hands massaged her ample chest.

"I'll be gentle, I promise," said Milli.

The woman's breath settled. "You're the renter on the ground floor. Right?"

"For now I am." If she were a real psychic, she would have used the past tense.

"You're quite a change from the Old Goat," Madame Sheeya tsked. "I warned him to make amends before it was too late. I even offered him a cat amulet to ward off negative energies. The geezer laughed at me. Look where it got him."

Dead, thought Milli. She'd better pay attention to this mega-sized Barbie. "Grenadine told me you could predict the future."

"That sidewinder doesn't know her ass from her elbow," sneered Madame Sheeya, wincing as Milli tugged at the brush. "Hey, it's attached, you know. Don't even think about cutting the brush out of my hair."

Milli worked methodically, one strand at a time. "So you're not a fortune teller?"

"Is that what Grenadine said? A common fortune teller?" The woman raised her three chins. "I'm a prophetess. I banish curses, eliminate spells, and expel evil spirits."

"So you're an exorcist?" asked Milli.

"In a way, but I'm not affiliated with any religion. My gift is innate, inborn. I see what hurts and I heal it."

Milli wondered if Madame Sheeya could have helped Leo after their son died. Oh what she would have given to cast out the spell that had lain over her husband. The doctors said he suffered from depression, but Milli suspected there was a devil devouring Leo's essence, destroying his bones, his skin, his aura. Her Leo turned into the shadow of a shadow's shadow.

Strand by yellow strand, the hairbrush finally released its grip. "Looks like we're done here," said Milli.

Madame Sheeya sighed. "I might lift curses, but you release strangleholds."

Milli thought about that word for a while before respond-ing. Keysi, Rashida and Bianca—the young women she had met recently—experienced strangleholds, like they were on their last breath. Kedrix too. Milli knew this was hyperbole, but she had expe-rienced the feeling. When she was in New Dawn, she felt strangled. Once she had been banished to the basement, the air closed in on her and her lungs barely expanded. But when she entered the Seaside Arboretum and sat on the bench beneath the lilacs and surrounded by daffodils, and experienced a vision of her husband and son, she felt like a balloon, able to rise and float on her own. *Is that what it feels like when a curse is expelled?* "I'm glad I could help," Milli finally said.

When Madame Sheeya held out her hand to thank Milli, the woman's face paled.

"You must sit down, right now," said Madame Sheeya and led Milli into the living room. "Your heart's aura is ashen gray. Something is gnawing at you."

"Old age?" said Milli.

"No, something worse. Something foreboding. Tell me, have you felt like a curse has been placed on you recently?"

Should I tell her the truth? That I escaped from an assisted living facility, that my photo is circulating on the news, and that I'm believed to have dementia. Milli hated the possibility of returning to New Dawn, but Grenadine was evicting her. Instead Milli chose to talk about the fun she'd had with Kedrix. "I rode the roller coaster and the Big Bamboo and the Fireball today and took a motorcycle ride and ate cotton candy and pretzels and pizza and ice cream. Maybe I'm still light-headed from all the excitement."

"Whoa, you're a regular spitfire. But woman, I see a shadow trespassing your heart, like a spirit is about to enter your body and do damage," said Madame Sheeya. "You need my help or you'll be a goner."

Milli didn't feel as if she were in imminent danger, but she didn't want to end up like the Old Goat. "I'm not averse to help."

Madame Sheeya grabbed a handful of rice and walked around Milli eleven times, tossing kernels and chanting *Bavanneer chattis jangir aagyavetal masna veer ll.* Watching this robed Amazon with wild yellow hair encircling her, Milli grew dizzy, and the pieces of rice stung like tiny bees.

"Stop, please!" cried Milli. "You're hurting me."

Madame Sheeya ceased her chanting. "I see what I see. Something is threatening you." Madame Sheeya raced into her kitchen returning with a jar of liquid that looked like apple juice but smelled like garlic. She dipped a spoon into the mixture. "Open up, Missy. Take one tablespoon every morning for seven days and your aura will be pink and pretty in no time."

Milli swallowed dutifully.

Madame Sheeya gave Milli the bottle and a bag of salt. "Now rub this all over your body tonight and then shower in hot water. You'll wake up tomorrow refreshed."

"Will whatever is endangering my heart be gone from my body?"

"I can't promise you anything, but if you do what I tell you to do, you'll have a running start." The voice followed Milli down the three flights of stairs. "You need to drink birchbark tea. It cleanses the pores and restores health. I'll bring you some in the morning."

When Milli returned to her apartment, she stared at her image in the bathroom mirror. The only color that bounced back was the droopy red in her hair. "The problem with my heart is the loves that it's lost."

Chapter Sixteen

In the morning, Milli heard heavy footsteps and then a brisk knock on her door.

"Yoo-hoo, I'm here with your birchbark tea," said the husky voice. "I'm coming in."

"The door is locked," said Milli.

"I have a key," said Madame Sheeya.

She's one nervy woman. Why does she have a key?

"The Old Goat gave it to me," Madam Sheeya said, having anticipated Milli's question. She sashayed into the room, teapot in hand. "In all the excitement, I didn't catch your name. I can't keep calling you Yoo-Hoo."

Milli wrapped herself in her blanket and sat up in bed. "Lately, I've chosen the name Ruby Tuesday. And now I'm thinking about changing it to, I don't know, Alice."

"Why Alice?"

"I need less complication in my life, and the name Alice reminds me of Wonderland and fantasy and kindness."

Madame Sheeya reached into her purse and brought out a thick pencil. She dotted Milli's forehead with a smudge of black. "I name this woman Alice Ruby Tuesday. The power of kohl will protect you from the evil eye." She waved her hands around Milli as if she were swirling smoke. Then she nodded three times, her chins totally involved in the process. "But the heart-curse is still hovering around you, Alice, so it's tea time."

Milli had to smile. She liked this woman, how confident she was, how sure of her convictions. "How about you? Do you have a special name that just your friends use?"

The woman's face crumpled, her long blonde hair practically fell limp and her cheeks drooped. "Friends? That's a laugh. No family. Lots of clients, but few friends." She plunked her rump bedside to Milli and handed her a teacup. "My parents named me Shirley Temple and paraded me around introducing me as The Real Shirley Temple. They billed me as her doppelgänger and pushed me onto the stage, singing, dancing, and telling dirty jokes that I didn't understand but got big laughs. My parents made a pretty penny at my expense."

Milli imagined this blonde dynamo as a petite tot with deep dimples, tap-dancing her way through childhood until a growth spurt changed her from a darling to a dirigible. "I'm so sorry," said Milli.

"No need. I had the last laugh. At thirteen when I grew these"— she shimmied her bosom—"I turned those dirty ditties into profitable titties and this time, I kept the cash. At eighteen, I divorced my parents, and legally changed my name from Shirley to Birdie."

Such a contradictory name for this large creature. Then again dinosaurs evolved into birds.

Birdie poured tea into Milli's cup and set the pot on the floor. She spotted the amber liquid bottle on the counter that she gave Milli the previous night and found a tablespoon. "Open up," she urged.

Milli obeyed, again recalling the sudden death of the Old Goat.

Birdie continued her story. "I know what you're thinking. The name Birdie? Such a weird choice."

The woman is psychic after all.

"I was flying away from home, so the name seemed totally appropriate."

Milli envisioned a pterodactyl with yellow feathers and a wide-wing span. If it could get off the ground, so could Birdie. As Milli sipped her tea, which tasted like wintergreen, she wondered how one went about divorcing her parents and was that why Birdie had no family?

"You know, my childhood was tough, but after emancipation from my parents, I was free to reinvent myself. It took me a while to figure out my calling, but once I did, I embraced it with all my heart."

"That's the only way to live, isn't it? In the moment. I'm beginning to understand that." Milli shook her head. "I've spent so many years waiting to join my husband and son in heaven."

"You're going to get your wish if you don't pay attention to your heart," said Birdie. "I've made you my mission. Once someone helps me, I'm committed to helping them."

Funny how close calls spur you into action. After being banished to the dungeon, I saw my life ending. But the vision of my family encouraging me to live turned me around. "I'm free to reinvent myself too. So Alice I am."

"Why the hell not!" said Birdie. "Up and at 'em, I say. How about you get dressed and let me show you what I do. Maybe by knowing me, you'll figure out you."

With so few clothes, it didn't take Milli long to outfit herself for the day.

"You need a scarf," said Birdie. "The neck is the gatekeeper of the heart. It must stay warm."

"And a hat, too," said Milli, reaching into her purse for Lionel's baseball cap.

"That's my girl," said Birdie, who slowed down to keep pace with Milli. Together, the women looked like a Great Dane and a chihuahua, walking in sync.

Milli settled into Birdie's van, a hippy-style Volkswagen, complete with dreamcatchers, peace signs, and archangels; shelves of candles, moonstones, tarot cards, and crystals; and strewn with pillows, shawls, and rag rugs. The smell of mint tickled Milli's nose.

"Good vibes, huh!" crooned Birdie. "My karma-mobile. I call her Little Flower. What do you think?"

"She's a trip," said Milli, channeling her '60s lingo. Imagine this woman seeking her approval, thought Milli. After what Birdie had been through, Milli was surprised she'd even care what others believed about her. But here she was, asking Milli what she thought of her life. That was the question, of course. Little Flower was the metaphor.

"First stop, Funland." She looked toward Milli. "Something's lighting up your aura."

The thought of riding the coaster again bolstered Milli's spirit. "So my heart's not gray anymore?"

"Your whole body is turning a sunny yellow. No grays visible. That birchbark tea is doing its job, all right. I know what's good for you, wouldn't you say?"

Milli rubbed her chest, her palm pressing into her heart.

At the amusement park, Birdie parked behind a row of stores. It was still early in the day, so to Milli's disappointment, the park was not open yet. They walked through a narrow alley to the boulevard, not far from where Milli had met up with Mr. Whiskers.

Birdie pointed to a purple and gold sign above a door: *Spiritualist Sheeya will set you on a positive path toward a brighter future.* "What do you think?"

"Catchy," said Milli, nodding approval.

Inside, the shop was the van on steroids—candles, incense, crystals, teas, necklaces, charms, rocks, dreamcatchers, cards, books, pillows, scarves, rugs, posters. In the middle of the room was a square table with a crystal ball in its center. On one side of the table was a wide-winged wicker chair draped with velvet and lace. Birdie sat down like a queen, transforming herself into royalty, and pointed to a plain wooden chair opposite her for Milli. She lit three candles, and swirled the air with floating fingertips. Her eyes lowered but her nostrils flared. When she spoke, her voice was like a bassoon, plaintive and penetrating. "The moment you came into my apartment to help me, I felt your presence. You've been carrying a heavy weight that's created waves of pain around you. I am here to dispel your burden."

Milli's flugelhorn kicked in—jazzy and brash—and her need to laugh bubbled up, but Birdie seemed so sincere, so concerned about Milli's well-being that Milli stifled the sound and went along with the medium's message. For so many years, Milli had buried her playful side along with Leo. But watching Birdie in action, lighting candles, swirling incense, talking about Milli's grief was more than she could bear. She had to redirect the conversation away from herself.

"Birdie," Milli began, "I appreciate your concern. Truly. And I know why my heart aches. Tell me though, how much of your psychic insights stem from your own sadness?"

Birdie leaned back in her chair. "So this doesn't do it for you? I get the feeling you're not buying into Madame Sheeya." She stood up and circled the small room three times, taking up all the space with her fulsome body.

Milli shielded herself from the rice that might batter her at any moment.

In a voice hushed and smooth, Birdie began to speak. "I rarely tell my story to anyone, but something about you has freed me. Maybe it's how your ears are shaped and the vibrations emanating from them."

Milli knew she was a good listener, but it had more to do with her heart than her ears. If her heart were failing, would her ears overcompensate?

Birdie leaned in, relaxing her shoulders this time, as if she were a different person with each new position. "Not everyone is a natural psychic. It's a skill to be learned. I've studied and observed and grown. From a painful childhood, I covered myself in darkness, head to toe. It's taken years to peel back the layers and expose my core. It's on fire to help others, like you."

A rap at the door interrupted their talk and a tall, bony woman with pixie brown hair and two bright dots of rouge on her cheeks bustled in. "Are you open for business? I hope so because I just have to talk to you, like right now. OK?"

"Doris! I'm always open for business for you."

The woman exuded a skunkiness that forced Milli to breathe through her mouth.

"Meet my assistant, Alice," said Birdie in a calm voice, nodding to Milli.

"Well aren't you a cute little Polly Pocket!" said Doris, waving with both hands. Milli responded with an airy bow.

Doris removed her sweater to reveal a shriveled necklace of garlic laced with ribbons and beads.

"How well did the charm work?" asked Birdie, unfolding a chair for Doris and setting it beside Milli.

"I can't believe it!" cried Doris. "Kippee's nowhere to be seen! He's vanished! Poof! Gone!"

It's no wonder Kippee vanished. Who would remain in close contact with someone who smells so rank? And no wonder the woman is rail-thin. All her energy goes into talking. Every word is an exclamation.

"Are you ready for the next talisman?" asked Birdie.

There's that word again: talisman. What magic is happening here? These people have so much faith in Birdie.

Doris removed the garland and handed it to Birdie, who wrapped it carefully in a cloth shroud. "I'll bury it later."

"I am so grateful to you. I can leave my house now and not be followed! My life is my own again!"

Doris babbled on about her ex-husband Kippee—how he stalked her, how he hid behind bushes and jumped out at her, how at every turn she saw his shadow and heard his voice and even smelled his after-shave. He was everywhere! she kept repeating, and now he was gone.

"You're a wonder, Madame Sheeya!"

Birdie gave Doris a beautifully wrapped box. "Open this on the threshold of your house when you get home. Then hang it above your front door either facing up or facing down. It doesn't matter which. Kippee will never cross your path again."

Doris' face radiated as she took the box and gave Birdie her credit card. She looked at Milli. "Worth every penny to have that man disappear forever!" she exclaimed and scooted out the door holding the box as if it were gold.

"Now that's a satisfied customer," said Milli. "What's in the box?"

"A horseshoe. It repels ghosts from entering a home," said Birdie.

"Ghosts? Kippee is a ghost?"

"A vindictive ghost, at that. Doris believes he wanted revenge for her killing him. The way she tells it, Kippee thinks she poisoned him. She didn't, of course, at least that's what she says. She had a habit of keeping food way past its expiration date. It wasn't her fault that he ate fish from a bloated can. She thought he was drunk, slurring his words, his eyes out of focus. By the time she drove him to the emergency room, about four hours later, it was too late."

"So he's dead?"

"Yup. She's been haunted by his ghost for three years and then she found me. I removed the curse and gave her back her life."

What advice would Milli have given Doris to remove the guilt she carried? It could never be as potent as the garlic wreath and the horseshoe. It was amazing to Milli how gullible people were when they searched for inner peace. Look at her own situation. If she hadn't been kicked out of her high rise, she might never have left New Dawn. She would have died there. And now? Was this living? Sitting in a psychic's shop surrounded by amulets and charms beside a blonde bombshell of a woman who believed in spirits and incantations. What was advice anyway but the bolstering of someone's self-confidence.

"Birdie, I'd like to finish our conversation. Do you think someone has innate psychic powers?"

"Everyone is born with psychic abilities. It's just a matter of tapping into them."

"So theoretically, you could teach me how to tap into my psychic powers?"

"Absolutely."

"And what about the ability to speak with the dead. Is that something you know about?"

"I can get rid of the dead, but I haven't had much success communing with them. Who would you like to talk to?"

"Everybody," said Milli.

During their conversation, a rotund man blustered in. "Patricia's back, Madame Sheeya. You're a miracle worker. My Patricia! She's back! Can you believe it!"

More exclamations, thought Milli. Birdie's clients sure had enthusiasm.

Birdie winked at Milli. "Damien! So happy to see you. I feel positive energy all around you."

"Patricia said she heard me call her. In the middle of the night! When there was a new moon! The chant! She heard the chant! *Om Koom Swaha.*"

"And what happened?" asked Birdie.

"She stormed through the door ready to do battle, but stopped short. 'The smell,' she said, 'The house smells like peace.'" The man caught his breath, inhaled deeply through his mouth, and let out the air so slowly through his nose that Milli could see his nostril hairs vibrate. "It was amazing." His voice sounded like home-baked bread. "She looked around and was astounded. Madame Sheeya, I did what you said. I swept the house daily with a corn broom and then buffed it with a soft cotton dust mop. I lit green candles and chanted the Gayatri Mantra. Then I walked through the house sprinkling lavender and lilac."

Lilac, thought Milli. No wonder springtime was so soothing. And housecleaning yielded positive energy? Boy, Patricia came home to a spotless home and a calm husband. No wonder she was flabbergasted.

The man whispered something to Birdie, then took out his wallet and handed her several bills. Birdie went to a highboy in the corner, reached into one of the drawers and withdrew a silk pouch. She placed it in Damien's palm. "Put this under your pillow and sleep with peace."

Damien hugged Birdie, his girth matching hers, like the embrace of two picture book elephants.

After he left, Birdie locked the front door. "We'll go out the rear entrance. I'm usually open from two to eight during high season. But when my clients see my lights on, they crowd on in."

Milli wanted to know more about Patricia and the silk purse, and she needed to know more about the clients she had seen on Friday—the man who heard weird noises in his store; the June-December couple who practically ran up the stairs; and the mother who set a terrible example for her children—but Birdie wasn't waiting around. She folded Milli and Doris' chairs, stacked them in the corner and led Milli through a beaded curtain, past a closet-sized room filled with boxes from floor to ceiling, and out a back door.

"The birchbark tea has had time to work its magic. Your mind should feel receptive and welcoming and your body ready for nourishment. Off to breakfast," said Birdie.

Thinking they'd go to a spiritual buffet brimming with wild rice-berry cakes, pomegranates and papayas, honey-bran muffins and lemongrass, Milli was shocked when Birdie pulled up to a McDonald's drive-through and ordered two sausage McMuffins with a side order of bacon and two coffees with milk and sugar. "Throw in two chocolate chip cookies."

Milli figured Birdie didn't get to be a two-ton Barbie on health-foods. "But what about my heart? Aren't those foods a recipe for clogged arteries?"

"Balance," Birdie said. "Everything's a matter of balance. The good and the bad. The yin and the yang. The dark and the light."

"The sad and the happy," Milli said, channeling the bar crowd's backwards sayings.

"Exactly. How would we understand happy if we've never been sad?" said Birdie.

Birdie parked her car at the ocean. With the ocean purring, the sun shining, and the seagulls waiting, they sat on a bench to eat their breakfast.

"You're a natural at what you do," said Milli.

"What I've learned to do is listen. It's taken me a while, but I've built a business on helping people help themselves."

"I understand. When my husband died, he lost his will to live. I tried cajoling him, yelling at him, soothing him, everything I could to dispel his sadness. But did I listen to him? I don't know. I'm a better listener lately by thinking less about myself and more about others." She thought about her three lovely ladies—Bianca, Rashida, and Keysi—and Kedrix, of course.

"That's key. When we put ourselves first, we are no good to others who need us," said Birdie. She looked at her phone. "The morning's gone by fast. I'll drop you back at your place and then I have to open up shop for the locals."

"Speaking of locals, I saw a few yesterday on their way to their appointments with you."

"Ah, Robert. Right? Nice man. Just overwhelmed with business."

"And a haunted clothing store," said Milli.

"He has this iron magnetism that attracts spirits. All I have to do is provide a repellent."

"So he's a basic 101. Not like that angry woman with the husband who was shot by the police."

Birdie sighed. "She wanted a potion that would hurt her husband so she could get her revenge. I just don't do that. I'm a healer."

"She stole money from you. I saw it," said Milli.

"I predicted that," Birdie laughed with parrot-squawks. "I left a roll of twenty-dollar bills on the table, but inside was paper money. In the center, I tucked a black tourmaline crystal that will protect her from negative thinking."

"Do you think it'll work?"

"No. I think she'll sell it, but it's worth a try. Some people just can't be helped."

Like my nephew. Milli knew Bernard had been in rehab and received therapy over the years. Milli's sister had said he was in recovery, but that wasn't true. Milli wished she had known about the power of crystals. It would have been worth a try.

"The happy-in-love couple was fun to watch," said Milli.

"He's her sugar daddy," whispered Birdie, even though no one was within earshot.

"So she's faking it?" asked Milli. "So your spell isn't true?"

"He thinks it is, so I count that as a win."

Milli was receiving mixed messages. On one hand, she liked Birdie, but then a creepy Birdie reared her head and Milli was not so sure. *Is that typical of all people? Being capricious? Being different from different angles? Am I like that?*

Birdie dropped Milli off on Porter Street. "Drink your birch-bark tea, salt your body, and then shower. Lie down for two hours surrounded by these candles." Birdie gave her a shopping bag with a dozen candles enclosed in glass holders. She included a box of wooden matches. "Put them on the floor around the bed. Don't blow them out. Allow them to burn down on their own. That's essential. Oh, by the way, there's an invoice in there for the candles, the tea, and the salts. Because you're my neighbor, I gave you a discount. I'd prefer cash to a credit card, if that's all right."

Flustered, Milli checked out the bill: $80.00. "But I didn't ask for any of this."

"Remember the Old Goat. He didn't listen to me and look what happened to him."

Milli reached into her bag and withdrew four twenties. "You know the old saying. Plan for the future but live for the moment."

Chapter Seventeen

Milli couldn't face the four walls of her apartment and she certainly didn't want to light a dozen candles and roll in salt. She needed to see the ocean. Walking to the corner, she saw a light on in Lila's Florist Shop for the first time since she moved in. She decided to investigate.

As she opened the door, bells jangled *Edelweiss*. The tune was familiar and comforting, but the shop smelled neglected. Ferns twisted up to the ceiling, mold clumped in corners, and plants languished. The dripping of water was the ever-present background noise. A young woman stood in front of a long table laden with a few buckets of leafy greens, yellow daffodils and purple lilacs. She had a picture clipped to a board of a flower bouquet with streaming white and yellow ribbons.

"Six bouquets and three vases in an hour. How am I going to get this done?" The young woman blubbered. "Darn blast it all. I knew I shouldn't have opened until after Memorial Day."

Milli looked through the shop expecting to see an employee or two, but no one else was there. "Looks like you have your hands full."

The girl swung around. "Oh, no. You're here already to pick them up. The customer on the phone said his aunt would be along to get them at eleven and it's only ten-thirty. Can you wait?"

"I'm not the aunt. I'm the new tenant in the apartment downstairs." Milli stood next to the girl whose face was blotchy and whose eyes were swollen.

"The customer is having an impromptu anniversary lunch for a bunch of his friends who got married in May. He wants a bouquet for each couple and a few vases to put around his house. I shouldn't have answered the darn phone!"

"I can help you arrange them, if you'd like. These flowers are my favorites."

The girl blew away strands of her hair with an upward breath. "Really? You'd do that?"

"All I have is time." Milli rolled up her sleeves.

"When I got the call, I ran home and picked these daffodils and cut the lilacs. That's the best I could do on short notice. If you can put the lilacs in the vases, I'll create the bouquets."

The sweetness of the flowers sent Milli into a daze.

"Are you all right?" asked the girl. "Maybe this is just too much. I'll call that man back and tell him to find another florist."

"No, no. I can do this. It's just that daffodils and lilacs are my reason for living." *Sure that's an exaggeration, sort of. But somehow, being here, in this shop, on this day is my destiny.*

As she worked, the girl looked like a child in a sandbox playing with toys. Milli, too, enjoyed the texture of the stems against her fingers, how they leaned into each other in the vases and gave off the fragrance of spring.

"It's good you did come in today," said Milli. "This is a sizable order for your shop." *And it sure needs it.*

"I love the flowers, but the job overwhelms me."

"Then why work here?" said Milli.

"It's a family business, and I'm the only family willing to put in any time."

"What about your folks?" Milli figured if it was a family business, they would be involved.

The girl twisted wires to keep the flowers stable. Then she wound stems around them, careful not to tear their tissues. "My mother and my uncle took over the shop from Grandma Victoria when she retired. But they aren't much interested. Don't tell Grandma though."

Milli frowned. "Me? Tell your Grandma? My lips are sealed. Does she drop in every so often?"

"Grandma lives in Maine now. Her vision is bad so she doesn't drive anymore. So nope, no Grandma. Believe me, if she did, she'd raise holy hell. My mother and uncle don't give a fig about the place, as you can see. I keep it running in the summers when I'm not in school."

"Where do you go to school?"

"Brewer College in West Hampton. My major is floral design."

"What a lovely pursuit. A flower is a smile from heaven," said Milli. As she looked at the blooming bouquets, she saw Leo and Lionel. They were calling to her.

"The store is mine when I graduate, so I might as well know what I'm doing."

"Why don't you have any help? Doesn't Grenadine work with you?"

The girl's face soured. "Grenadine was Grandma's housecleaner for years. They used to have cocktails together in the afternoon and gossip about the locals. Grandma got a hoot out of her, but I thought she was a busybody. When Grandma retired, she insisted mom keep her on to tidy up the downstairs apartment and keep an eye on the shop in the off-season."

Clearly, she only did half the job. "Grenadine rented me the apartment for four weeks."

The girl stopped weaving the ribbons through the stems. "Doesn't Randolph LaCross live there?"

"I heard he died."

"That doesn't sound right. No one told me, but I can't say I miss the Old Goat."

"Madame Sheeya calls him that too."

The girl laughed. "She and I made up the name for him together."

"He must have been a character."

"He hit on every woman he saw, including me. Even when I was a pre-teen. Disgusting. I wonder if my mom knows that he died and forgot to tell me."

The girl went into the back room for more supplies while Milli arranged the flowers in the vases. The bones of the store were solid, but the neglect was obvious. On the wall near the cash register was a framed photo of an attractive older woman sitting in the Seaside Arboretum surrounded by lilac bushes. Milli's heart skipped. She supposed that wasn't such a coincidence, after all the Arboretum was nearby and it boasted an annual lilac festival.

The girl returned with shallow boxes to carry the bouquets and vases.

"Is the store named Lila for your grandmother?" asked Milli, pointing to the photo.

"No, the store is named for her favorite flower, lilacs. Her name is Victoria. I'm named after her."

"Lilacs are my favorite too," said Milli, veering off into reverie, but the presence of the young girl brought Milli back to the moment. "Your grandmother is lucky to have such a lovely granddaughter."

"I miss my grandma terribly. My mom and uncle are too busy to even think about her."

It was clear that the mom and uncle didn't spend any time in the shop.

Victoria anticipated Milli's next question. "They're real estate agents for the coastal towns around here. Lots of beachfront property. They buy houses and flip them."

"What about your dad?" asked Milli.

"He's a lawyer in Boston. Even though he's not a real estate lawyer, he oversees all the closings."

So there was the answer. The family kept the floral shop because of Victoria, both older and younger.

"So Grenadine works for them?"

"Sort of. Grandma lives in Maine but the house is still in her name. Grenadine checks on it once a week and is responsible for keeping the downstairs apartment clean. That's all my mom trusts her to do."

The tune of *Edelweiss* chimed through the shop. A flawless woman dressed to the nines, probably in her mid-sixties, sauntered in. "Oh, how pretty," she said, admiring the completed bouquets. "The flowers look scrumptious. My Freddie will be delighted." She took out a credit card and handed it to Milli, who gave it to Victoria.

"She's a whiz at floral decorations," said Milli.

"I can see that." She looked at Victoria with an air of privilege. "You know, I could use someone to spruce up my house. Are you available?"

"What would it involve?" asked Victoria.

"Probably an hour every few days. Fresh flowers. Pretty arrangements. If your creations are as beautiful as these, I'll pay you well." The woman gave Victoria her business card and Victoria beamed with pride.

When the woman left the store with the floral arrangements, Victoria sighed with relief.

"I don't know what I would have done without you," she said to Milli as they cleaned up. "My Grandma Victoria has an expression. We don't meet people by accident. They are meant to cross our paths. Seems to me my Grandma sent you."

"You would have managed without me. I'm confident of that. You're smart, determined, and creative, a winning combination."

"My mother doesn't think so. She says I'm wasting my time and brain getting a floral design license. But Grandma Victoria supported the idea and it makes her happy, so it pleases me."

Milli knew that Lionel would have been similar to this girl: thinking about others, wanting the best for them, embarking on a path of success. It wasn't the fact that she'd have a floral design degree, it was the fact that she was pursuing a passion and doing it for a good reason.

Milli needed to sit, but looking around the store, there was nowhere to put her backside.

"Does floral design include store design? This shop needs a make-over. In my younger years, I painted houses."

"Like on canvas?"

"Like on ladders," said Milli.

Victoria discreetly looked Milli over from head to toe. "Maybe you shouldn't be climbing ladders?"

"How about I'll take the middle of the walls. You can do the highs and lows."

Victoria grabbed a pad of paper and began a list: paint, brushes, rollers, pans. "What else?"

"Some furniture might help. And, oh yes, a plumber to fix the water leak."

"I'm on it," she said.

"And how about candles? I have a few we can put on the window ledges." Milli smiled thinking that Madame Sheeya might offer design tips. Filling up space was her specialty.

Chapter Eighteen

It had been a busy morning—first the visit from Madame Sheeya and then the arrangement of flowers for Victoria. Milli returned to her apartment, changed into her capris and sandals, got her wide-brimmed hat and sunglasses, and walked to the Mirage Café where she bought lunch and the daily *Globe*. She crossed the avenue to the steel bench on the boardwalk, cushioned her bottom with a pillow and sat.

Absorbing the sea and sun was a dream come true, but niggling thoughts crept into her peace. Bernard's betrayal. Banishment to the basement. Imminent eviction from the walk-in apartment. *Stop it. Stop that right now.* She opened a corner of her mind to the experiences of the last few days: Kedrix and the motorcycle ride, the roller coaster, and the freedom of speed; the trio of young women; the crazy clients of Madame Sheeya; and her new goal—helping Victoria with the floral shop. *What happened to One Day at a Time? Take it as it comes. Go with the flow.*

So deep in thought, Milli neglected to see the bratty boy Apollo take a seat on the bench beside her.

"Got an apple for me?" he asked. "Please?"

"Will a chocolate chip cookie suffice?" she said, reaching into the paper sack.

"I never had no cookie and ice. Is that like a slush puppy?"

"Suffice. It means sufficient, adequate, acceptable."

Apollo lowered his head. "I don't know much words."

"Many words," Milli corrected him. "You can change the course of your life with words, and reading them lets you dream with your eyes open."

Apollo bit into the cookie. "Mama says books are a waste of time, and daddy says school is overrated. The streets are the way to go if I want to be educated. But my pop is in jail and won't be out for a long time." Apollo chewed slowly as if the cookie were his only meal of the day. "Wow, I'd sure say that this suffice."

"Suffices," said Milli.

The boy rose to leave. "I'm a dumb shit. Everyone says so, including you."

Milli reached for *The Boston Globe*. "I'll bet you two more cookies that you're capable of reading and enjoying it."

"I know my letters. It's how the words go together that screws me up."

They began with Milli pointing out positive phrases in the newspaper—*Finding hope, Going the extra mile, Animal wisdom*—and chatting about their meaning.

"These are easy to understand. Find me tough ones."

"Let's read some headlines." Milli opened to random pages. *The surprising benefits to eating mushrooms. Would you swim with sharks for $100,000. I'm being bullied by a fish tank.* He and Milli read through a dozen other headlines, laughing and making up stories that went along with them.

After an hour, the boy stretched out, rubbed his eyes and stood. "Know what? I never sat that long reading anything. Mom gives me workbooks, and I have to fill in answers and boring stuff." He shuffled his feet. "I know I'm not dumb. But I never thought I'd have fun reading words. By the way, how do I spell dumb?"

"The final letter is silent. D - U - M - B."

"A dumb spelling for a dumb word," he laughed. "Can I come back on Monday?"

"Aren't you in school?"

Apollo kicked the base of the bench. "Nah. My Daddy thinks public school is a government plot to make kids slaves to society. My mom teaches me sometimes, but she's busy with my little sister. Besides, she's always tired."

Milli wondered if any special services were involved in his upbringing. There must be some sort of check on Apollo's progress by the state. But having seen the mother and heard about the father, she knew Apollo's education was low on their list of priorities.

Milli nodded. "I don't want to interfere with your mother's homeschooling."

"We don't do nothing on Sunday. It's our day off."

Milli refrained from correcting his grammar. "Perfect. Come by at noon tomorrow and we'll spend some day-off time together. I'll make us some lunch and we'll work on reading articles in the newspaper as well as headlines."

"But we did that today."

"Newspapers change daily. Today's news is tomorrow's history."

"Seriously?"

"Would I lie to you?"

"You're the only one who wouldn't." He high-fived her from a distance, then sailed off down the boardwalk like a man with a plan.

Chapter Nineteen

By the time Milli left the boardwalk, the sun was a quarter way down in the sky. Three o'clock, she figured. Time for a nap. When she entered her apartment, she noticed the closet door was open. Milli never left closet doors open. It was a cat-thing. When she was young, she had a beautiful tabby named Frieda who gave birth to five kittens. The kittens had a habit of wandering and Frieda would fret until each was found. One day, one was missing. Milli and her sister scoured the house with no luck. Finally, they opened the closet and there she was, barely breathing. They rushed her to Frieda, who cradled the kitten into her body until it was able to nurse.

From then on, she and Linda Mae made it a ritual to check the closet before they left the house. "No kitten left behind" became their mantra. So when Milli saw the closet door ajar, she knew someone had been snooping. *Grenadine or Birdie? Someone from New Dawn? Maybe Victoria?* Milli figured she must have a key too.

Milli checked every corner in the closet and the shelf too, but nothing was amiss. Very little had been in there—her hat, her sweater, and a few trash bags. She looked into the pockets of the cardigan, making sure they were empty.

Even though she was exhausted, Milli couldn't relax. If someone had been in the apartment, she wanted to know who and why. She walked to the front entrance of the flower shop. *Eidelweiss* greeted her and Victoria gave her a deep-dimpled smile. Before Milli could ask whether Victoria had been in her flat, the girl piped up. "I called my mom about the Old Goat. She was shocked, I mean, jaw-dropping shocked. I could hear it over the phone even."

Why wouldn't Grenadine have told Victoria's mother that the Old Goat died?

"My mom called Grenadine. She said it slipped her mind. But how does someone forget something as big as that? I don't understand," said Victoria.

"How long ago did you speak with your mom?"

"This morning after you left. I told her all about how you live downstairs and how you'll help me update the shop."

"Does she come by to check on the store?"

"My mom? No, never. She keeps her distance. She says it reminds her of her childhood, slaving away day-in day-out at the flower shop. Just the smell of lilacs makes her gag."

How could anyone hate the smell of lilacs? Could such a woman be trusted? "Did you happen to see Grenadine or Madame Sheeya this morning?"

"No, neither."

Milli decided not to mention that someone was in her apartment. Why worry Victoria needlessly.

"Since you're here, let me show you the color palette I've chosen." Victoria opened a site on her computer where the entire store was laid out to scale. Two walls were lavender, two were yellow. "Lilacs and daffodils. What do you think?"

"Perfect," said Milli, but her mind drifted to why someone would have been in her place. There was nothing to steal. She carried her purse with her, so there was no money hidden anywhere, but the intruder wouldn't know that.

Milli returned to her apartment and boiled some water for Birdie's special birchbark tea. Then she sat at her little table and swept her eyes through the open space, pretty much seeing everything at a glance. *What's amiss besides the closet door?* And then she spotted it tucked under the radiator: a miniature rag doll. She didn't want to touch it, but her curiosity got the better of her.

What stunned her first was its smell: woodsy like pine, clean like lemon. The doll had gray hair with red streaks, wore sweatpants and a short-sleeved jersey, and sported oversized sunglasses: a replica of Milli. A yellow pin was clasped to its heart. The doll didn't look sinister; in fact, it was darn cute. When Milli turned it over, the tiny sweatpants dipped below the doll's belly to reveal a supple bay leaf wrapped around a kernel of corn. *It must have healing powers and Birdie left it to protect me. She's looking out for me, but do I want that? Do I need more caretakers?*

Milli returned the doll to its hiding place, but propped it up, like it was watching the room. She suspected that voodoo had its positive energies, at least that was what she chose to believe.

Milli was so exhausted, she crawled into bed for a much needed nap. She awoke hours later to Birdie fluttering around her apartment lighting candles and brewing tea. "Why didn't you light these? I gave you absolute instructions. Do you want to end up like the Old Goat?"

"Birdie," said Milli, sitting up in bed, "I value my privacy, so next time, please knock."

"I didn't want to disturb you. Besides, your health is fragile and I know what will benefit you."

Milli shook her head. *This will not do.* "What benefits me is undisturbed rest. If you can't honor my wishes, I would like you to return my key, please."

Birdie's face turned to chalk. Her hands flew to her chest, which she massaged with both palms and deep sighs. "I knew you wouldn't do what I suggested. I just knew it. Listen, Alice Ruby Tuesday, do you want to live another year? How old are you anyway?"

"Eighty-four until June fifth."

"Then surrender yourself to me. I will protect you," insisted Birdie.

"And that includes your coming in here any time night or day without an invitation? I appreciate your concern, truly, but I can't allow that," Milli said, using the sternest voice she could muster. She had hated when the aides bustled into her New Dawn room like they owned her.

"Think of me as your private nurse."

"No. No. No and more no."

"Fine," shouted Birdie, her nostrils flaring. "See if I care." She slammed down the key on the nightstand and stomped out in a full-blown huff, shaking the bed frame and Milli with it.

Milli endured enough people ordering her around; she didn't need another, not at her age. When she was in her thirties after her automobile accident, she was hospitalized for weeks, inundated by doctors and nurses day after day. When she returned to her parents' home and her childhood bedroom to recuperate, healthcare work-ers made regular visits. Once she recovered, her parents became ill and she became their primary caretaker, taking them to doctors' appointments, preparing meals, and keeping them and their home clean. They treated her like their servant, cook, nurse, and child all mixed together. Never a please. Never a kind word. Just do this. Do that. What Milli now realized was she never talked back to them. She did whatever they said, including bathing her father top to toe as he became more and more disabled. She didn't mind so much doing this for her mother, but her dad? They'd had enough people in their home, refusing to let anyone else help and they wouldn't think of asking Linda Mae.

Heat boiled through Milli, but she isolated it deep inside. Maybe that was why Milli kept rubbing her chest; she was redistributing the anger. Birdie was not going to control her and she would not feel remorse for speaking up.

Milli slept poorly and woke at dawn with dark thoughts about her future. To dispel her frustration, Milli walked to Mirage for breakfast and bought the Sunday newspaper for her lesson with Apollo, hopeful that he'd show up. She overheard the mother who wanted $10,000 from her son swearing into her cell phone so that the whole Café tuned in. *What is wrong with that woman? Drama. Drama. Drama. Always looking for an argument. Are people born that way?* Milli avoided the woman, hoping that her wrath wasn't contagious.

Milli stopped at the supermarket to buy sub sandwiches for her and Apollo and then had an aha moment. In the baking aisle, she selected a cake mix, cocoa and powdered sugar. In the refrigerated section, she found eggs, milk, and butter. If that didn't provide incentive for Apollo to enjoy reading, she didn't know what would—and they'd both reap the reward.

Returning home, she put her groceries away and ate her breakfast on the forlorn patio. She could hear Birdie on her landing saying goodbye to one of her clients.

"Now don't disappoint me," Birdie said, in a voice overly loud, seemingly for Milli's benefit. "I'm counting on you to drink the tea and take salt showers. They reduce negativity and draw out stress."

So someone else was in the same dire health as Milli, but when the woman skipped down the stairs, she wasn't old and feeble, but young and limber. On her face, however, were worry lines that etched into her youth.

Milli called out "Have a nice day" as much to Birdie as to the girl.

"That's not going to happen," squeaked the girl, who clutched a stuffed blue dolphin to her chest, and dangled a paper bag from her fingertips.

"Do you want to talk about it?" offered Milli.

The girl squinted in Milli's direction. "Unless you're a masochist, why would you want to talk to me?"

"Sometimes we all need to be heard and I'm a good listener," said Milli, wondering if Birdie was eavesdropping. But she had heard Birdie's door slam after the girl descended the stairs.

The girl took the seat beside Milli. She held tight to the dolphin and the paper sack. "Madame Sheeya is a great listener too. At first, I thought she'd be cuckoo, you know, a psychic and all. But her advice is better than my last three therapists combined."

Milli had never been to a counselor, although she should have. Maybe then she wouldn't have been robotic after Leo died, and maybe then she would have flagged Bernard as a phony.

"Why so many therapists, if you don't mind my asking," said Milli.

"I like to spend my daddy's money."

"But weren't you being helped?"

"I have a classic borderline personality disorder, or so I've been told. Seems to me though, if my daddy spent less money and more time with me, I wouldn't be seeking his attention so much," said the girl, hardly taking an extra breath.

"Have you had this conversation with your father?"

"Hell, no. What fun would that be? He'd just throw more money at me and tell me to buy a dress. A dress? Honestly, he just doesn't get me."

"What if you did buy a dress and then asked him to take you to dinner?"

"He eats like a horse, just shovels the food in. He's in too much of a hurry to eat properly or even sit down to dinner."

"What if you cooked him dinner?"

"Now you're just making fun of me. Do you see me? I'm unfit to cook. I have fingers that fly all over my face and I can't sit still for two minutes, never mind read a recipe to cook something. Besides, my grandmother won't let me in the kitchen. It's her sacred place. She passes food out through a hole in the wall. Crazy, huh?"

Milli figured there was no mom in the girl's life, just a nutty grandmother and a neglectful father. To get attention, she exaggerated everything. *How can I help this child?* "Tell me about the dolphin," Milli said.

"Cute, isn't he? I've named her Karana, after the girl in *The Island of the Blue Dolphins*. Have you ever read that story? Or seen the movie? I did, both, many times. It's about this girl who lived alone on an island for umpteen years and made friends with birds and dogs and had to survive on octopus and fish. She didn't eat dolphins though. In fact, I don't think there were any dolphins in the book, just the name of the book, because that was the name of the island."

The girl took a breath and snuggled tighter to the stuffed dolphin.

"Madame Sheeya said dolphins are lucky and will protect me from evil spirits and they guide lost people to safety." She took another breath and peeked into the bag. "She gave me this too." She withdrew a pouch of birchbark tea, a bag of salts, and a bottle with a few pieces of sea glass in it. "Madame Sheeya told me to drink the tea in the morning after my bath with the salts and then walk the beach and fill the bottle with more sea glass. When it's full, I should visit her again and she'll show me how to create a mosaic using the pieces. She says I can pick the design."

Milli whistled inside. *Smart woman, that Birdie.* She gave the girl a project that was reasonable to accomplish and one that gave her something tangible. Besides that, the dolphin provided security and companionship.

"I'm going to start collecting sea glass right now. Do you want to come with me? You look like you have eagle eyes."

"I'm helping a young man with his reading today, but I'd be happy to join you tomorrow afternoon. I'm pretty slow on my walking skills though."

"Then I'll run circles around you. I'm good at that. Everyone says so."

"Okay, then. We have a date. Meet me at Lila's Florist Shop around one o'clock. But I don't know your name. So how about a formal introduction." Milli held out her hand to the girl. "My name is Millicent, but my friends call me Milli." *Oh, oh,* thought Milli. But the name had already escaped into space.

The girl shifted the dolphin so that one hand was free. "My name is Philippa, Pippa for short. Just don't call me Pipsqueak. If you do, we can't be friends. But Pips is okay."

"I know a poem about a girl named Pippa Passes," said Milli. Pippa piped up in a sing-song voice:

> The Year's at the spring
> And Day's at the morn;
> Morning's at seven;
> The hill-side's dew pearled;
> The lark's on the wing;
> The snail's on the thorn:
> God's in his heaven,
> All's right with the world.

"I've been reciting that since I was knee-high to a grasshopper," she said. "My pre-school teacher taught it to me."

"Have you ever read the full poem?" asked Milli.

"Should I?"

Milli wasn't sure if she should. The girl in the poem believed that all was right with the world, but it was a misconception. Bad things were happening in all the places that she passed, but she was unaware of them. What an appropriate name for this girl sitting next to her holding tight to her dolphin and searching for ways to understand her place in the world. Why burst that bubble?

"Maybe after our beach excursion, I can read it to you?" said Milli. She'd love to get a library card, but she'd have to admit to being Millicent Tarnover. "You have a library card, right?"

"Sure, somewhere," said Pippa.

"Pippa Passes was written by Robert Browning in the 1800s. Let's see if we can find it," said Milli.

"The library is in the center of town, not so far. We can go there tomorrow afternoon after we hunt for sea glass."

"I like your attitude," said Milli.

"Funny thing. No one else has ever said that to me. Imagine that. Two listeners in one day! Must be some kinda record. And I agree with them both." Pippa saluted Milli and skipped away, her legs long and lanky like a heron's.

Apollo showed up precisely when the sun hit its apex. A paper bag was tucked under his arm. "Got you a surprise," he said.

Milli glowed.

He reached in the bag and brought out a large nondescript rock and handed it to her.

She figured she'd better feign delight until she noticed the lettering on its surface. "Thank you for being my teacher." The words were painted with bright yellow and purple markers, each letter carefully blocked. "I mean it," said Apollo. "You rock. Get it!"

"Thank you. Sincerely," said Milli, delighted that every word was spelled correctly. "It's nice to be a good teacher, but it's better to have a good student."

Apollo did an aw shucks movement with his feet.

"Now I have a surprise for you. Follow me." They went into the kitchen where Milli had set up a worktable for baking. The Old Goat must have used the oven because there were some supplies in the cabinet like measuring cups and spatulas. "I hope you like cake."

"Do I? Do I!"

"But before we bake, we need to read the directions. Ready?"

A few words were problematic and fractions were new to him, but he was a fast study. He worked with a steady hand and measured the oil precisely. He'd never cracked an egg before, so that was a bit messy, but he was adept at picking the shells out of the bowl. When the cake finally went into the oven, he let out such a sigh of relief that Milli laughed. Oh to bake with joy again, something she used to do with Leo, a professional baker. He was the one to teach Lionel as she snapped their picture. Those photographs were in a box under her bed in New Dawn. *How could I just have left them there? Because I never intended to leave forever?* She definitely needed to retrieve them.

Milli set the timer on the stove for thirty-five minutes while they whipped up a chocolate frosting. This time, Milli dictated the directions to Apollo as he wrote them down. Then he followed through on preparing it. By the time he finished, the cake was cool enough to frost.

They set the table together and Milli brought out the sub sandwiches and poured them each a large glass of chocolate milk. They didn't talk much as they ate—Apollo devouring every morsel of his meal including an enormous slice of cake—but the silence between them was friendly.

Around one-thirty, Apollo said he had to skedaddle. His mother had hired him out to mow lawns in the afternoon.

"When would you like another lesson?" Milli asked.

Apollo scratched his head. "I can come Tuesday morning. Will that be all right?"

"Sure. But here's the thing. Once you begin to read, you have to practice. I've bought today's newspaper for you to look at on your own."

"Like homework?" he said wide-eyed. "Like a normal kid?"

She pointed out a headline on the front page of dogs chasing gulls and racing into the water. It read: *No Dogs Allowed on Boston Beaches after June 1.* "What does it say and why is it important?"

"That's easy," said Apollo. "There are a lot of people using the beach in the summer and they don't want poop all over their feet."

"Exactly," said Milli. "Cut out four articles that interest you. Write down what each is about and why it's newsworthy. We'll talk about them on Tuesday." She wrapped a piece of cake and handed it to him. "There'll be more for you in the morning."

"More than OK. Props, Milli. You really rock," he said as he waved goodbye.

DURING MILLI'S NAP, she heard banging at the door. At first she thought she was dreaming, but the sound shuddered through the open space.

"Millicent Tarnover or Minnie Yanover, whatever you call yourself. Are you in there? I need to speak with you," said a voice like sandpaper.

Milli pulled the blanket over her head and shrank into the bed.

"Come to the door. I have something to show you."

Milli barely breathed. She could hear Grenadine trying the door-knob. She had a key, but that would be trespassing, wouldn't it? And Milli knew Grenadine did not own this property, so she had no legal right to enter. She could feel the woman at the side window, cupping her eyes and peering in. But the angle would be wrong for seeing the bed in the corner and there was no other peeking spot. Milli counted to one hundred, letting the numbers dominate her thoughts. By the time she finished, she felt that Grenadine was no longer at the door, but she didn't dare check. She could be lying in wait on the patio.

Milli was afraid to leave her apartment, so she sat at the kitchen table eating cake and drinking birchbark tea to calm her nerves. An hour later, another rap came at the door, but it wasn't hard and insistent, more like a rat-a-tap-tap. She crept toward the door and saw Apollo.

"I didn't expect you until Tuesday. Maybe you'd like a little more cake?"

The boy rushed into the room and spread the newspaper out on the table. He flipped to the Metro section, to a page that Milli had missed entirely when she skimmed the paper before giving it to Apollo for homework.

"Look, look at this!"

Milli saw a small photo of herself with the headline *Elderly Woman believed to be the victim of foul play.* She collapsed into a chair to read the article.

> Oldham—The clothing of Millicent Tarnover, an elderly woman missing for one week from the New Dawn Retirement Village, has been found stashed under a bush in the Seaside Arboretum.

Mrs. Tarnover vanished Tuesday morning after being dropped off by a livery service at a dentist's office on Main Street. There is no record of her meeting with any physician. She is eighty-five years old, five feet tall, and gray haired. She has difficulty walking and is easily confused.

A down coat, gloves, and wool cap were found rolled up and hidden under a grove of bushes. Police fear that she was abducted against her will and was a victim of foul play although her body has not been found.

Oldham police interviewed two teenaged boys who said they last saw her standing beside a golf buggy. Mrs. Tarnover was crying and was in a yelling match with the driver and his passenger. The boys said they admonished the men to leave her alone, but did not stay to find out what happened next.

The police are searching for the two men, described as in their seventies, white haired, overweight, and driving an electronic golf cart.

If you have any information about the whereabouts of Millicent Tarnover, please contact the Oldham police.

"Except for your red hair, that picture sure looks like you!" said Apollo. "Is she your sister? Are you in trouble?"

Milli didn't want to lie to Apollo and she didn't want him to worry, so she put on a calm face. "There's just been a misunderstanding. I'll take care of it."

"My Daddy said that and he's in the hoosegow. And I don't know when I'll see him again. Is that what will happen to you?"

"No, no way. I did nothing illegal," Milli said, hoping that was true.

"Sure," said Apollo, like a boy who knew about lies. "Is your real name Millicent Tarnover, like it says in the newspaper?"

"I'm afraid so," she said, knowing that no matter how much she wanted to reinvent herself, her past would not allow it. "Apollo, the newspaper article has some truth to it. But I'm not ready to inform the police yet about my whereabouts."

"Yeah, I get it," he said with twisted lips.

"Thank you for showing this to me. I'm so proud of you and your reading abilities." Milli's eyes drooped and she sighed with exhaustion. "Tell you what, Apollo, come back on Tuesday like we planned and I'll explain more then."

After Apollo left, Milli put on a pot of water to boil. Then she knocked on the pipes. "Birdie? Are you there? Please, could you come down for tea? I really need your help."

Within ten minutes, Birdie sat across from Milli at the kitchen table reading the newspaper article.

"What's going on?" she asked, rubbing her chest.

"I hated how I ended up in a basement room in New Dawn waiting to die. So I left without telling anyone. I just wanted to get out by myself for a few hours. At first, I meant to go back. But I'm finding myself again and it feels good."

"I understand," said Birdie. "So what are we going to do about it?"

Milli nearly fainted at her use of 'we.' "I guess I have to tell them that I'm alive and well."

Birdie's jaw moved like a puppet's as she gave this thought. "I knew you had darkness in your chest. I just couldn't figure out its cause. Seems like birchbark tea and salts are not your remedy. Who are the two men they're talking about in the article?"

"Comb Over and Hairy Ears. Two old jerks who made fun of me. I gave them a what-all and a whither-for!"

Birdie honked with laughter. "A curse on their houses! How did you end up hanging with them?"

"They gave me a ride in their golf buggy at the Arboretum where I slept the first night after I left New Dawn. I don't know their real names."

"Did they threaten you?"

Milli shook her head. "Not directly. They were loud-mouthed bullies out for laughs at my expense, but I didn't think they would hurt me physically."

Birdie leaned back. "What did the golf buggy look like?"

Milli's mouth stretched left. "Ah, white with an orange stripe on its hood."

"That should be easy enough to spot," said Birdie. "I give you credit, Alice Millicent Milli Ruby Tuesday Tarnover. You've got chutzpah, balls, big kahoonas. But you're playing with fire here."

"There's something else. Grenadine suspects I'm Millicent Tarnover. I'm convinced she wants to turn me in because I tricked her into thinking I was Minnie Yanover."

"You're full of surprises, Alice-Minnie-Milli."

"I'm worried about Grenadine. She seems vindictive, especially against you. She said you gave her bad advice."

"Baloney! A few years ago, Grenadine came around collecting the rent and I noticed a yellow hue around her face, like something sinister lurked below her skin. She asked what she should do about it and I told her to stop smoking, take Vitamin A, and meditate. I packaged up a mineral tea with instructions to sip it daily, something like I made for you. She laughed at me, saying I didn't know anything about her health. I was a quack and shouldn't be practicing medicine."

"But you were only trying to help."

"I come on too strong. Some people like it. Clearly, Grenadine didn't. It's like I insulted her," said Birdie, downing the last of her tea.

Milli had the same impression of Birdie when she first saw her in the bathroom with that brush stuck in her hair—loud and overbearing. *Are first impressions that powerful and inaccurate? What can be done about that?*

Milli flashed on the Wizard of Oz and the appearance of power, how people relied on their instincts for insight, but were often tricked, how an entire nation worshipped a man whose facade projected strength. He professed to rely on his gut to provide the best answers. In truth, his gut was filled with parasites that poisoned his brain, his heart, and his soul, and left him like a bombastic cavity of pus. Too bad he didn't have Madame Sheeya to help him grow.

"Relax your bones. I'll do some snooping for you. Stay close to the house. Okay?" said Birdie.

"I told Virginia I'd help her paint the store tomorrow morning. And you know your client Pippa? I said I'd collect sea glass with her during the day. We planned to go to the library afterwards. And Apollo is coming on Tuesday for a reading lesson. I have people depending on me. Don't you see? I don't want to go back."

"And I don't want you to leave," said Birdie.

Milli wanted to hug her, but for such a bulky woman, she made a fast exit. Milli heard her heavy feet on the stairwell and some stomping around in her flat. Then she heard Birdie's van start remotely as she bustled down the stairs. *How can Birdie help me? Will she make matters worse?*

Milli rubbed salt over her body and then took a hot shower, no sense wasting a possible cure for her ills.

Chapter Twenty

On Monday morning, Milli woke, dressed, peeked out the door, saw no one there, and walked stealthily to Lila's Florist shop. *Eidelweiss* greeted her once again.

"Good morning! I was hoping you'd come by early," said Virginia, her dimples deep. "It's kind of weird of me to ask, especially since we spent lots of time together the other day, but I don't know your name."

Milli gulped. *Which name would I give her? Alice? Minnie? Millicent? Ruby Tuesday?* "My friends call me Milli."

"Then Milli it is. I sure could use your help."

Milli surveyed the room to see what she could do. On the long table was a pan of lavender paint and a roller.

"That color's for the two corner walls. Thoughtful and calm," said Victoria, who was painting the other two walls a butterscotch yellow. "I'm going for cheery and bright."

"All anyone needs is a smile like yours to light up a room," said Milli as she put on latex gloves and an apron, and got to work.

"It's funny," said Victoria. "I was thinking the same thing about you. You have a welcoming smile. I knew you were a good person the minute I saw you in the store. You bring a sense of peace. My grandma was a thunderstorm. When she entered a room, everyone swirled to please her. They got so busy, there was no place to rest. My mom takes after her."

"I'd like to meet your mom," said Milli, more to be polite than to be honest.

"She credits you with the idea to redecorate the store. She's investing in my future, she says."

Leo had dreams for Lionel, to be the owner of a bakery, not just a lowly blueberry muffin man. Lionel learned measurements before he knew his alphabet. Teaspoon, tablespoon, cup, quart, gallon. Cracking eggs was his specialty, even at age four, not a shell in the bowl. Milli wondered if Victoria had learned about flowers at her grandmother's knee.

"Did you begin your job yet with Freddie's aunt?" asked Milli, recalling the elegant woman who commissioned Virginia to work for her.

Virginia nodded. "Her house is amazing. Views of the ocean from every window. No wonder she asked for greens, yellows, and blues. It's like bringing the outside in."

"What an opportunity. Did you run it by your mom?"

"If I'm making money, she's making money."

As they talked, the walls gained color and the room grew bright.

"And how about your grandmother? What did she say about redecorating and the new job?"

"Grandma Victoria doesn't say much lately. Once she was a force of nature and it seemed like overnight she was barely the wind. Why does that happen?"

"I'm sorry, Victoria. Age has a way of creeping up on us. I wish I could tell you that your grandmother will get stronger, but that won't be the case. Some of us have arteries that clog up and forget how to work. From what you've said, your grandmother's are in her mental capacity. Madame Sheeya thinks mine are in my heart."

"Which is worse? Having your mind and not your body or your

body and not your mind?" asked Victoria. "My mom says we can't have it both ways."

Milli stood back and admired her wall. Granted, she couldn't reach the highest sections and Victoria forbade her from using a ladder, but the middle of the wall was evenly glossed. "I guess the best we can do is appreciate one day at a time. Sure, we can plan for the future, but we need to live in the day however our bodies and our minds allow."

Victoria completed Milli's wall and they both went out to the back patio while the first coat dried. In addition to a bag full of doughnut holes, she brought her computer and showed Milli the graphics for the finishing touches in the shop: new long tables, a deep sink for cutting and washing, two refrigerated cases, shelves, a desk, a two-person wicker bench and two chairs around a coffee table, scattered with home beautiful magazines and flower books. Victoria had pictured it from beginning to end.

"It's your vision, Victoria, and you'll make it happen," said Milli.

"You jump-started me, just like my grandma would have done." Victoria strode off to check the paint and to order more supplies just as Pippa strode in to the patio.

"Are you ready to find sea glass?" she asked.

Pippa had brought Milli a small glass jar of her own.

"Let's be off," said Milli, lifting herself from the chair, refusing to let age interfere. But after they crossed the street, Milli made a beeline for the boardwalk bench. "I'm going to set my old bones down and survey the land for a few minutes."

Pippa pranced around the bench. "I'm going to check out a square of beach while you catch your breath. Be right back."

Milli watched Pippa study the sand. Each time she found a shard of sea glass, her face lit up with sunshine. When she returned to Milli, she showed off a few pieces. "This green one looks like a heart. And the white one is one of those boxy states in the midwest, like North Dakota. And this one," she held out a milky chunk of yellow, "is a sleepy sun."

"The beach is a treasure chest," said Milli. Pippa looped her arm beneath Milli's, and they set off down the ramp. "I'm going to need a cane pretty soon."

"I'll be your cane." Pippa stood stick-straight like a soldier. "Lean on me."

For the next hour, the two of them were dots on the sand, side by side, searching, finding, glowing, adding color and form to the bottles. Pippa walked Milli back to her apartment, both of them bone-tired but happy.

"Pippa, would you knock on Madame Sheeya's door to see if she's home? She'll want to see what we've collected."

Triple-stepping the stairs, Pippa gave three knocks and a howdy, but no one answered. "Not home. I'm going to leave my sun-chunk of sea glass for her. She'll know it was me."

"Let's save our trip to the library for the next time we meet," said Milli.

"How's tomorrow? I have an appointment with Madame Sheeya in the morning. We could go afterwards."

"Sounds like a plan, Stan," said Milli.

"God's in his heaven. All's right with the world," sang Pippa, as she danced her way onto Porter Street.

Chapter Twenty-One

Milli heard Birdie banging around in her apartment in the middle of the night, but she was nowhere to be found in the morning. Milli figured Birdie was working her booth at Funland, but dinnertime came and went and still no Birdie. Putting on her new jeans, a pink t-shirt, and sneakers, Milli considered adding red to her hair again as it had faded in the shower, but she decided to go *au natural*. She set out for the D-Note on the boulevard, her step slower and her mind restless.

The place was just as she left it. Two pony-tailed men sat angled toward each other at the bar. A couple canoodled in a corner. The same woman as last time sat alone. There was no live band, but head-banging music blared from speakers around the room and a few couples gyrated on the dance floor.

"If it isn't the Lady Young. Coke and rum coming right up," said the bartender.

Milli felt like she was in an episode of *Cheers*.

"Sip it slowly," said the woman who had helped Milli. "We want you to stick around for Karaoke. I bet you sing a mean Sinatra."

Milli's eyes misted. "My husband and I used to sing a heartfelt *Don't Stop Believin'* by Journey." Milli crooned softly, "*Some will win, some will lose, some were born to sing the blues. Oh the movie never ends, it goes on and on and on and on."*

But it hadn't gone on and on like Leo promised. Birdie was right about Milli's dark aura. The sadness remained. Milli removed the straw from her cocktail and tossed back the drink.

"Oh, oh. Time to find Kedrix," said the woman, her face wrinkling into worry. "You're going to need your knight in shining armor."

And just like that, Kedrix appeared. "What gives, Milli? What's going on?"

Milli swiveled on her bar stool. She parroted the words from Marvin Gaye's song. *"Come on talk to me, so you can see what's going on, what's going on, tell me what's going on."*

Kedrix frowned. "I think you could use some fresh air. Is there somewhere you'd like to go?"

Thinking so deeply that her chin fell onto her neck, Milli's face popped up and brightened, "How about Monmouth?"

"Isn't that where that New Dawn place is? You want to go back there?"

Milli shook her head so hard, her hair trembled. "No. No. Pine Hill Cemetery overlooks the retirement village. Can you take me there?" Another thought creased Milli's forehead with a dozen lines. "Where can we get flowers at this time of night?"

"I know just the place," said Kedrix. "Let's go."

Milli knew the drill, but she was a little light-headed from the coke and rum. She had a feeling, though, that the bartender went easy on the alcohol. He didn't want an old lady lying flat on the floor. Kedrix helped her onto the back of the bike and strapped on her helmet.

"Hold on," he said and they revved away.

It was still light enough to see a field of daffodils from a distance and the bordering lilac trees at the base of the Arboretum. Kedrix pulled alongside a fertile area. "You stay put, Ruby Tuesday. I'll do the picking."

Milli didn't argue. She closed her eyes and rested. Milli's nose awoke as Kedrix returned with purple boughs and yellow trumpets. He wrapped the flowers in a towel and placed them gently into a side pannier. Even as they rode, the sweet smell bounced around the air and calmed her worries.

The cemetery was high on a hill. On one side was wooded conservation area, on the other a panoramic view of the New Dawn complex.

"See that place down there? It's where life ends and waiting begins," said Milli, pointing to dozens of buildings and landscaped grounds. "Tonight I'm in limbo land." Milli directed Kedrix through the gates of Pine Hill Cemetery, past a gazebo and an obelisk until he came to a fenced-in plot. "You can park here."

Kedrix helped Milli off the bike and handed her the flowers. Milli cupped her ear, tuning in to her surroundings. "I hear them! My family didn't expect me and they're overjoyed that I've come."

Beside the fence was a tall maple tree, newly green, with its leaves shiny and full. Kedrix leaned against the trunk and gave Milli her space.

The gravestones were not inside the fence, but in the open under the shade of the tree. Milli didn't want Leo to see that she had arrived on a motorcycle.

She set all the flowers down in a space to the right of the five gravestones, then stood in front of the one that said, *In Loving Memory of Leo Tarnover, 1930–2005, Age 75. Beloved husband and father. May he rest in peace.*

Milli didn't cry as she caressed his name. "Oh Leo, my Love. You came to me in a dream last night, all sugary from baking. Flour covered you like a second skin. I brushed it off with a feather duster and you giggled that it tickled. Then we hugged and I felt so safe. I'm no longer upset that you left me the way you did. I know you chose a quiet way. No gunshot. No blood. Just ingesting a chemical potion. Pesticide poisoning, the doctors said. I don't blame myself anymore. I understand that now. But Leo, why didn't you think about how bereft

I'd be when you left me? You became so sad and frail and removed. You said I deserved better. But Leo there is no one better than you for me. You're my one and only true love."

Milli wrapped her arms around herself as she felt Leo reach out to embrace her.

"Now let me finish, will you? After you died, I worked at the bank for a few more years, but I was numb and robotic, I tell you. When I retired, Bernard sold the house, and I moved into New Dawn. At first I felt comfortable there. You were close by and I could visit you often. I made a friend, Anne Marie, and life resumed for me. Until she died. Then, poof. Pill time." Milli glanced to her right. "You recently got a neighbor, our nephew Bernard. He screwed me over, Leo. Stealing our money to pay for his pills, landing me in the Downtown Dungeon. Then something wild happened. In my dreams, I smelled lilacs. I smelled daffodils. And I needed to go where I could enjoy them freely, where we had been alive together. So that's exactly what I did. And here's the truth, Leo my love." Milli held the bouquet of flowers close to her heart. "I'm beginning a new journey without you. Sure, you're on my mind and in my heart, but I must go on alone to live the rest of my days making new friendships and having new adventures, and even, if I may be so bold, ride on a motorcycle."

Milli placed branches with deep purple lilacs and stems of smiling daffodils on his grave. She waited for Leo's response as heat moved up her body, wove around her legs and torso, then settled in her heart. She bowed her head and said, "Rest in peace, my love."

She moved to Lionel's grave. From her purse, she withdrew his favorite cap, the one with the sun emblazoned on it. She smelled under its brim, but too many years had passed and that musky sweetness had dissipated. She put it on her head and waited to hear him, his just-changing voice crackling hello. Milli closed her eyes and imagined their hug, his bony arms around her, him on his tiptoes to appear taller, just as he was at thirteen, with a ready smile and bright snapping eyes. "You'll grow," she told him all the time, although Leo wasn't much over 5'6", with small hands, small ears, and small feet. Milli glanced over at Leo's grave again. "Your dad made up for his height with his breadth of heart," she said aloud.

Milli gazed at Lionel's inscription: *Lionel Davis Tarnover, beloved son of Millicent and Leo, 1984–1997, Our Souls Will Never Say Good-Bye.* "I'm helping a young boy to love the written word and it's so rewarding for me. Do you remember all the books we read together? The three of us, cuddled in bed. You always had so many questions and I loved that. So curious. So filled with wonder about everything. Lionel, you know I'll be joining you and Daddy soon, but I thought I'd stay on earth a few extra years, if that's all right. Not just to tutor Apollo, but for lots of Apollos. And for Virginia. She's just about the age you'd be now. No. That's not right. No matter. You'd be her handsome older man and you'd be madly in love. After all, Daddy was thirteen years older than I was and look how well matched we were."

Again Milli looked to Leo. "But I couldn't help you, Leo. Not in the end. I'm sorry." Returning to Lionel, she kissed her fingers and touched his name. "I'm still learning about life and forgiveness." She told him she loved him as she laid the flowers on his grave.

She moved to the right: *Linda Mae Davis Monk, 1938–2012. Beloved Mother, Sister, and Friend.* There was a round mound of earth in the center of her plot where Bernard's urn had been buried. A rectangular plate read: *Bernard Monk, 1974–2022, Age 48.* Milli vaguely recalled signing the papers for the funeral home. She guessed Ms. Fagan had made all the arrangements and that she had been here when he was laid to rest. But the hours fogged in her mind, like many of those hazy pill-filled days. "What can I say? I love you both, but Bernard, you did me wrong." She forced herself to remember Thanksgivings or birthdays when the family was together and healthy. She saw them all at the beach, then skiing Sugarloaf, then skating. Seeing the good erased the bad. That was the only way to experience their love. She set the flowers out for them. "Take care of each other," she said.

Finally, her parents lay together under one stone. They died within six months of each other, her dad first. It was tougher to think of happy days with them. She had to go way back to childhood when she and her sister opened Christmas presents and sang carols throughout the neighborhood. Her father and mother harmonized like pros and enjoyed the tradition until Linda Mae eloped right out of high school and rarely returned to the family home even when their parents' health spiraled. Milli focused on the peaceful images of *Silent Night* and *O Come All Ye Faithful*, hot cocoa afterwards, and Midnight Mass. That would have to do.

She left flowers on their graves, and placed an extra few on Lionel's. The sweetest for the sweetest.

"I'm ready to go home now," she called to Kedrix, as she removed Lionel's hat and put it in her purse.

"I've been watching you, Ruby Tuesday. You got a lot of sadness in you. Do you feel better now?"

"More than better. Renewed. Ready to move on."

Chapter Twenty-Two

After Kedrix dropped Milli at her apartment, she banged on the pipes to see if Birdie was home. No reply. It was only 9:15, but Milli was tired. She decided to go to sleep and check with Birdie in the morning.

The next day, Apollo knocked earlier than expected and Milli wasn't quite ready for him.

"Make yourself at home," she said. Then she rued the choice of words. Home was not a pleasant place for Apollo. "There's cake on the counter. Milk's in the fridge. I'll be with you in a few minutes."

When she finally sat down beside him, Milli saw the crumple of his face.

"I been thinking about the story in the newspaper." Questions streamed out of Apollo. "Why were your clothes found at the Arboretum? And did those two men hurt you? What does abduct mean? What does admonish mean?"

Milli folded her hands in front of her and took a deep breath. "Abduct means to kidnap, to take someone against their will. So no, I was not abducted. Admonish means to warn. And yes, those two teen-aged boys did warn the two men who drove the buggy to be nicer to me." That part was easy to explain. "My clothes were in the Arboretum because I didn't want to be burdened with them for the day. I thought I would return to retrieve them." That was the truth. "But most of all, Apollo, I've done something I should not have done."

Apollo angled toward Milli. His eyes were so focused on her, she felt their drill.

"Do you know what claustrophobia is?" she asked.

"I can guess," Apollo said. "My daddy might say it's when you have to hide in a closet because people are following you."

Milli didn't laugh. "Claustrophobia means the fear of living in a small, closed in place."

"Like a jail cell?"

"Yes."

"Then my daddy must have claustrophobia."

Milli took another deep breath. "I lived in a tiny room with little windows that had a view of trash cans. The hallways were noisy and I rarely had enough time that I could call my own."

"That sounds like my house," said Apollo.

"So I left the place without letting anyone know where I was going. That was wrong of me."

"But you left for a good reason, right?" asked Apollo.

"That doesn't matter. Good people are worried about me, and they fear that I'm injured."

"You can keep on running. I can hide you," said Apollo.

"Is that the right thing to do?" asked Milli.

Milli could see Apollo's wheels spinning, weighing what he knew about telling the truth and its consequences. "If my dad had skedaddled, he wouldn't be in prison now."

"But he'd never be able to come home. He'd always be on the run."

Apollo nodded. "But claustrophobia must be like being strangled. It's better to run away, even if you have to leave everyone behind."

"But you'd always be looking over your shoulder. Every day, you'd live with the fear of being discovered. Even though I didn't like living in that tiny room, there were other ways I could have handled the situation."

Milli wished she had thought out her choices. She could have left New Dawn freely. Given notice. Found a new retirement village. But being close to the cemetery where Leo and Lionel rested was a strong pull and she felt so overwhelmed by Bernard's death and his bad judgment that she just swallowed her fate, quite literally. Her best bet now was to apologize for her actions, pack her photographs and belongings, leave New Dawn, and return to her rented apartment. Then she recalled Grenadine and the letter of eviction. Victoria's mother would intervene, wouldn't she? But if money were the woman's motivation, then Grenadine's tenant would win out.

"I don't know what the future will bring, Apollo. But I do know that telling the truth is the only way to move forward."

"What if they put you in prison?" asked Apollo.

"I didn't do anything wrong legally, just morally. Do you know the difference?"

Apollo's eyes roamed the room without finding a place to rest. "My father can legally hit me, but it is not morally right."

Milli's eyes welled. "You're a smart young man with a bright future. Doing what is morally right can be difficult. I did what was morally wrong and now I have to correct my mistake."

"My dad says that when he gets out of prison, he's going to be a better man and a better father. I want to believe him."

"You put a lot of faith in your father. I hope he lives up to your expectations. As in all things, time will tell," said Milli. "Now, it's time for me to face the music, but first I want to give you something that means a lot to me." Milli reached into her purse for Lionel's hat. "This belonged to my son, the light of my life. You are a lot like him. Curious and kind."

Apollo traced the logo of the sun.

"One of the mythical Apollo's daily chores was to harness his chariot with four horses and drive the sun across the sky," said Milli.

"Without him, there'd be no sun. So let this hat be a reminder for you to do what is needed to make the world a brighter place."

"Maybe you need it more than I do," said Apollo.

Milli laughed. "How about you keep it for a while to remind you to read and learn and seek out knowledge. Apollo is also the god of truth and light."

"He's a superman."

"And so are you."

A commotion outside drew their attention to the patio. Two police officers had come into the yard and paused at Milli's door. She wanted to hide, but she took Apollo by the hand and they walked outside. But the officers went up the stairs instead and knocked on Birdie's door.

"Madame Sheeya? Police. We'd like to speak with you."

Milli and Apollo stood at the base of the stairs, their mouths agape.

"What's going on?" asked Birdie who came to the door all dolled up. Her hair was in curls, her makeup blazing.

"We have a complaint lodged against you by an Anthony Rizzo and a Carl Smith. They said you tampered with their golf buggy's engine and it won't start. We'd like to take you to the station for questioning."

"Am I under arrest?"

"No ma'am. We'd just like to talk to you about the charges."

Birdie came down the stairs with the officers. "Give me a few minutes. I need to talk to my friend first."

Birdie drew Milli aside. "I put a curse on that golf cart that belongs to Comb Over and Hairy Ears. They won't be bothering you again."

"Is that why the police are questioning you?"

"Well, I planted a doll under the hood of their vehicle," she whispered.

"Like the one you put in my closet?"

"Not exactly. This one had long red pins in its heart and in its eyes.

Those men have lost all power over women. Forevermore," declared Birdie.

"A doll is not a crime," said Milli.

"True, but I spray painted the engine. They'll never have a restful sleep again. I tell you, it was my best curse ever."

The police officer approached the two women, but he addressed Milli. "Might you tell me your name, Ma'am? You resemble a person we have on file."

Milli looked over at Apollo, who looked like he was going to cry. Before Milli could reply, a van pulled up to the apartment with New Dawn Retirement Village in bold-letters on its side. Grenadine escorted two people into the yard: Alexis Fagan, the social worker; and the burly man who accompanied Ms. Fagan the last time they came looking for Milli.

"I believe this is your missing person, Millicent Tarnover," cackled Grenadine.

The police officer raised his eyebrows. "Yes, that's exactly what I thought."

Milli bound her wrists together and offered them up. "Guilty as charged. I am Millicent Tarnover, alive and well. I'm ready to return to New Dawn now."

For Milli, the next ten minutes were a whirlwind of chaos. Apollo sobbed. Birdie spewed curses on Grenadine. Virginia ran down from the Floral Shop asking what she could do to help. Pippa showed up for her appointment with Birdie just as one of the policemen was putting her into the squad car. Grenadine emerged from the apartment carrying a green trash bag with Milli's belongings spilling out. The other officer and the burly man exchanged information.

Ms. Fagan took Milli by the elbow and escorted her to the van. "The case is solved, Officers." She handed the policeman her business card. "You probably have questions for Mrs. Tarnover, but she's been through enough. I'll be available to discuss her case." To Milli, she cooed, "Come along, Dear. We'll take good care of you."

Milli's eyes clouded over and her hearing went deaf. All action took place outside her sphere and she watched it like a movie.

Grenadine threw the trash bag into the van and retreated. Apollo waved his hat in Milli's direction. Virginia shouted into her cell phone as Birdie settled into the squad car. Pippa stood stock still, probably for the first time ever.

Moral? Legal? What difference did it make now? thought Milli, as she sat in the back of the windowless van, claustrophobia setting in.

PART TWO

Chapter Twenty-Three

"Who on earth are you?" asked Milli, pointing to the burly man driving the windowless van.

Ms. Fagan swung around in her seat. "This is Basil Grasin, Dear, the controller at New Dawn."

"So you're in charge of my millions? The one who stuffed me into that Downtown Dungeon?"

Grasin stared into the rear view mirror. "Mrs. Tarnover, I'll have you know, we've been scouring the area for you for the last week. Your health and well-being are in our hands." His voice was gruff like a bulldog's.

Ms. Fagan raised her eyebrows. "Millicent Dear, We're just glad you're well and able to return to New Dawn intact."

Intact? What does that mean? Has my mind escaped my body and is it running around outside of itself? "I'll have you know, I am in complete control of my faculties."

"Of course, Dear," said Ms. Fagan. "That is exactly what we'll be deciding. You know, Dear, we thought you were kidnapped. We interviewed the two gentlemen who recognized you from the newspaper. They said you were belligerent and aggressive toward them."

"Comb Over and Hairy Ears, scoundrels, both of them." Milli wanted to spit.

Mr. Grasin murmured under his breath. "She's nuts, I tell you. Off her rocker."

"Mr. Grasin, those men tried to take advantage of me. If it weren't for the teenaged boys who came along, who knows what those perverted geezers would have done."

"Delusional," growled Mr. Grasin.

Ms. Fagan smiled at Milli as if she were a child. "My Dear, you've had a rough week, not knowing where your next meal would come from, not knowing where you'd sleep. You were lucky Grenadine sheltered you."

"That woman is a witch," said Milli, her voice pounding out the words.

"The other one, that Madame Seer, she's the witch," mumbled Mr. Grasin.

"Madame Sheeya is my friend, and she's a healer, not a witch," said Milli.

"Of course. But why would a healer place a voodoo doll with pins in it under the hood of those men's vehicle. Isn't that dubious behavior?" said Ms. Fagan.

"She was trying to help me." Milli's body began a slow burn, creeping up her legs and into her heart. She tried to settle her breath by counting to one hundred, but by fifty, she had trouble breathing. She closed her eyes and tried to imagine an idyllic field of flowers, but all she could see were bare branches and burnt grass.

"What were you thinking, Dear?" asked Ms. Fagan.

"She wasn't, that's the problem. Nothing up there," said Mr. Grasin, his fingers whirling around his head in a cuckoo motion.

Milli wanted to tell them she had duped them when she went off on the motorcycle with Kedrix. How she said that her best friend Minnie Yanover lived in that apartment, not Millicent Tarnover. And they believed her, didn't they? *Minnie Hah Hah on them!*

"Did that Grenadine psychopath tell you I was out of my mind?" Milli mimicked Mr. Grasin's rotating fingers.

"She didn't have to, Dear. When that motorcycle woman with the crazy red hair told us about a woman parading up and down the street yelling in a foreign language, we thought it could be you. We followed that lead and thank God, with Grenadine's help, we found you."

They thought motorcycle Milli was an entirely different person than she. *Well, I certainly fooled them. Maybe I shouldn't have said anything! I thought I was being so clever, but my arrogance might have done me in.* What could she say now that would convince them of her sanity and her motives?

"What if I told you I'm Ruby Tuesday, the woman on the motorcycle?"

Ms. Fagan smiled. "Of course you weren't Dear. I spoke directly to that woman. She was perky and strong-legged. Why she hopped on that motorcycle like a teenager. I know you'd like to think you were she, but that's unlikely."

Milli's heart constricted. "Ms. Fagan, I left New Dawn last Tuesday. The car service took me to a dentist's office in Oldham. I slipped out the back door and walked to the Seaside Arboretum where I spent the night sleeping on a bench. The next morning, I met a lovely young woman named Keysi, whom I helped by offering advice, and then I walked toward the ocean. That's when those two men picked me up and harassed me."

"Do you mean Mr. Smith and Mr. Rizzo?" asked Mr. Grasin.

"Exactly," Milli said. Hairy Ears and Comb Over she said in her mind. Neither deserved the dignity of a real name.

"Yes, we spoke with them, as did the police. It seems you were disoriented and confused and began a verbal argument with them. They seemed like perfectly civil gentlemen to us," said Ms. Fagan. "They certainly didn't deserve a voodoo doll in their engine."

Mr. Grasin stage-whispered, "Why are you persevering with this conversation? She's clearly out of her gourd."

"In my line of work, it helps the patient to tell reality from fantasy if we go over the facts together," said Ms. Fagan.

"The fact is I am neither delusional nor incompetent. I just wanted to be on my own. Is that so hard to understand?" cried Milli.

"Now Dear. Don't get upset. We'll straighten this whole thing out as soon as we get to New Dawn."

"Mr. Grasin, do you own your own house?" asked Milli in an even tone.

He pulled the van up to the curb in front of a sheltered wing of New Dawn's Retirement Village. "I certainly do."

"And do you have more than one room?"

The man rolled his eyes. "There are seven rooms in my house."

"How would you like to be confined to only one room?" asked Milli.

"I wouldn't like it at all, but that is neither here nor there, is it? New Dawn is a vast center for senior living. We accommodate all our residents with top of the line work-out spaces, eateries, entertainment rooms, and we provide around-the-clock nursing services for those who need them. Are you saying, Mrs. Tarnover, that New Dawn imprisoned you?"

"That's exactly what I'm saying."

"I told you the woman is daft. Alexis, schedule Mrs. Tarnover's evaluation. Then we can decide what to do after the results are confirmed."

"Mrs. Tarnover, Dear, come with me, please."

Milli saw no alternative but to allow Ms. Fagan to lead her into New Dawn.

Ms. Fagan signed them in and led Milli down a narrow corridor that she had never seen before. As she walked, she heard a door click behind her. Milli entered a small room with its own bathroom and shower. The room had no windows, a narrow bed, a folding chair, a bureau with shelves and drawers on one side and a rod for hanging clothes on the other, a closet, and eight cardboard boxes stacked against a wall. Each had Milli's name on it.

"We didn't know whether you were alive or dead, so we cleared out your Downtown Crossing room. I'll bring you the bag that Grenadine put in our van," said Ms. Fagan.

"What's going to happen to me?" asked Milli.

Ms. Fagan patted the bed for her to sit and opened the chair. "Millicent, Dear, we need to assess your state of mind, so we'll be doing a few routine tests over the next few days."

"Days?" said Milli. "My state of mind is clear as a bell. That's all you need to know."

"May I ask, what is today's date?"

Milli didn't hesitate, recalling the date on Apollo's newspaper. "May 24."

"And what day of the week is it?"

"Wednesday."

"The truth is, today is Tuesday, May 23, 2023."

"So I got the day and date wrong. What does that prove?"

Ms. Fagan shook her head. "I get the date wrong all the time and it doesn't mean I'm confused or not living in the real world. But you have shown yourself to be unreliable and inconsistent. We need to get to the bottom of this before we can trust you to be on your own again. We are responsible for you, Millicent Dear. You must see that."

"What I see is a man and a woman who are unable to admit that someone might hate being in this place." Milli stood up to pace the small room, but her legs shook in anger. She leaned against the bed.

"Why don't you rest for a while. The aide will bring you lunch." Ms. Fagan fluffed Milli's pillow. "Now you just lie back and don't worry about a thing. You're safe now."

"I want out of here immediately," said Milli. "I have my rights." *Or do I? Have I relinquished them the minute I got into the van with Ms. Fagan and Bulldog Basil?*

Ms. Fagan left the room and Milli heard the clack of her shoes along the hall. The door clicked, but Milli opened it and poked her head out, trying to figure out where on earth she had landed. There were about ten rooms, five on each side of the corridor. At the end was a red exit sign. *Aha! That's where I'm going. Out of here.* But first she needed a specific plan, not the dreamy goal of lilacs and daffodils. She would think this out, not helter-skelter, but with a serious defense that could not be refuted.

THE AIDE BROUGHT MILLI'S LUNCH: tuna and cheese on wholewheat bread, a salad, a chocolate milkshake, and an oatmeal cookie. At least there was no green Jello. Milli devoured every crumb. Then she felt strong enough to explore this new prison. Two rooms down was a sitting area with two couches and a television. She might as well make herself comfortable, she decided, and watched a rerun of *I Love Lucy*. Another woman joined her.

"Ricky Ricardo! My favorite. Such a great singer," said the woman, who did a shuffling cha-cha before sitting down.

"I'm an Ethel Mertz fan myself," said Milli.

"Do you live here? I haven't seen you before," said the woman.

"Just visiting," said Milli, hoping it was true.

The women watched an episode of *Happy Days* and hummed the theme song together.

"I'm going to get a glass of water," said the woman. "Would you like one?"

"No thank you," said Milli. "Is there a kitchen nearby?"

The woman didn't answer. She exited the room with a flourish, "And away we go."

Milli stayed to watch a half hour of *The Mary Tyler Moore Show* and enjoyed the nostalgia of a bygone era. When it was over, she checked out other rooms on the floor. In one, a woman sat in a rocker flipping through a *People* magazine. In another, a man listened to a ball game on the radio. There was an alcove with a refrigerator and some snacks. Milli chose crackers and a ginger ale. In the next room was the I-Love-Lucy woman.

"Hi again," said Milli.

The woman looked at Milli with a wide smile. "Hi there. Are you new here?" she asked. "I haven't seen you before."

"We just watched television together," said Milli.

"That must have been fun," she said.

It didn't take Milli long to realize this ward was for men and women who had memory issues. She made her way to the nurses' station at the end of the hall.

"I'd like to take a walk outside," she told the nurse. "Is there a log book for me to sign?"

The nurse looked up. "You're Millicent Tarnover, correct?"

"The one and only." Milli should have said the only and one.

"I'm sorry. There's no attendant to take you out at the moment. Perhaps in an hour or so."

"I'm capable of being outside by myself," Milli said.

The nurse set down her pen and came around the desk to stand beside Milli. "You've been through a traumatic experience recently. It's in your best interest to walk with an aide who can help you if you can't recall the unit you're housed in. Trust us, Millicent." She put her arm through Milli's and escorted her back to her room.

Milli sat on her bed, stewing. *I've been to the mountain, don't they know that? I am perfectly capable of living on my own.* To hell with a specific plan, Milli wanted out, and fast. She peeked out her room again and saw that no one was at the nurses' station. She scurried to the door, tried the latch, and an alarm sounded.

The nurse hurried toward her. "We have rules, Mrs. Tarnover. We understand that you'd like to go outside, but that's not possible now."

An aide rushed to help the nurse. "Do we need to restrain her?"

Milli fully understood what they were saying and wanted to tell them to take a hike or worse, but she knew that would get her nowhere. "Tell me. Do you have a written set of rules? Something I can read?"

The nurse shook her head. "I can certainly ask Ms. Fagan. She'll be checking in with us tomorrow. In the meantime, Mrs. Tarnover, I can prescribe medication to help you relax."

"How about a beer?"

The aide laughed, but the nurse remained stone-faced. "I'll tell you what. I'll have one of our volunteers come to your room to read you a story. Would you like that?"

"Yes. Please. Thank you," said Milli and returned to her room on her own.

After half an hour of staring at boxes, Milli selected one to see what was inside. Like a child, she sat on the floor and sorted through an assortment of random clothes, papers and knick-knacks tossed together with no thought to organization. *Is this what happens when people die? Their lives are stacked carelessly inside cardboard?*

She found five jerseys, four pairs of sweatpants, and two pairs of pjs—she piled them on her bureau; a poster signed by her bank colleagues wished her well in retirement—she barely recalled their names; and a folder contained birthday cards from Leo, Lionel, Linda Mae, and Bernard—she ran a finger over their signatures and rubbed them into her skin with her thumb. At the bottom of the box was a pouch of rings and earrings, all costume jewelry, and the book *New Passages* by Gail Sheehy. *Wow! Again! I never did get a chance to read the one on Porter Street. Maybe it's a sign, hey, Madame Sheeya?*

Milli flipped to the section called *Sharpening Up for the Sage Seventies and Beyond.* She read the line, "They do all kinds of things they wouldn't have dared at earlier stages. They have nothing left to lose." *How true is that? How much more would I dare to do? Swim in the ocean. Explore a foreign country. Take a cruise. Volunteer in a school. Put on one of those virtual gizmos and fly. Break out of this place and head for the ocean.*

But the line that resonated the most was the last one in the chapter: "If every day is an awakening, you will never grow old. You will just keep growing."

Chapter Twenty-Four

Late that afternoon, a tall, bone-thin, dark-skinned man with stooped shoulders entered her room.

"I've come to read to you," he said in a quiet yet distinctive voice.

"Can we read outside?" asked Milli.

"Let me check."

The man returned shaking his head. "I'm sorry, Mrs. Tarnover. The nurse on duty said you're a flight risk. Those were her exact words. Apparently, they don't think I'm quick enough to subdue you," he laughed and his eyes twinkled.

"There you have it. I'm a felon. A criminal. A real-deal prisoner. Do I look dangerous to you?" Milli pulled back her shoulders and jutted out her chin, like she was posing for a mug shot. "Now what?"

The man sat and opened a dog-eared book. *Please, not a Bible, and please, none of those self-help books.* Milli radiated sunshine when the man recited a poem:

> *My Journey*
> *By Rachel Rousso*
>
> *The path winds along a river*
> *That flows south, as I trod north.*

Along the bank, waters flow downhill.
My climb is steep; the way choppy.
I cross a bridge and veer west.
Hills, plateaus, dips and ruts,
Grassy knolls, fields and farms,
Caves and crevices, palaces and shacks.
Keep moving. Witness more.
Shall I choose Robert Frost's less traveled?
Or stay the familiar?
Or forge a new path?
My choice. My journey. My way.

Like a harp, the man plucked each word rhythmically and with precision. Each had its own identity; each spoke its separate truth. As he read, Milli felt a calm rush over her. She lay back on her bed and closed her eyes. When he finished, she clapped silently.

"I guess I chose the right poem. Why did it have such an effect on you?"

"It tells me that if I trust in myself and follow the path of my choice, I'll be all right."

"It's interesting. I've read this poem to many residents on this wing. No one has had your reaction."

"I don't belong on this wing," said Milli.

"You're Millicent Tarnover, aren't you? I read about your disappearance. I'm so sorry you were abducted against your will. I hope your captors didn't disrespect you."

His words were so old-fashioned, like Leo's. The man took such care with language, like Leo did with sugar and flour and butter. "I was not abducted. I escaped."

The man stifled a chuckle. "But this wing is locked."

"I lived in the Assisted Living section of New Dawn. They let us out for good behavior."

"So no one took you or wronged you. What landed you here, if I may ask?"

"To tell you the truth, I'm not sure," said Milli. "I'm told I need to be evaluated to see if I have dementia or if I will harm myself. Nothing in my history supports this, and yet here I am."

"Have you no recourse?" he asked.

"Maybe you know someone adept at advocating for the elderly?"

When Milli said this, the man's face broke into pieces. He closed his book of poems and rose to leave. "I wish you luck, Mrs. Tarnover. I'm sure the powers that be will realize they've made a mistake."

"So you cannot help me?"

He came closer to Milli. "My wife died a year ago from this horrid disease of Alzheimer's. It takes many forms. One day she was perfectly lucid, like you. And the next, she couldn't remember that I was her soulmate. The pain of watching her deteriorate destroyed me. To experience that again is untenable."

"I'm so sorry about your wife. Tell me. What's your name?"

"Call me Joe. I've found it the easiest name for patients to recall."

"Poetry Joe, that will be my name for you. I guarantee I'll remember it even months from now."

"I hope you're right. You're a lovely woman of substance and I would like to get to know you better. But I am fearful of what tomorrow may bring."

When Poetry Joe left, Milli rummaged through another box. Her family photos. *Talk about painful, huh, Joe?* She could barely look at Leo's beautiful smile and Lionel's toothless baby-grin. She wanted to rip up all pictures of Bernard, and upon seeing Linda Mae's radiant face, she gave herself up to tears.

"Mrs. Tarnover, Dear, I've come to check on you," said Ms. Fagan. "Oh, my, what's wrong? Don't cry."

Milli accepted the tissues Ms. Fagan offered and gained control of her emotions. "What's wrong? What's wrong! You know perfectly well I don't belong in a locked ward. I don't need constant supervision. I am an eighty-four year old powerhouse of independence and I demand a lawyer."

"Now, now, Dear. I understand your frustration. First things first. I've scheduled a meeting tomorrow for you with Dr. Boothbury. He will assess your capacity to understand your situation."

Milli knew full well that she was at one-hundred percent capacity. "How is this test conducted?"

"The doctor will ask you a series of questions to discover your ability to make decisions."

"And then what?"

"If he's satisfied that you can understand, appreciate, and reason, you'll be free to make your own choices. If not, New Dawn will advocate for you." Ms. Fagan fluffed Milli's pillows for the second time that day. "We'd like you to get a good night's sleep, Dear, so you'll be refreshed in the morning. The nurse on duty will be in shortly with your dinner. Are you all right with these decisions so far?"

"Do I have a choice?" asked Milli.

The answer, of course, was no.

The nurse came in with dinner—meatloaf, brown gravy, potatoes, creamed corn, this time followed by green Jello with a dollop of whipped cream—and she returned an hour later to prepare Milli for bed. "The doctor has requested you take two pills with warm milk so you won't be up all night fretting about the procedure tomorrow."

Milli knew she'd have a tough time sleeping, but should she risk being groggy in the morning? The nurse assured her the pills were mild and stood beside her as she swallowed. Sleep came fast and with it vivid dreams: Apollo wearing Lionel's hat as he drove Kedrix's motorcycle; Grenadine dropping daffodil petals into boiling water; Ms. Fagan spoon-feeding Milli mashed blueberry muffins. In the early morning, Milli woke with stomach pains. Good thing she had her own bathroom. For hours, she suffered and before long, she was wrapped in sweat.

When the aide came in, Milli was a dish rag. A nurse quickly followed.

"My, my. What's the matter, Lovey?"

"Bad night," she said. "The pills did not agree with me." *Or maybe it was the Jello.*

The nurse took Milli's vital signs and jotted them down on a chart. "You have a low-grade fever, Lovey. Can you tell me how you're feeling?"

"My stomach's in a knot and my mouth is dry," squeaked Milli.

"Let's get you a cup of coffee and toast. Then we'll check in with the doctor," said the nurse.

"Coffee and I don't get along. Could I have tea instead?" asked Milli.

The aide brought Milli tea and toast; she helped her into new pajamas, changed the bedding, and settled Milli back in bed.

"Thank you." Milli read her badge, Reshma Ramirez. "Reshma, how lovely."

The aide's face widened into a smile as if Milli had given her sunshine on a platter.

"You remind me of a kind young woman I met recently. Even your names sound alike. Reshma, Rashida. I'm lucky to be in your care," said Milli.

Reshma took both of Milli's hands in hers. "I pray for your return to good health." The nurse returned and Reshma left the room. "I have a call into the doctor, Lovey. In the meantime, see if you can get some sleep."

"No more sleeping pills. They upset my stomach."

"It's unlikely the pills were the cause, Lovey," she said tight-lipped. "Let's wait for the doctor's diagnosis. He knows best."

Just like *Father Knows Best,* thought Milli. Where did that get her? Her own father knew least and cared less. Milli tumbled into a restless sleep. What pulsed through her mind was the truth of Poetry Joe's poem: *Be determined to save the only life you can save. Your own.*

The nurse took Milli's vital signs again, and seeing that her temperature had spiked, she called the doctor. "No evaluation for you today. Bedrest, fluids, and acetaminophen."

"Does the doctor know I won't be taking his test today because I'm not feeling well, not because I'm incapacitated mentally?"

"Ms. Fagan is on it. She'll be by later to check on you."

Milli knew what later meant, hours and hours would pass. She might as well go back to sleep. Around noon, Reshma stopped by.

"I'm sorry, Mrs. Tarnover, but the doctor left a message for you. He is not available again until next Tuesday. It's Memorial Day weekend, and he's off with his family for a few days."

Milli sat up right quickly. "I'm fine now. Call him back. I'm ready to roll." She stood, but cramps in her belly doubled her over.

"Sorry, Mrs. Tarnover, but you'll have to wait until Tuesday."

And be stuck in the memory-care ward for five days? Milli stifled the urge to scream really really loud, but she knew it would be a sign of diminished capacity. She'd have to obey the rules. *How will I survive?*

Chapter Twenty-Five

Often Milli experienced a day that was lost and never retrieved, especially after Lionel passed and both she and Leo grieved. Milli tried to work around Leo's debilitating sorrow so that it wouldn't sink them both.

Depression was the clinical term, but for Leo suicide was the result. Milli didn't blame herself, but she also didn't absolve herself. What else could she have done? They saw doctors. He took medication. She made his favorite meals. She kept the house spotless and tried to anticipate his mood swings. But Leo's inertia resulted in lost work hours, salty blueberry muffins, flat cakes, and bland cookies, and ultimately lost him his job. It was up to Milli to pick up the slack, so she was hired as a teller at a downtown bank.

Leo didn't complain, but then again, she left him alone all day. He said he kept busy and put on a smile when she came home, but Milli knew his soul was starved. Bernard came by and played cards with Leo, but that ended when Leo caught him pocketing oxycodone. Milli had told her sister about the thefts, which had occurred regularly in small doses, but Linda Mae refused to accept that her son was at fault. She blamed it on Leo's depression, and made Milli feel guilty that they accused Bernard.

Milli went along trying to take a sunny approach. In retrospect, Milli saw it as denial, but at the time, she got through her days. When Leo suffered a mild stroke, Milli nursed him back to health, and still she disregarded the signs of imminent demise. It was only after she found Leo wrapped in a blanket, his face stone-cold, did she understand the depth of his sorrow. She had found empty bottles of insecticide in his study, in his shop, and in the garage and knew this wasn't a random act. In his letter to her, he apologized. He told her he was in a better place and to carry on. He knew she was strong and would find peace on her own.

But that wasn't true. She was not strong. And now it felt as if her freedom were being taken away from her, again. As Milli spiraled, she shrouded herself in darkness and allowed no light to penetrate. Every extremity on her body reminded her that she was going nowhere. Her lilac and daffodil days had ended and she was reduced to Groundhog Day reruns for real.

When the sun rose on Saturday, she felt more like the worn-out, sorrowful Millicent Tarnover, and less like the what's-around-the-corner Milli or the devil-may-care Ruby Tuesday. Bitterness simmered toward Bernard. Anger roiled at Leo for taking his own life. The early demise of her only child stabbed so deeply, she couldn't move. And she had no one to talk to. Her friend Anne Marie was gone, along with her sister Linda Mae. Her new friends in Oldham were unreachable.

When Ms. Fagan checked on her, Milli feigned sleep. She had no interest in speaking with that woman, someone she now regarded as the enemy. Only Reshma lifted her spirits when she brought her hot soup and crackers and sat beside her as she slurped.

Poetry Joe made his rounds, but Milli couldn't let him see her in the state she was in. She understood his pain in losing his wife to Alzheimer's. If she and Poetry Joe shared words, hers would be garbled and disjointed, like her mind. She knew she wasn't incapacitated, but she wasn't the same woman who swooned over the Rachel Rousso poem only two days ago.

On Sunday morning, Reshma propped up a letter on Milli's breakfast tray. "Special delivery," she said. "But first, you must take a shower and have something to eat. Only after that can you enjoy your surprise."

Milli didn't stir.

"Okay. I'll give you a hint. A certain young man and his mother came to visit you yesterday, but we told them you were not feeling well. The boy asked if he could write you a letter."

Milli opened one eye. "Was he wearing a hat?"

"Indeed he was."

Milli opened both eyes. "What was on the hat?"

"I couldn't really say. Something yellow, I think. Does that sound familiar?"

Milli reached for the letter.

"First things first," said Reshma, hiding the letter behind her. "Up and at 'em. Then your reward."

"Is this how you treat all the patients on this floor? Like little kids?" grumbled Milli.

Reshma tsked. "Now that's the Millicent Tarnover I recall from Wednesday. Nice to see you back in the real world."

Milli understood that if she accepted defeat, she'd die in this room. She got out of bed and allowed Reshma to help her begin again. "Satisfied?" she asked after all Reshma's requirements were met.

"I'll leave you to it."

Milli studied the words on the envelope.

FOR MILLICENT TURNOVER.

The letters were big and blocky, but written with strong strokes. She could picture Apollo's tongue working away with each letter. No matter that her name was misspelled—she kind of liked the implication of the word, Turnover, like a new leaf.

The letter was folded in threes and neatly tucked into the envelope.

She wasn't sure what she expected, but was thrilled that it was more than one sentence.

> *Dear Mrs. Milli How are you? I am fine. You be happy I am reading the newspaper like you tot me. I hope you feel better. When can I see you again?*
>
> *From your frend Apollo*

The tears came fast, falling like rain. She had to hold the letter against her heart so the ink wouldn't blur. How could she again allow herself to deny life? How had she sunk so fast into the abyss? Didn't she have any recollection of her recent days with Apollo, Victoria, Pippa, Kedrix and Birdie? What about the three young women with whom she'd had lunch: Bianca, Keysi, and Rashida. A real luncheon date! Didn't that prove she was still functioning, still able to experience life, still meaningful? What business did she have tempting death? Or worse, inviting it, like Leo.

She had no way to contact Apollo, no phone number, no address. But she could find Victoria by calling the florist shop. Even a prisoner got one phone call.

When Reshma returned, Milli wiped away her tears. "Do you think I can make a telephone call?"

"I'll ask the nurse on duty," said Reshma.

Milli paced the room, trying to regain circulation in her legs. It was slow going, but at least she felt her heart pumping and her mind whirring, something she had wished would stop even as she awoke that morning.

Reshma shook her head when she entered the room. "You'll need Ms. Fagan's permission. She's not working this weekend because it's a holiday. It looks as if you'll have to wait until Tuesday. I'm sorry."

"What if you called for me?"

Reshma's face scrunched. "Mrs. Tarnover, I'd lose my job if I went against the rules. As much as I'd like to help you, I can't."

Milli didn't chide or scold or whine or coerce. She honored Reshma's work ethic and wouldn't compromise it. "Thank you anyway, Reshma. I understand."

Exhausted just from rising and facing the day, Milli lay back in bed, but she didn't want to think. She decided to distract her mind from her worries yet engage her brain. She recalled the alphabet scavenger hunt game she and Lionel made up together when he was learning to read. Their goal was to seek out something for every letter of the alphabet in order. Her self-imposed rule: it had to be outside the confines of her room and it had to be an object, not a letter in a word.

A. She went to the kitchen first looking for apple juice. Nope. But she did see an ant.

B. A waste-paper basket stood in the corner.

C. Cabinets were in the kitchen area.

D. The obvious, a door.

E. This was tougher. No eggs were in the refrigerator. She went to the TV room. Nothing caught her attention. She cruised past the nurses' station, glad that the nurse on duty just gave her a brief nod. On her desk was a pencil with an eraser. Eraser!

Reshma saw Milli wandering the hall. "I'm getting some exercise," Milli told her.

"Glad to see you up and about," said Reshma. "You go, Girl."

F. On the desk was a vase of flowers. Unfortunately, they were plastic.

G. Knowing her side of the hall had no windows, she figured the other side might overlook a courtyard. She poked her head into a room and saw only dark walls. The resident was in her bed. Her glasses had slipped down her nose. G. Glasses.

The woman in bed waved. "I'm so glad you're here. I'm ready," she said.

"How can I help you?" asked Milli.

"Aren't you going to paint my nails now?" She held out her hands.

Milli wanted to count hands as her H, but that was cheating. The H had to be an object. Milli noticed the hairbrush on the woman's bureau. "What if I brushed your hair instead? Would that make you happy?"

The woman removed a barrette and her hair flowed long but thin. Milli ran the brush through it as the woman purred. *Such a simple act brought such joy,* thought Milli. As Milli stroked the woman's hair, she scanned the room for an object that began with I. Nothing appeared that she could see. When the woman's eyes closed and she snored lightly, Milli laid the brush down and tiptoed from the room.

Off to the kitchen again, she opened the freezer and found ice cubes. On the counter, she found a juice box and in the refrigerator, packets of ketchup. For L, she saw a lamp; for M, she noticed a magazine; for N, there were napkins; an O for oven, and a P for a pen. The Q was always a problem for her and Lionel. But as she poked her head into rooms, she saw that some residents had quilts on their beds. Homemade, in fact. She wondered if they had brought them with them from a former life.

Shelves were everywhere as were tables. Could she count the U as nurses' uniforms? But these nurses were more modern, no white caps or white shoes or white shirtwaist dresses. She hoped U wouldn't be a problem. When she passed the room where the man had been listening to the radio, she saw a stack of laundry on his bureau with his underwear folded neatly on the top. Technically boxer shorts, but still underwear.

She thought V would be problematic too, but the vacuum was right there in the open closet waiting to be used. A water bottle sufficed for W, but the X was impossible. However, she was, after all, in a medical establishment. If she looked long enough she could probably find someone's X-ray. She decided that would have to do. Unless there was a Xerox machine at the nurses' station. But there wasn't, so she wondered how she would have squared it with Lionel.

"If the word sounds like it starts with X, we can use it," she remembered telling him. So when she found the fire extinguisher on the wall, she almost swooned.

Y for yogurt and Z for zipper. Zipper rhymes with Pippa, and suddenly Milli flashed an image of Pippa combing the beach for sea glass, how comforting the act of finding the shards of glass was for her, how good the advice was that Birdie offered. This silly alphabet game had worked the same magic. It took Milli's mind off her frustrations and focused it on something else. And it made her feel less strange in a strange place. So simple.

Milli went back to her own room and poured through another box. In this one, she found Leo's flannel shirt, and Lionel's baseball card collection. She put on the shirt and instantly felt stronger. The collection would be for Apollo when she saw him, and she was determined to see him. Digging deeper into the box, she discovered a journal from her pre-teen years, one of those narrow-spaced books with a lock and key, although she didn't need to use the key. It opened easily. Most pages were empty, but a few had her childish scrawl.

> *Daddy yelled at me today for putting the milk away behind the juice so when he went to get it, he had to take everything out to find it. I have to be more careful.*
>
> *Linda Mae told on me that I read her letter from Richard. I got sent to my room without dinner.*
>
> *Harold kissed me. I love Harold.*
>
> *Miss Tatro let me clap the erasers and wash the board. I want to be a janitor.*
>
> *I rode my bike all by myself to the penny candy store. Harold saw me and waved. I love Harold.*
>
> *I drew blue leaves and Miss Soul told me there was no such thing. I hate Miss Soul.*
>
> *Mommy and I cut lilacs from the tree in the backyard and put them in vases all over the house. They smelled so sweet.*

How lovely to be naive, thought Milli. But hiding behind the words were her father's rage, her sister's dominance, and her mother's gentleness. What did it tell her about herself? Low expectations? Easily distracted? A black and white outlook? She wished she had kept more journals to replay her life, but she knew no matter how many boxes she explored, there wouldn't be any other written remnants. It was never too late though. She wondered if Reshma could dig up a notepad for her.

Milli peeked out the doorway but Reshma was not there. She went from room to room looking for her and ended up at the nurses' station.

"I'm looking for Reshma," she told the nurse on duty.

"She left. Can I help you?"

"I wonder if you have a spare notepad or a pad of paper that I may use, and a pen, please."

"For what purpose?" asked the nurse.

"I'd like to begin a journal."

"What a fun activity. I'll see what I can find and I'll bring it to you in your room, Mrs. Tarnover. Will that be all right?"

Again, Milli felt like a child. Talked down to. Patronized. She wanted to tell this nurse that she wrote newsletters for the Parent Teachers Association, and compiled a book of recipes for Leo, complete with photos. And what about all the Christmas letters sent to friends, catching them up on her family from year to year, at least until Lionel died. She was praised for her writing skills at the bank when the tellers filed a formal complaint. And she had even penned an award-winning poem back in seventh grade. She could be trusted with pen and paper.

About an hour later, the nurse brought Milli a few pieces of white computer paper folded down the middle, along with crayons, and a pen. "I have an idea of what you could write about," said the nurse. "Ms. Fagan told me you'll be seeing the doctor for your evaluation on Tuesday. He'd be impressed if you shared some of your experiences with him, perhaps even drawing them. If you prefer, you can dictate your stories to an aide."

Milli couldn't begin to answer. Somehow the idea of a journal had lost its appeal. Instead, she constructed an arsenal of paper airplanes and began sailing them down the hallway, inviting other patients to join her. That didn't go over well with Nurse Ratchet. "But look how pretty they are?" Milli told her. "I stayed in the lines when I colored them."

Poetry Joe made his rounds in mid-afternoon.

"I could really use some fresh air. I'd be deeply grateful if you can arrange that." As an afterthought, Milli added, "I promise I won't escape."

Chapter Twenty-Six

Outside at last. Although it was an ordeal. The begging. The cajoling. The assurance that Poetry Joe wouldn't have to chase her down. The promissory note for New Dawn to say she would come back. As if she were a criminal.

But it was worth the effort. Milli breathed in the late spring air. Every inch of her came alive like a wilted flower receiving water. The return to life was instantaneous.

"Poetry Joe, do you know how thankful I am to be present, right here, right now? Not at New Dawn, of course, but part of the air?"

Joe stared down at Milli. He must have been a full foot taller, at least. "My wife was afraid to go outside for the last few years of her life."

"Why?" asked Milli.

"I think it was a combination of fears. At first, it was just being in public places. So we stopped going to the movies or out to dinner. As the Alzheimer's progressed, she refused to cross the threshold of our house. Just stepping near the door, she'd break into a sweat."

"That must have been very difficult for you," said Milli.

"I didn't understand what was happening to her. She had been so adventurous, so daring. The first in line to bungie jump or zip-line.

She was on the dance floor the minute the music began. The disease was gradual. I figured she was just getting older and more cautious."

"So much of life sneaks up on us," said Milli.

"Yer darn tootin."

Poetry Joe and Milli were quiet for a while as they strolled the grounds of New Dawn. Neither was in a hurry. Neither needed to be anywhere but where they were. The day was warm, but not humid. Sunny, with wispy clouds. Milli's mother would have called it a 'go-out' day.

"What was your wife's name?" asked Milli.

"Rosalie."

"That which we call a rose, by any other name would smell as sweet," said Milli.

"If I found a rose every time I thought of my dear wife, I'd be picking roses for a lifetime."

"Take time to smell the roses," said Milli.

"You know, Mrs. Tarnover, all my Rosalie was left with were thorns. How unfair was that?"

"Thorns and roses grow on the same shrub," said Milli. "Isn't that what life's all about? The Yin and the Yang. The Black and the White."

"In sickness and in health," said Poetry Joe.

"Exactly," said Milli.

The exchanges of words were short, but each utterance had substance. Milli felt like she had known Poetry Joe forever. He spoke to her in a way that turned life into living, something she dearly needed.

They had come to a bench in front of a small pond, a place Milli had never been, although it reminded her of the view from her balcony apartment.

"Let's sit a bit," said Milli, scanning the grounds for daffodils and lilacs, although their season was on the wane. "Tell me, is Joe your real name, or did you really choose it because it was easier for the patients to recall?"

"My birth name was Louis Joseph Jefferson, but I took up boxing in high school and my friends nicknamed me Joe Louis. Mind you, I was a scrawny kid, but I never gave up a match. I had a tough time working through my anger until I met my Rosalie. It was she who introduced me to poetry and turned my life around." He closed his eyes and steadied his voice and a thrum of his soul emerged:

A Golden Day

I found you and I lost you,
All on a gleaming day.
The day was filled with sunshine,
And the land was full of May.
A golden bird was singing
Its melody divine,
I found you and I loved you,
And all the world was mine.
I found you and I lost you,
All on a golden day,
But when I dream of you, dear,
It is always brimming May.

"She's been gone one year this month. Paul Dunbar's poem says it all."

"Rosalie was a lucky woman."

"I was a lucky man."

"Do you have children?"

"Rosalie and I never had children together, although I have a daughter from a previous marriage."

Milli wanted to ask more about his private life, but a dark haze blunted his eyes so Milli changed the subject.

"Do you write your own poetry?" asked Milli.

"I've been known to dabble."

To Milli, this man was a lot like Leo. Leo had been married before he met Milli but didn't like to talk about it except to say that he was too young and had made bad decisions. The good that came of his failed marriage was measurable. He listened when Milli spoke and carried through on promises. She could tell that Poetry Joe had matured because of an unsuccessful relationship too. People who have come through adversity show a special strength.

"May I ask a favor of you?" asked Milli. "You can say no if it makes you uncomfortable."

Poetry Joe angled toward her. "You can ask."

"I want to make a phone call, but the staff at New Dawn won't allow it until I've been evaluated by the physician on Tuesday. If you have a cell phone, could you help me?"

"What's the evaluation supposed to prove?" asked Poetry Joe.

"Whether or not I'm capable of making my own decisions and deciding my fate," said Milli.

"You've got to control your own destiny or someone else will." Poetry Joe handed his phone to Milli.

Milli scrunched up her face. She had done a great deal of thinking about whom to call when she had a chance. She didn't know Birdie's legal surname and she didn't want to call Madame Sheeya's hotline. Apollo was out of the question, and she didn't know how to reach Kedrix. "Do you think you could find a number for me first?"

Milli gave him Lila's Florist Shop info and he plugged the details into his cell. Within minutes, the connection was made. Poetry Joe left Milli alone on the bench and sat under a tree.

"Hello, Lila's Florist Shop." The voice sounded like butter.

"Victoria? It's Millicent Tarnover. I could use your help." And then Milli heard: "I'm sorry we cannot come to the phone right now. Leave your message after the beep." *What should I say? Come get me? Your father's a lawyer, can he do anything for me?* Frustrated and flustered, Milli dropped the phone and it snapped shut.

Milli returned Poetry Joe's phone. "No luck. I guess I'm on my own."

"I wish I could help you in some way, but I don't know what you're up against."

She didn't quite know herself. If her evaluation went awry, she'd become a Ward of the State. New Dawn would declare her incompetent and take over the role of caretaker, which meant that all her assets would go to them. She still had some secret wads of cash in her purse, but certainly not enough to live on. Forced to live at New Dawn, she'd be dependent on the State and the whims of the Retirement Village.

"On Tuesday, I have to prove that I'm mentally competent to make my own choices for my future."

"I'm assuming that your disappearance has something to do with this," said Poetry Joe.

Milli shrugged. "At first, I just wanted a day to myself. Was that too much to ask? One thing led to another, and I lied about who I was and got my friend Birdie into hot water and disappointed my young friend Apollo." Milli felt herself rambling, but she couldn't control her tongue. "Was it so wrong to leave New Dawn and start all over again?"

"Perhaps the question I would ask if I were the doctor is were you in control of your actions when you were on your own?"

"Yes, I thought so. But sometimes I was watching myself and I couldn't believe I was doing what I was doing. Like riding on a motorcycle or drinking coke and rum at a bar or sleeping on a wooden bench." Milli watched the man raise his eyebrows. "But I was perfectly safe. At least I thought so."

"What about the argument you had with the men in the park? The men who were in the newspaper?"

So Poetry Joe knew her story anyway. "Those men were derelicts determined to ridicule me. I wasn't going to allow that."

"You seem to know your own mind. I wish my Rosalie had."

As Milli and Joe made their way back to her building, she stopped short when she saw the lilac tree. Its purple buds had shriveled and its leaves had withered. *How could that have happened in only a few weeks' time? And where had the daffodils gone?*

Chapter Twenty-Seven

Monday was a holiday so the staff on the floor were few and far between, and Reshma was nowhere to be seen. When breakfast didn't arrive by 8:15, Milli went to the small kitchen and helped herself. As she walked past other rooms, she noticed that other residents were waiting for their meals with no results. Milli checked at the nurses' station.

"Why is breakfast so late this morning?" she asked.

The nurse was on the phone and instructing an aide at the same time. "Busy, busy morning, Mrs. Tarnover."

"What can I do to help?" asked Milli.

The nurse hung up the phone and the aide stared at Milli with a puppet mouth.

"I'm capable and competent and these folks are hungry. Dementia patients do poorly when their bellies grumble. You're in for rebellion soon if breakfast isn't served."

The nurse nodded to the aide. "Let her set down the trays and pour the milk or juice. I'll follow with the pills. Go ahead. It'll be all right."

Milli stayed close to the aide and followed her instructions. At each room, Milli took a minute to fluff a pillow or put slippers on a patient or tie a bib. She hummed *I've Been Working on the Railroad*, knowing that familiar tunes settled the soul. The time passed quickly and with Milli's help, all the patients' tummies were filled by nine o'clock, no worse for wear.

The nurse breathed a sigh of relief. "You came to our rescue this morning, Mrs. Tarnover. It's rare that a resident of this ward realizes a way to solve a problem. I'm grateful for your help."

"Where's Reshma? And the others? Usually there are a dozen workers." Milli looked around. "I see four."

"For starters, it's a holiday. Then, there's some sort of stomach bug circulating. After the pandemic, we have a strict policy if workers are not feeling well, they must stay home. Our patients are a vulnerable population, so safety first. Sometimes, we'll have temporaries from other sections of New Dawn fill in, but for some reason, our inter-communications broke down this morning, and we weren't in touch soon enough with the higher-ups."

"Then I'm glad I could help," said Milli. Instead of going back to her room, she popped into random rooms to chat with the residents. She would be their Poetry Joe for the day, as she knew he had plans to be with his daughter.

By lunchtime, the floor buzzed with workers as New Dawn shifted its staff. Milli's only job now was to wait out the day and anticipate Tuesday's test. What would they ask? She was a crackerjack speller. Numbers were never a problem. She'd received individual recognition from the bank several times for her accurate balances and attention to detail. She had a knack for remembering names and making associations. There was no way she could be deemed incompetent.

Late in the afternoon, Ms. Fagan stopped by Milli's room just as she was about to nap. "I hear you've been a busy bee, Dear. So nice of you to come to our rescue. However, the nurse on duty has been reprimanded for allowing you to interfere. In the future, refrain from taking on duties related to other patients. We have rules, Dear. Rules."

"Well, that's a slap in the face, Dear," Milli replied. "Helping others is the way we help ourselves. I heard that on the Oprah Show."

"You don't have to tell me. I'm in the business of helping others. For twenty years, I've walked these hallways and given my time and energies to making our residents comfortable."

"And I'm sure they're infinitely grateful," said Milli.

Ms. Fagan's face pruned. "All I get is sass and complaints. Just the fall out from your escapade almost cost me my job, as if your vanishing act had been my fault. Do you know how many sleepless nights I had worrying about you and how many extra hours I put in looking for you? When I found your clothes in the woods, I thought you had died and I was to blame."

Milli was reminded of Mr. Whiskers' owner, Corazon Wolff, how she overused the pronoun I, how everything revolved around her needs. Could a social worker have the same malady? *But I've been selfish too, thinking no one at New Dawn would care about me. It's true I put Ms. Fagan through a hellish week, but she seems hell-bent on locking me up forever. Why?*

"Ms. Fagan, I don't need this evaluation tomorrow. I have shown myself to be alert, rational, and competent. I demand my right to be released."

The woman unfolded the chair in the room and pulled it close to Milli's bed. "You gave up your independence when you entered New Dawn's Memory Care Unit on Tuesday. Therefore, the evaluation will take place as planned."

Is this legal? Even a prisoner is read his rights! I don't understand, or is that the whole point of having landed here?

"I'd like to talk you through what you can expect, Dear."

That's the least this woman could do.

"First, evidence will be shown concerning the state of your mental health."

"What kind of evidence?"

"Mr. Grasin has canvassed people who know you. It will be their testimony."

Milli breathed easier. Mr. Grasin must have been back to the apartment and talked with Victoria and Birdie. Maybe Birdie wasn't the best character witness though, considering she put the voodoo doll in Comb Over and Hairy Ears' golf caddy. Then an image of Grenadine loomed. But even Grenadine knew Milli could take care of herself. She might not like her, but she wouldn't condemn her to a sealed ward for the rest of her life.

"Has Mr. Grasin spoken with Reshma?"

"You mean the aide?"

"Yes, the lovely woman who works on this floor, the one with the long braid and the smiling eyes."

"She is no longer employed here."

"As of when?" asked Milli.

"That is not your concern, Dear."

Of course it was her concern. Reshma could attest to Milli's sentience. But Milli knew she couldn't pursue the issue. There are rules, Dear, she could hear Ms. Fagan say in that haughty stuck-up tone. "Has Mr. Grasin spoken with Joe Louis, the volunteer?"

"No. Should he?"

"Well, yes. Joe Louis and I have spent several delightful hours together talking about poetry."

Ms. Fagan made a note of this. "I'll let Mr. Grasin know."

"And what about the nurse on duty at the front desk at Downtown Crossing? She can attest to my mental state?"

"Do you mean the day you wrote that you had a medical appointment, but didn't? I imagine she'd be a hostile witness."

"But there are others with whom I interacted. What about them?"

"Yes, Dear, we'll make sure we gather sufficient information."

"And what happens after Mr. Grasin is finished?" asked Milli.

"Then the doctor will administer a short test. Once all is completed, you'll return to your room and enjoy the rest of your day. On Tuesday there's a sing-along. It promises to be great fun."

"Ms. Fagan, tell me the truth, please. Do you honestly think my brain is bananas?"

The woman neatened up the papers in her folder, put them in a briefcase, sat back in the chair and crossed her arms and legs. "If you recall, Millicent Dear, we had a meeting after your nephew died and your monetary circumstances changed. Are you familiar with the word 'affect'?"

"Yes, it means influence, like when I was on my own, I tutored a boy named Apollo. I affected him in a positive way."

"Ah, yes, but there's also the noun, *affect*, the first syllable accented. In psychology, it is the outward show of emotion. I have been trained to measure someone's affect. A flat affect is when a person shows no emotion, which is a red flag for mental instability. In my experience, Millicent Dear, you displayed no affect upon learning that your nephew was no longer alive and your estate had been squandered."

"That isn't true. I collapsed when you gave me the news. I stayed in the hospital for two days."

Ms. Fagan pursed her flat lips. "Your immediate reaction was shock. Subsequently, when we met, you displayed no emotion. You just sat back and let me take over for you."

"So I should have cried and torn out my hair? See I have affect now!" Milli contorted her face.

"That's not the point, Mrs. Tarnover. We are examining your overall behavior from the time you moved into New Dawn to now. We need to determine if you comprehend the impact of your decisions. That's the key to your future. Do you understand, Dear?"

All too clearly, thought Milli.

That evening, the nurse on duty suggested Milli take a sleeping pill, but Milli remembered the stomach cramps and fever from last week. "No, no thank you. I'll tough it out."

Chapter Twenty-Eight

At precisely 10:00 on Tuesday morning, Ms. Fagan accompanied Milli to a small conference room in the main building of New Dawn. She felt like she needed handcuffs or something official to show she was her prisoner. Maybe she should have worn orange. Ms. Fagan had finally delivered the green trash bag that Grenadine had thrown in the van on the day of Milli's capture. Milli found her new jeans, the pink t-shirt she'd bought at the thrift store, and her white sandals. She spiked her hair, even though none of the red highlights remained. She dabbed on lipstick which added to the allure. Just right for sanity, she decided.

Mr. Grasin met them at the door. The doctor rose when the trio walked in. Milli recognized Dr. Boothbury immediately. He looked like his name, kind of blue-veined with a thin pencil-line of a mouth. Milli supposed he was a compassionate man who watched out for his patients, although in the back of her mind she recalled seeing his name on so many of her prescriptions, too many perhaps?

Milli extended her hand to the doctor, but he went straight for Mr. Grasin and pounded his shoulder like old buddies. "Good to see you, Asa. Thanks for doing the legwork. You've saved us a lot of time." He directed Milli to a chair, poured coffee for the foursome and brought over a tray of croissants. "Let food be your medicine," he said before sitting opposite her.

Milli spoke up. "We've met before, Doctor. My nephew Bernard and I had several appointments with you. You prescribed anti-depressants and mood enhancers for me. Your name was on all my pill bottles. Remember?"

Dr. Boothbury peered over his glasses. "I see hundreds of patients, Mrs. Tarnover, and I prescribe a great number of medications. Now, enjoy the repast, and let's get started."

But Milli insisted. "You and Bernard talked on the phone too. Tall, dark hair, thin, with quiet eyes and a crooked smile. And jug-ears. You even commented on them. You said you knew a doctor who could pin them back. The two of you laughed and he said, 'Powerful men have big ears.' How can you not recall him?"

Ms. Fagan interrupted. "That is not the reason we are here today, Millicent Dear. Dr. Boothbury is a busy man with many responsibilities. Surely you can't expect him to remember everyone who comes through his door."

"Bernard wasn't everyone. He died from an overdose of opioids. How many of your patients have you lost over the years?"

Mr. Grasin scowled. "The woman is confusing the issues. Her nephew was not your patient, she is. So let's get on with this."

Milli folded her arms across her chest, red-heat rising. A terrible burden sat on her heart and somehow these three people put it there.

Dr. Boothbury removed his glasses. His eyes met Milli's. "I'm so sorry about your nephew. I have a vague recollection of the young man. Big ears and long black hair? Yes, like that actor Adam Driver. Such a shame." The doctor put his glasses back on. "Mrs. Tarnover, I understand how worrisome this process must be for you. Taking up all the space in your mind, I'm sure. It's time you put your nephew's tragedy behind you and move forward. Don't you agree?"

Bernard's death had changed the course of Milli's life. His aura jumped out at her. See me, it shouted. The gangly man with big ears

and long hair lay like a corpse between them. She swept his body off
the table and onto her lap. He sat heavy and caused her body to sink
into her chair.

"Drink your coffee, Mrs. Tarnover, and relax. We're here to help
you," said the doctor.

Milli didn't want coffee, but she sipped dutifully. She needed to
show them she was in compliance and fully present.

Dr. Boothbury picked up the thick folder and read aloud from
the first few pages.

- Millicent Tarnover. Date of Birth, June 5, 1943.
  Resident of New Dawn Retirement Village since
  2007. Relocated from High Rise Haven to Downtown Crossing in 2022 due to a lack of funds.
- In November 2022, the decision was made to apply
  to Medicaid so Millicent Tarnover could remain in
  New Dawn. Social worker Alexis Fagan completed
  the paperwork, as the resident was unable to fill
  out the applications on her own.
- On Tuesday, May 16, 2023 at 10:00 a.m., Millicent
  Tarnover signed out of New Dawn and was driven
  by The Friendly Ride Transportation service to a
  dentist's office on Main Street in Oldham. An investigation showed there had been no appointment.
- On May 17, 2023, two gentlemen at the Seaside
  Arboretum had a belligerent encounter with Millicent Tarnover.

The doctor raised his brow and looked at Mr. Grasin. "Am I correct that you have additional information on this confrontation?"

"Indeed I do."

Milli piped up. "Those two men verbally assaulted me. I feared
for my life."

Ms. Fagan patted her hand. "Yes, Dear, we'll get to that."
The doctor continued.

⬩ From Wednesday, May 17 to Tuesday, May 23, Ms.
Grenadine Graziella reported that she took pity on
Millicent Tarnover, who was roaming the streets
of Oldham, and provided her with shelter in an
apartment that she managed. She said the woman
had given her a false name: Minnie Yanover. At
first, Ms. Graziella had no reason to question this,
but when she saw Millicent Tarnover's photo in the
newspaper article, she was sure of her true identity.
When she attempted to confront her, the door was
locked and Ms. Graziella refused to trespass.

"That's not entirely true," said Milli, jutting out her chin. As she
spoke, a fog passed before her eyes like a morning mist. "I object,"
she murmured. The words came out damp, like they'd been dipped
in dew. Milli wondered if a sedative had been stirred into her coffee.
The doctor smiled with a pouty puff of lip, his eyebrows arched.
Milli sank into her chair, her muscles limp. He went on.

⬩ On Tuesday, May 23, Mr. Asa Grasin and Ms.
Alexis Fagan apprehended Millicent Tarnover at
said apartment.

"You've left out essential details," said Milli, the words slow and
exaggerated. Her tongue felt like a wad of cotton.
Dr. Boothbury looked up. "Mrs. Tarnover, you'll have your chance
to respond. Now is not the time." He turned his attention to Mr. Grasin. "Asa, you have reconstructed her movements through personal
interviews. Might you share them with us?"
"Yes, Doctor. I returned to Porter Street and canvassed a number

of people who interacted with Millicent Tarnover between May 17 and May 23."

Mr. Grasin read from the papers in his folder:

- My first interview was with Corazon Wolff, a resident of Mayfield whose dog got loose and was returned by Mrs. Tarnover. Mrs. Wolff said, "The woman was unbearably aggressive, implying I was selfish and negligent. She told me to get over myself. The nerve of her! I went along with her babble because I thought she was off her rocker. My daughter and I even bought her ice cream, we felt so bad for her."
- My next interview was with a regular patron at The D-Note, a nightclub on the boulevard. Ms. Queenie Karl said, "This old woman came in like she was from another planet, looking around the place like it was a foreign country. I mean it's a bar, you know. Then she ordered a coke and rum. We all thought that was hilarious. Before we knew it, she had passed out. I helped her to a chair until I found someone to take her home. She returned another time, and seemed confused about why she was there. She didn't stay long and asked a young man for his help."
- A young boy's mother also weighed in on her perception of Millicent Tarnover. She and her son had come to New Dawn to visit, but were unable to because Mrs. Tarnover was ill. "The woman put a spell on my son, like that horrible Madame Sheeya. My sweet Apollo changed into a know-it-all, telling me I was stupid and didn't know anything about reading. Then he called his father a thug and

tyrant. She taught him that word tyrant! Imagine that woman turning my boy against me." When I asked why she had consented to bring her son to visit, she replied, and I quote, "'If I didn't, Apollo said he'd run away and I'd never see him again.'"

+ Finally, I spoke with the two men from the Seaside Arboretum, whose golf caddy had been vandalized by Mrs. Tarnover's friend.

"Is this true, Mrs. Tarnover? A friend of yours took the law into her own hands?"

Milli's head wobbled. She felt like she was underwater and sinking. "I need some air. Might I step outside for a moment?"

"Answer the question first," said Mr. Grasin.

Milli stood up, holding on to the edge of the table. "I will respond when I can breathe." She left the room unsteady on her feet.

"That woman needs to be monitored," said Mr. Grasin.

"I'll keep an eye on her," said Ms. Fagan.

Milli made it out the front door just in time to retch up her breakfast.

"There, there, Dear. This is just too much for you. I'll take you back to your room. We can resume this on another day."

"No. No way. My stomach reacts badly to coffee. I should know better than to drink it. I was being polite. But I'm fine now," Milli said, her hands jittery and her face ashen. "Let's go back."

Dr. Boothbury pulled out Milli's chair for her. "Please, take a moment. Drink some water. That should help."

Milli had the feeling she was way beyond help.

Mr. Grasin proceeded with his testimony. "Anthony Rizzo and Carl Smith, the men whom Mrs. Tarnover encountered in the Arboretum, said she threatened them. 'She lunged at us like a crazy woman,' said Mr. Rizzo. 'And bared her teeth. We feared for our lives,' said Mr. Smith."

"Those men provoked me," said Milli, feeling her strength return.

"So you admit to malicious intent?" said Mr. Grasin.

"I said no such thing," countered Milli, pointing her finger at the man. "You're twisting my words."

"You see, Dr. Boothbury, Millicent Tarnover is incapable of living in civilized society. She has a record of abusing others. I have several other statements including a woman in the local coffee shop who found Mrs. Tarnover, and again I quote, 'insufferable.'" Mr. Grasin passed the notes to the doctor, who nodded as he read them.

Milli stood, her hair on fire. "These are my character witnesses? How dare you? What about Victoria? Or Kedrix? Or Joe Louis, the volunteer at the lock-up ward? You're maligning me for your own evil purposes and I don't understand why."

Ms. Fagan shushed her. "You'll have your turn, Dear. For now, just be quiet and let us conduct this meeting."

"But I have my rights," Milli shouted.

The doctor's eyes widened. "Mrs. Tarnover, I must insist on your silence. I need to listen to Mr. Grasin's research without interruption. Do you understand?"

Milli folded her arms and blew out steam. "I demand a lawyer."

"Now, now, Dear. This is not a trial. It's an airing of information."

"Your selective information," said Milli. "When do I get a chance to participate?"

Dr. Boothbury opened a bottle of pills. "Take one of these, Mrs. Tarnover. It will calm your nerves."

The audacity of the man. So this is how he operates. Medicate to sedate. The weight of her nephew's treachery slammed into her. Milli took the yellow pill and set it in her lap. "There you go, Bernard," she said.

Dr. Boothbury's lips flattened into a grim line and his eyes shifted to Mr. Grasin. "Asa, do you have anything else to add?"

"I do, doctor. There were two people who offered positive testimony."

At last, thought Milli.

"However, one is Madame Sheeya who was apprehended by the Oldham police for vandalizing the golf caddy. Grenadine Graziella, the woman who helped us locate Mrs. Tarnover said that the fortune teller was, and I quote, 'a hussy who takes advantage of human weaknesses.' The other person whose acquaintance seemed constant was a man named Kedrix Forsythe. His reputation in Oldham as a gang motorcycle member is suspect, but not confirmed."

"Kedrix is a lovely young man with tremendous potential," said Milli, standing to defend him.

"Mrs. Tarnover, sit down," said the doctor, shaking his index finger at her. "Alexis, do you have any other testimony to add?"

"Yes, sir," said Ms. Fagan, with a side-smirk toward Milli. "I spoke with several of Mrs. Tarnover's neighbors in her former high-rise living quarters and at Downtown Crossing. They said she always muttered to herself and seemed distracted. Although she participated in enrichment activities, she sat alone. A volunteer who facilitated the exercise hour recalled Mrs. Tarnover's correction of others if they didn't stand properly or if they moved in the wrong direction. Also, at mealtime in the commons room, servers reported that she never had a regular table, as most residents did. She floated from group to group, barely intermingling."

Milli moved her head from side to side, feeling the darkness creep into the corners of her eyes. "I was grieving for Anne Marie. Don't you see that? She was my friend and she died. And when I was stuffed in that room in Downtown Crossing, I was frustrated and upset over the loss of my nephew. But I turned a corner and began taking control of my life." How could they get it so wrong? Not one of those testimonies spoke about her kindness, her deep interest in others' well-being, the advice she offered. In exercise class, she tried to help others, not offend them. A faulty move could injure the body! And what about Victoria? Why hadn't anyone spoken to her? And those three lovely young women with whom she had lunch? Why had these people actively pursued the negative.

Unless that is who I am. Could it be me who has it all wrong? Am I a surly old curmudgeon who looks for ways to undermine others. Is my judgment that impaired? Maybe I deserve to be locked up if that's what the world thinks of me.

"Now, Dear, it's your turn. We're going to let you have some private time with the doctor," said Ms. Fagan. "Mr. Grasin has to return to his duties, but I'll be right outside the door and will accompany you to your room when you are finished."

A deep growl escaped from Milli's throat. She wanted to kick the woman in the shins and whip that Grasin man in the butt. But she silently counted to one hundred and waited for them to leave.

"Before we begin, Doctor, I must speak in my defense. Mr. Grasin and Ms. Fagan missed many positive people to interview."

"No doubt," he said, "but they are the authorities in this case, and their research holds weight."

And mine doesn't? "Do I seem unstable?" Milli enunciated her words. "Dr. Boothbury, why are we going through this charade? I didn't hurt anyone. I only wanted some independence. Why am I being treated like a criminal?"

"Mrs. Tarnover, you don't seem to grasp the seriousness of your escapade and therein lies the problem. We care about your well-being and your ability to behave rationally. I've watched how you've reacted to Mr. Grasin. I see deep-seated anger, the kind that escalates. Notice how your body rebelled and you had to leave the room. Your aggression during these proceedings is detrimental to your health. We're here to help you, truly."

"Like when you offered me that little yellow pill and how you think pain killers and opioids are therapeutic?"

"That's exactly what we're talking about, Mrs. Tarnover. You're just plain looking to get under my skin and I'm not going to fall for it."

Milli breathed in Leo's name and breathed out Lionel's. She needed to dispel the tension. "Tell me, Doctor. What is your first name? I like to know with whom I'm speaking."

The doctor softened. "That's a reasonable request. My first name is Boris, but my friends call me Birch."

"Birch, like the tree?" *And Birdie's curative tea!* "Did you know that there are a dozen varieties of birch trees? I learned that last week when I worked at Lila's Florist Shop." She emphasized the word 'work' hoping he'd catch her meaning.

The doctor scratched his temple. "I've heard of the Japanese white birch, the silver birch, the yellow birch and the dwarf birch, but son-of-a-gun, I didn't know the birch was so prolific."

"Maybe that's why your friends named you Birch? You're multi-faceted?"

"No, they thought I was a tall, skinny white guy with thin skin, who looked like a birch tree."

Milli and the doctor shared a laugh.

"If my memory serves me correctly," said Milli, matter-of-factly, "the birch tree is also known for its medicinal properties."

"You don't say." The doctor leaned in.

Milli had learned this tidbit from Birdie, but she wouldn't tell the good doctor that. "Yes, crushed birch leaves have been used in tea to cleanse the system. Quite tasty, too. I think your friends were prescient."

"Prescient?" said the doctor.

"Yes, farsighted, perceptive. Qualities you seem to possess," said Milli, nodding her head. Nodding was a trick she had discovered. Others tended to be more agreeable when her head bobbed up and down.

"Well, yes, Mrs. Tarnover. But let's discuss the reason you're here today—an evaluation to determine your ability to make your own decisions. Shall we begin?"

Milli sat straighter, pushing Bernard to the floor. "Yes, Doctor, I'm ready."

"Would you state your name please."

Milli almost laughed until she saw those straight-pencil lips stretched tight.

"Millicent Davis Tarnover."

"What is today's date?" he asked.

"Today is Tuesday, May 28."

"And the year is?"

"2023."

"Please listen carefully. I'm going to name four objects. Later on in our meeting, I'll ask you to repeat them. Do you understand?"

"Yes, you're going to say four objects and I'm to repeat them later when you ask."

"Exactly. Bicycle. Tiger. Umbrella. Shoes."

Milli tried hard to cement the words, erasing the fury in her head and concentrating on the moment. *Bicycle, tiger, umbrella, shoes.* The doctor held a piece of paper. "Please take this with your right hand. Fold it in half and then in quarters. When finished, place it in the middle of the table."

Milli reached out for the paper. She'd always been proud of being ambidextrous. When she was little, she had a freckle on her right thumb, which was how she remembered right from left. But age had a way of turning freckles into wrinkled skin. She hoped she used the right hand to take the paper. Beyond that, she followed the instructions perfectly.

"Thank you, Mrs. Tarnover. Now I'd like you to recite the alphabet backwards."

Milli sat up straight. She thought about each letter as she said it. "Z, Y, X, W, V, U, T, S, R, Q, P, O, N, M, L, K, J, I, H, G, F, E, D, C, B, A."

"Very good. Now repeat the alphabet backwards again, but faster."

"Z, Y, X, W, V, U, T, S, R, Q, P, O, N, M, L, J, I, H, G, F, E, D, C, B, A."

"This time, Mrs. Tarnover, I'd like you to repeat the alphabet backwards skipping every other letter beginning with Y."

Milli took a deep breath. "Y, W, U, S, Q, O, M, K, I, G, E, C, A."

"Thank you, Mrs. Tarnover. Now, I'd like you to count backwards from fifty by sixes."

Milli took a deep breath. "Fifty, forty-four, thirty-eight, thirty-two, twenty-seven, twenty-one, fifteen, nine, three."

"Thank you, Mrs. Tarnover. Now I'd like you to draw a picture of two pentagons that intersect." He handed her paper and a pencil with an eraser.

She knew a pentagon had five sides and she understood the word intersect. Taking the pencil, she pressed down too hard and the lead snapped.

"Click on the eraser for more lead," said the doctor.

Milli clicked, but nothing happened. She tried again. Still nothing.

The doctor gave her an old-fashioned pencil. "Try this one instead."

This time the pencil cooperated, but Milli's hand shook just a tad so the lines on the pentagon were wavy. She didn't like the way it looked, so she erased them. However, the eraser was stiff, so everything smudged. Remaining calm, she turned the paper over and began again. This time she drew two pentagons but forgot to intersect them.

"Do you have another piece of paper?" she asked. "Third time's a charm."

Dr. Boothbury shook his head. "Your efforts are sufficient to tell me what I need to know. Now, I wonder, Millicent, can you repeat back the four words I told you at the beginning of our session?"

Milli perked up. "Umbrella, lion, no tiger, and," Milli couldn't remember. She thought it might be a tree, but maybe she was confusing their birch conversation with the word. It was an object, a common object. Then the word popped into her mind as clear as day, "shoes."

"Thank you, Mrs. Tarnover. We're all set."

Ms. Fagan practically fell in the door when the doctor opened it.

"I'll be back in touch," said Dr. Boothbury.

"What? That's it? What about my defense? Where's the justice here? I've done everything you've asked of me. When do I get my turn?" asked Milli.

Ms. Fagan shushed her. "Thank you so much for your time, Doctor. I have office hours today from four to five. Shall I expect a call then?"

Dr. Boothbury checked his calendar. "Oh my," he said, rushing to his desk. "I totally forgot. I have baseball tickets today. Red Sox against Cleveland." He looked at his watch. "Game time is four o'clock. I have to fly."

"So my fate rests with the Red Sox?" cried Milli.

"I'll call you tomorrow, Alexis." Dr. Boothbury turned to Milli. "Now don't you give it a second thought, Little Lady. You did just fine." He smiled and pulled the door shut.

"How fair is that?" asked Milli. "First he takes off with his family for four days and now he's watching a baseball game while my life hangs in the balance."

"Aren't we being a bit dramatic, Dear? You have the whole day to relax, have a nice lunch, sing some songs, and visit with your neighbors."

"Oh joy," said Milli, her voice like a razor. "Tell me, did you speak with Poetry Joe?"

"Do you mean the volunteer who reads to our patients?"

"Yes, I'd like him to speak on my behalf."

"Oh, my Dear, no."

The woman side-stared at Milli for the second time, a slight grin crossing her face. "I called the number he had on file, but no one answered. I'm afraid the hearing is now closed. Dr. Boothbury is a fair and impartial judge. I'm sure he'll come to a satisfactory decision."

For whom? thought Milli.

Chapter Twenty-Nine

Milli couldn't believe that only last week she had been on her own in Oldham, riding a motorcycle, visiting with Leo and Lionel, and embarking on a new beginning. *Now look at me.* With the covers over her head, she lay in bed unwilling to rise.

An aide brought her breakfast, but she had no appetite. She started to scold herself. *Millicent Davis Tarnover, get your body up. Stop this pity party. Ms. Fagan will show up soon and you'll be what? Released? And then what? Returned to the basement apartment? And be guarded? Or locked up forever on this floor with no windows and no hope? Or kicked out of New Dawn and forced to live on my own? How wonderful would that be?*

When the aide brought Milli's lunch, she still wasn't hungry, but knew not eating was dumb. D-U-M-B. Not long ago, she had spelled the word for Apollo. The silent B. The sneaky B. The dumb B. *How will I survive this nonsense? Who will help me?*

In the dayroom, there was a musician singing Bob Dylan songs. His harmonica interludes tickled Milli's memory of her high school boyfriend Fabian, who played harmonica swing jazz. Lionel had given the kazoo a few tries, but he tried way too hard and it sounded buzzy. Leo could strum the guitar well enough to play basic Elvis, but it was her first husband, that jerk Brian who won her heart with the fiddle and an agile Irish two-step. As Milli watched the residents in the dayroom, she understood how music lit an eternal flame.

Back in her room, she considered going through more boxes, but she lacked the energy. The hours dragged on and Ms. Fagan was a no-show. Milli shuffled to the nurses' station and requested to use the phone to call her.

"I'm sorry," said the nurse. "You need permission and I am not authorized to grant it."

"But it's Ms. Fagan whom I want to call and she's the one to grant permission. Doesn't that seem backwards?" But the nurse was too busy to acknowledge the irony.

Milli stopped in the television room where reruns of *Scooby-Doo* played, followed by *Gilligan's Island*. She wondered if oldies were the only shows allowed. *Would I be subjected to sit-coms and cartoons forever?*

That night Milli scrolled through a list of old TV shows beginning with A and proceeding up the alphabet until she fell asleep: *Andy Griffith, Beverly Hillbillies, Carol Burnett, Dragnet, Mr. Ed, F Troop, Green Acres, I Love Lucy.* She avoided the crime shows. She had enough drama in her life.

In the morning, she considered reading to pass the time. Maybe there was a shelf of books somewhere that she could peruse. She went to the nurses' station.

"By any chance, do you have some reading material?" Milli asked.

"We sure do, Lovey," said the nurse, who led Milli to a shelf in a closet-sized room that she hadn't explored.

Combing through the selection, Milli found several Dr. Seuss books, a stack of *National Geographic* magazines, *Treasure Island, National Velvet*, an anthology of short stories, and a slim volume of Rachel Rousso poetry with Joe Louis Jefferson's name on the inside cover. She clutched it to her heart and brought it back to her room. She propped herself on her bed and flipped through the pages until she stopped when she saw the word 'flower' mid-page. She almost passed it by because the title was *On the Doorstep of Death* and she really didn't want to confront that, but she was curious about the flowers. So she read the poem slowly, each word a treasure:

> *When my days are done and death arrives*
> *I will enter its door with open eyes.*
> *And think:*
> *What will happen next within this space of forever?*
> *Will time have stopped and continued without consequence?*
> *Will eternity consist of flowers and music*
> *Or the stillness of stone?*
> *When my days are done, I want to say*
> *I have experienced life:*
> *the awe of the silences between*
> *And the veins within.*
> *Pumping wonder and lust*
> *With pinches of bitter*
> *Dabs of anger*
> *Wallops of kindness.*
> *Let me enter that place knowing I have lived.*

The words spoke to Milli. How she thought of life as a flower. How she wanted to step into the next phase of her life with wonder and curiosity, how she took the world into her arms. And most of all, after squandering so many years, she didn't want the next decade—if she lived that long—to pass her by.

Maybe that was not what others may have gotten from the poem, but it brought solace to Milli. She made up her mind right then and there to take the high road. If Dr. Boothbury decided she was not in control of her own future, she would defy his decision internally. Milli would not return to being a shell of a person going through the motions of life.

She got out of bed, showered, combed her hair, and put on lipstick. She found a cute pair of culottes that Leo liked because they highlighted her round tush. The top she chose had flowers in reds, yellows, and whites—bright and cheerful. In five days, she would turn eighty-five. She needed to live each day as if it were her last, because when death came for her, she would not sigh or argue or be frightened. She would have been an active participant in this world.

Milli started her new attitude at the nurses' station with a "good afternoon" and proceeded down the hallway visiting each resident. Some said hello, some stared vacantly, one handed her a candy bar, and another sang her a song. She made herself useful when she could: straightening eye glasses, pulling up socks, raising the back of a bed, peeling an orange, holding a straw, and drying a tear.

Ms. Fagan neither visited nor called, but Milli put disappointment deep in a corner of her soul and chose not to address it. She spent her evening reading *National Velvet* to a circle of residents and the next morning making the rounds after breakfast, singing a selection of songs she found soothing: *You are My Sunshine, Somewhere over the Rainbow* and *What a Wonderful World*. Just singing aloud and with pizzazz made Milli feel alive.

When the aide brought Milli her lunch, there was a note on the tray:

June 2, 2023
Dear Mrs. Tarnover,
    I regret to tell you that Dr. Boothbury has not made his final decision yet. I will be contact you after the weekend.
                                    Sincerely,
                            Alexis Fagan, MSW

After the weekend? Monday is June 5! How ironic is it that my fate will be decided on my birthday. Milli's stomach churned with the news, but she chose to swallow the bile. She had no choice but to wait. She concentrated on her birthday instead. *How should I celebrate? Making paper planes? Singing all day? Asking for cake? Burning down the place with eighty-six candles?*

Turning eighty-five was a threshold and symbolic of her new start. A different idea whirled through her mind. Leo's demise. Choosing to end one's life was, after all, a choice. To die on one's eighty-fifth birthday wouldn't be so bad. *How would I do it? Pills are the only way out in a place like this. How would I get hold of them? Maybe I'll ask for sleeping pills for the next few days and have enough saved to put me to sleep permanently? It's a possibility.*

Milli breathed hard. *How could Ms. Fagan's letter turn me around so quickly? Am I that fragile? That hopeless? Who can I speak with? Who can help me?* Perhaps she should write her own letter, or maybe a poem? Milli wanted to disappear under her covers, but the words from *What a Wonderful World* thrummed through her: "*I see trees of green, red roses too, I see them bloom for me and you, and I think to myself what a wonderful world.*" Flowers again! Red roses. *How can I die never seeing another lilac or daffodil in bloom?*

Milli tore up Ms. Fagan's letter and flushed it. No one was in charge of her fate but herself.

In the afternoon, an aide brought her a beautiful bouquet of lemon-yellow flowers. Milli beamed with surprise. "For me?" The buds looked so much like daffodils, but hardier and more fragrant, with trumpet petals and long reedy stems. She opened the envelope that accompanied them, noticing that the seal had been broken. *Had Ms. Fagan read the note? But she hasn't been around? Maybe it was the nurse on duty?*

> Dear Milli,
> I hope you are feeling better and I look forward to seeing you soon. May the lilies cheer you up.
> Your friend, Victoria
> P.S. Call when you can! I tried reaching you but the number wasn't available.

Such a lovely child. So thoughtful. But why doesn't this unit have phone access for its residents? Am I so deeply hidden that I'm not even a number?

Even so, she loved the flowers and was pleased Victoria had thought about her. To add to Milli's optimism, Poetry Joe paid her a visit after lunch.

"Such beautiful flowers. I spoke with Victoria yesterday."

"How did you know who she was?"

"Ah, the beauty of modern technology. Her phone number was still on my mobile after you tried to reach her, so I gave it a shot and connected with a lovely young woman. I told her you wanted to speak with her and that you were at the New Dawn Retirement Village's Special Care Unit. That's the best I could do."

What a thoughtful man to have called Victoria. "Thank you."

Poetry Joe shrugged. "I'm just trying to help a friend in need. What have you found out about the evaluation?"

"According to Ms. Fagan, I won't hear my fate until next Monday." She didn't tell him it was her birthday. No need for him to pity her. "I think I did all right on the test, but I can't be sure."

"Ms. Fagan? The social worker?"

Milli nodded.

"Rosalie never liked that woman. When she came into her room, Rosalie shivered. It was like that with the money man, Mr. Grasin, too. They talk like nice people, but underneath there's something unsavory about them."

"It's like we're numbers to them, statistics, not real people," said Milli.

"And yet they spew about what's best for their residents. When I discussed with Ms. Fagan about taking Rosalie home, she said Rosalie's life was in jeopardy without New Dawn's meticulous care. I just thought home would be a better setting for her, you know, surrounded by what was familiar."

"Why would she object? Being with family would have comforted all of you," said Milli, thinking of the last days she spent with Linda Mae.

Poetry Joe's chin jutted and his eyes narrowed. "I regret my decision. When Rosalie passed, they cleared out her room before her body was cold. Heartless. That's what it was. She was here for two years. You'd think they'd show her body some respect. But no. Out within the hour."

"And yet you continue to visit. The place must feel so empty for you," said Milli.

"It seems to me that the patients are neglected on a personal level. Sure, they have cognitive impairment, but that doesn't mean they don't experience joy or sadness or excitement. When Rosalie was here, we'd walk the floor together and visit other residents. I know it brought all of us pleasure."

"I hardly see any other visitors," said Milli.

"I feel like it's discouraged."

"It would be really hard to prove that the administrators have anything but their residents' best interest at heart," said Milli. "You know, I asked Ms. Fagan to speak with you about our poetry discussions, so you could tell her I have strong opinions and know my own mind. But she never got around to it and now it's too late."

Poetry Joe pinched his nose. "'Every guilty person is his own hangman,' so said Seneca, the Roman philosopher."

Milli gave that a lot of thought. Did it mean that if Ms. Fagan and Mr. Grasin were up to no good, that they'd sink themselves eventually?

Poetry Joe shifted gears and asked which poems Milli enjoyed most in Rachel Rousso's book. Milli pointed out phrases that resonated with her in the poem *On the Doorstep of Death*. They discussed each line and came to the conclusion that Rachel Rousso was a glass-half-full kind of person and made the most of every day. When Poetry Joe rose to leave, Milli tried to return his book.

"Keep it for yourself," he said. "Poetry has brought you the same joy I shared with Rosalie. It speaks to the soul."

Chapter Thirty

On Saturday, Milli awoke to the morning-march of aides and nurses.

"Millicent," said the nurse on duty, "It's time for your morning pills."

Three pills sat in the cup, none of which she had ever seen before.

"You must have the wrong patient. I take a few vitamins, but nothing else," said Milli.

"That's unlikely, Lovey. You're eighty-four years old. Everyone that age takes an abundance of pills." The nurse showed Milli her name on the day's print-out. "Millicent Tarnover, that's you, correct?"

"Yes."

"Dr. Boothbury prescribed these medications. His name is right there beside yours. I insist you take them."

"And what if I don't?"

"Lovey, this is for your benefit. Let me explain. The yellow pill is to reduce anxiety. The white one is to lower your blood pressure. And the small orange one is to regulate your moods. Now doesn't that sound reasonable?"

Milli knew what was happening. Pills induced a state of malleability. She'd become docile and stop chatting with the patients and singing to them. Her activity over the last few days had caused a stir, one that had been reported and discussed. She was to be stifled, handled, stopped. So Dr. Boothbury was around to dispense medication, but not to give her an answer about her future? Where was the justice in that?

Milli took the pills and did the old pretend-to-swallow trick. When she was alone, she spit them out and saved them in a tissue. *Will I have enough by my birthday to make the day my final celebration? Maybe I'll sing a little louder and dance in the hallways so that my dosage is increased.*

Milli didn't expect to see Ms. Fagan on the floor, so she was surprised to hear the woman's voice raised to an angry level.

"Ronald Dempsey is to be separated from Margaret Patterson at night. Each has a room, no cohabitation. Do you understand?"

"But they cry out for each other and the nurse on night duty doesn't understand why they can't be together," said the nurse.

"Because we have rules. And that's the final word on this subject," said Ms. Fagan. "Issue additional sedation for both of them and make sure the night nurse follows instructions."

Whispering ensued that Milli couldn't hear, then another explosion of voices. "Follow the instructions on the chart. Do you understand?"

More hissing and whispering.

"Continue hospice care for Corinne Blanchard," said Ms. Fagan.

"But she shows tremendous progress," said the nurse.

"I am in charge here and those are my orders," said Ms. Fagan.

"Now I know why Reshma isn't here any longer. She had the nerve to stand up to you. I see things that contradict my training," said the nurse on duty.

"You're new here, Ms. Hildebrand. You'll either catch on or you'll be gone too. Are we clear?"

It sounded like a threat to Milli, who had shuffled closer to the conversation. Ms. Fagan practically backed into her.

"Oh, Millicent, Dear, I didn't see you," Ms. Fagan stammered.

"Lovey, you should be in your room. Breakfast is coming around soon," said Nurse Hildebrand.

A current of tension sizzled in the air and Milli felt it. "I just love those pills that Dr. Blothy-bury prescribed. I feel like I'm floating." Milli twirled with her eyes closed.

Ms. Fagan took her by the arm. "Yes, Dear. That's very good. Now let's get you back to your room."

"Ms. Fagan, I heard I'll be released on Monday. Isn't that wonderful?"

"Who told you that?"

"That nice nurse with whom you were speaking. She's a honey, so gentle and kind," said Milli.

Ms. Fagan signaled an aide. "Take Mrs. Tarnover to her room now, please. And see that she stays there. Her medication is making her light-headed, so strap her down for self-protection."

Milli didn't see that coming. "Oh, that's not necessary. I'll be a good girl and stay put." She bowed to Ms. Fagan and shuffled back to her room.

Ms. Fagan returned to the nurses' station. "What did you tell that woman about leaving on Monday?" Milli heard her say.

Milli stifled a laugh. If she had to stay in this place, she would make it entertaining.

Within seconds, Ms. Fagan appeared at Milli's door. "Dear, you are causing trouble. Are you aware of that?"

"Are you aware that Dr. Boothbury was supposed to issue his verdict two days ago? That to me is troubling."

"I have addressed that with you. His decision cannot be rushed," said Ms. Fagan, her lips tight and her eyes piercing.

Milli raised her fists. "You're angering me and I have had just about enough of your mistreatment." Instead of lunging for Ms. Fagan, which she dearly wanted to do, she punched the wall, not hard enough to hurt herself, but enough to make the woman jump. "I demand to meet with the doctor. You're keeping me here against my will. I object."

Ms. Fagan left the room and returned with the nurse and a burly aide. The aide strong-armed Milli onto the bed, holding her tight until the nurse administered a needle in her arm.

"I'm sorry. We cannot have our patients out of control. This is for your own good," said Ms. Fagan.

Milli curled into a ball. The aide arranged her in the bed and covered her with a blanket. They all left, closing the door behind them.

The scent of the day lilies invaded Milli's dreams, catapulting her into the V of a tree, perching her there like a chickadee. In her haze, she saw Poetry Joe enter the room.

"Millicent, are you all right?"

"Help me," she said, but her voice devolved into chirps. From her branch, she watched him lean over her, take her pulse, and shake his head.

A nurse appeared and ruffled Milli's feathers. Milli tried to spread her wings, but she was stuck to the branch and unable to move.

Images of sand and waves floated around the room and she swam with orcas and sharks. A daffodil bloomed on the water and lilacs petaled around her. Leo and Lionel splashed and called to her; Apollo and Birdie beckoned. Milli's neck rotated like Regan's in the *Exorcist*.

Chapter Thirty-One

Milli woke with a stiff neck, an aching arm, and blurred vision but her limbs were free to move on her own accord; she was no longer restrained to the bed. The lack of sounds in the hallway indicated it was the middle of the night.

Shaky but determined, she made her way toward the door and peeked out. The hallway was dark except for the nurses' station. She closed her door, turned on the light in her bathroom and splashed water on her face and brushed her teeth. She kept the water to a trickle so it wouldn't make much noise. She had no intention of drawing attention to herself.

Refreshed, she put on sweats and a t-shirt, combed her hair and sat on the edge of the bed deciding what to do next. There was a tray on the nightstand with her evening meal: meatloaf, potatoes, string beans, Jello and a carton of milk. She picked at the beans, drank the milk and suffered through the Jello.

Clarity was what she needed, so she worked at breathing in to Leo's name and out to Lionel's. She practiced until her thoughts melted into the air and her body relaxed. After twenty minutes or so, she opened her mind to the present and confronted her new reality. *I need to get out of here, one way or another.*

She put on her sneakers and found a light sweater in one of the boxes. She checked the lining of her purse to make sure her secret stash was still intact, which it was. She turned off the bathroom light and snuck out of the room away from the nurses' station.

As she made her way down the hallway, she was amazed at how quiet it was. In one room lay a white-haired woman whose left eye was wide open, and whose mouth drooped on the right. Milli read the information on her chart: Hermione Zaccardi, age 91. There was a list of her meds and the times they were administered, as well as a list of scheduled appointments from a physical therapist, an occupational therapist, a speech therapist, a massage therapist and a cognitive behavioral therapist.

"You're one busy lady," whispered Milli as she neared the woman, who seemed to be awake. "With all that therapy, you must be making great strides."

Hermione followed Milli with her good eye and responded with a grunt. When Milli got even closer, she realized that Hermione was missing her right leg from her knee down.

"I'm so sorry. I didn't realize you couldn't walk."

Hermione grunted again.

Milli understood why Hermione might need a massage therapist, although if she had dementia as well as a stroke, as Milli suspected, she seemed way beyond a therapist's help. Milli pulled up a chair and sang the Beatles' song *Blackbird* to her in a soft and gentle voice.

> *Blackbird singing in the dead of night*
> *Take these broken wings and learn to fly*
> *All your life*
> *You were only waiting for this moment to arise*
> *Blackbird fly, blackbird fly*
> *Into the light of the dark black night.*

Before Milli knew it, Hermione's left eye closed and her breathing steadied.

Milli peeked into other rooms. Most residents were asleep, but down the hall, a painfully thin old man with wispy white hair and a bony nose stretched out in a recliner. His irises were a hazy blue ringed with gray. "Thirsty," he called out, so Milli held a straw to his parched lips as he sipped water from the cup on a nightstand. His chart identified him as Rodney Patrick, 87, and on his white board in large letters was written RISK OF FALLING. The room was stuffed with ambulatory equipment: walkers, canes, fall mats, a lift chair, a lift swing, and a wheelchair. Milli couldn't imagine why one person needed so many devices.

In the next room was Margaret Patterson. Milli recognized her name as the woman who wanted to cozy up with Robert Dempsey during the night. She was strapped into her bed, its hospital sides high like a newborn's. In Robert Dempsey's room, he was subjected to the same restraints. Milli recalled Ms. Fagan's orders: "Issue additional sedation for both of them and make sure the night nurse follows instructions."

In the last room before the locked exit door, Milli recognized the familiar face of Katia Bridges, a former neighbor from the high rise. After Anne Marie died, Katia sent Milli a sympathy card. It was so considerate of her that when Milli felt strong enough to knock on the woman's door a few weeks later, she was surprised when a stranger answered.

"I'm looking for Katia," said Milli.

"The woman who lived here? She's been relocated," said a dapper gentleman.

"To where?" asked Milli.

"No one told me, but I'm thinking the Special Care Unit."

"Why? What was wrong with her?"

"She fell and broke her hip."

"But won't she be back? Won't she return to her apartment?"

"Nope," said the man. "Seems like she can't be on her own anymore."

Milli felt bad at the time, but didn't give it much thought until she saw the woman in the bed with iron railings, like an adult crib. Milli crept closer and noticed that Katia's eyes were open.

"Katia?" asked Milli.

"Who wants to know?"

"It's Millicent Tarnover. We were neighbors in the high rise. I was Anne Marie's friend. Do you remember me?"

Katia stretched out her chin, her lower lip practically touching her pointy nose like a wicked witch. Then her face softened and she wet her lips. "Anne Marie, now she was a hot ticket. Kept me laughing for hours with those parrot jokes." Katia squawked, "Put away the beads, boys, our prayers have been answered." She shook her head. "That was the punch line. Can't recall the rest of it though." The woman's face fell back into the witch pose.

"I came for a visit but you had already moved. I'm sorry about your hip," said Milli.

"Hip, shmip. Nothing wrong with my hip. It's my bank account that went kaphooey. Landed me here in this hell hole."

Milli was confused. "What do you mean?"

"Mean? I'm not mean. I'm a sweet little old lady. Wouldn't harm a flea. Or is that a fly? What did you say your name was?"

"Millicent. Milli. You sent me a note when Anne Marie died and I wanted to thank you for your kindness."

Katia shut her eyes. "Too late. It's too late Baby, now it's too late. I really did try to make it. Something inside has died and I can't hide and I just can't fake it." She mumbled the words and nodded off.

Milli looked at Katia's chart before she left the room. The woman's meds were a page long with Dr. Boothbury's name everywhere. There were two areas highlighted in yellow: Delusional and Falling Risk.

That poor woman. Milli wondered if she had been in this ward for the last four years. *Will I be strapped down and overmedicated for the remainder of my days too, pills in the morning, shots at night? No, just plain no.* Milli decided a talk with the night nurse was in order. She hoped she was more like Reshma and Nurse Hildebrand and less like Ms. Fagan.

Milli approached the nurses' station where she saw the backside of a full-figured woman who sat clicking and typing at a computer. Unlike most of the workers, she wore a white uniform, white stockings, and white rubber-soled shoes. There was a nameplate on the desk: Magda Manowicz, RN.

Milli cleared her voice to get her attention. "Good evening, Nurse Manowicz. I wonder if you have a few minutes to chat?"

Startled, the nurse turned in her chair. Milli was surprised at the abundance of chins and the fat that rolled like bracelets down her arms. The woman exuded a heaviness beyond her pounds like she carried weights on her cheeks, her shoulders, and her chest that sagged her entire body.

"Well, I'll be." Contrary to her size, her voice was Minnie-Mouse high. "What can I do for you? Mrs. Tarnover?"

"So my reputation precedes me?"

"It's my job to know my patients." Magda pulled a folder off her desk. "I've read your file." She stared at Milli with narrowed eyes. "I've been told that you are a danger to yourself and others. So far, you haven't given me any trouble. You've been sound asleep every time I check on you." She flipped through several pages in the folder. "How can a mite like you cause so many problems?"

Milli was about to weave a wonderful story about her supernatural powers and how she put curses on people, but her attention was distracted by the scent of wintergreen. "I smell something heavenly, like sweet mint. Am I right?"

"You have a strong sniffer," said Magda. "Indeed. I'm brewing a special tea. Perhaps you'd like some?"

Milli recalled teatime with Birdie and Apollo. The tea Nurse Magda was making had the same minty scent. *Birchbark?*

"Tell me, Nurse Magda. Where did you get this wonderful tea? It's my favorite," said Milli.

"There's a woman in Oldham who sells it," she said.

Milli assessed Magda, her anxious eyes, her round body, her droopy shoulders and wondered what was causing such sadness and if Birdie had helped with a cure.

"Have you worked here long?"

Magda pouted. "This is my ninth month. Graveyard shift. Midnight to dawn."

Milli laughed. "Night shift would be a better word; after all, we're all such ancient people. The word graveyard is all too appropriate."

The woman actually tee-hee'd.

"The man who hired me decided I'm well suited for the overnight schedule. He calls me his Burly Bouncer." Under her breath, she said, "Is that grounds for harassment?"

Milli saw red sparks bubble up around the woman's chest.

"If there were trouble, he claims I'm the perfect person to handle it."

"And is there ever trouble when you're on duty?"

"The worst that happens is a patient falls out of bed." She patted her bicep. "Nothing is too heavy for these guns."

"So every night is like this?" Milli marveled at the peace on the ward.

"Yes, quiet, very quiet."

At the nurses' station, wheelchairs were lined up. Patients sat there for hours during the day to pass the time and to be watched. "May I sit here for a bit?" asked Milli.

"Of course," squeaked Magda. "I rarely have company, especially someone who actually converses. So by all means, take a seat."

Milli went one step further. She brought the wheelchair around the counter to sit alongside the nurse. *Now we're on equal footing.*

The nurse angled her chair toward Milli, and readied the tea.

"Do you like working here?" Milli asked.

Nurse Magda looked around. "To tell you the truth, I don't feel much like a nurse. I receive my orders when I arrive, check on my patients and administer their meds. I clean them up if need be, wipe a few tears, and talk gently to calm any fears. I submit my report when I leave. I'm more like a robot."

"You must do your job so superbly that you're trusted without question," said Milli.

"I never thought of it like that. But you're right. I've never missed a shift, I'm never late, and I've never lost a patient. So why do I feel under-appreciated?"

The woman wasn't really addressing Milli. It was more like she was speaking to the air and Milli just happened to be there.

"How do you spend your time away from the job?" asked Milli.

"Have you taken a look at me? How do you think? I eat. A lot. And I sleep. A lot."

"What about family and friends?"

"I have two cats, Amber and Mopsie. They're my friends and family." Magda clicked on the computer to a screen shot of her felines.

"Oh, so cute," said Milli. "I had a pet sitting service when I was younger. We had a galumphing golden retriever, but no cats. My Leo was allergic to them."

"You know, I don't understand the information about you in your file." She took out the cover sheet. "'Millicent Tarnover does not engage in conversation. She stays to herself and avoids contact with all others. She is highly belligerent when she does interact.'" Nurse Magda shook her head. "This description can't possibly be you."

"What else does it say?"

"Nothing good, I'm afraid. It's as if the nursing staff has been warned to keep their distance from you or else subdue you whenever possible. I've been curious to meet you and see for myself. And here you are." The nurse held the folder with both hands and ran her fingers over Milli's medical chart. "It says you were born in 1943."

"I'll be eighty-five on Monday," said Milli.

The nurse sat straighter in her chair, her brows knitted together and her lips twisted. "I don't usually break the rules. You have to understand that, but I feel we are entitled to read what is written about us, and you're of an age where you deserve to know what it says." Magda hunched her broad shoulders and lowered her head. "I smell something very wrong here. I've been smelling it for quite a while, but most patients in this unit don't interact, so I rarely know what they're thinking. But this floor has a secret and somehow, you're a part of it." Magda handed Milli the folder. "I have to make my rounds now. You can sit here and read. Just don't cross anything out or spit on it or anything. All right?"

All right? All right!

Milli breathed in Leo, breathed out Lionel and dug in. The first few pages were details about Milli's life: age, weight, family history, medications, and general impressions. Subsequent pages included a day-to-day investigation into Milli's disappearance, accompanied by newspaper clippings and random interviews. Milli laughed when she saw the quote by the woman named Ruby Tuesday on Porter Street discussing a disoriented woman babbling in the streets. *That really was me!*

There were also printouts of the correspondence between Mr. Grasin and Ms. Fagan which implied business, but Milli caught a double-edged tone, like the words were in code. She read a hand-written memo from Grasin decrying the negative publicity caused by Millicent Tarnover's disappearance, and how it would uncover any misconduct, which would do irreparable harm.

What she hadn't expected to see were financial statements from her luxury high rise and documents signed by Bernard Monk, her nephew. Inexplicably, there was the deed to Milli's house, with a note attached listing Bernard Monk's assets. In addition, Bernard's death certificate was among the papers. Cause of death: heart failure. Milli knew he had overdosed, so the official reason—the stopping of his heart—made sense. There were notes by Ms. Fagan about Milli's social security and pension, and photocopies of Milli's application to Medicaid.

On the last page was a handwritten memo from Ms. Fagan: *Keep this patient under control. She is a danger to herself and others.* Milli knew one thing for certain after reading the file: she was destined to live out her days in the New Dawn Special Care Unit.

WHEN NURSE MAGDA RETURNED from making her rounds, her face was pale and her hands shook. "When I read the chart on your door, it said you had received a sedative at nine o'clock a.m. and again at six p.m. I was supposed to administer it again at three a.m., even if you were asleep. It's already four thirty."

Milli shrank back, expecting the woman to yank her out of the wheelchair and throw her into her room. Instead the nurse sank into her chair.

"A lesson I learned in nursing school was the doctrine of double effect, where a treatment intended for good unintentionally causes harm. It seems to me, if I had come into your room as scheduled, I would have done as instructed. If you had struggled, I would have held you down and administered the sedative with more resolve. I've done that with other patients and I've never questioned it." Nurse Magda's face creased into folds. Her shoulders lifted into her neck. Then she heaved with sobs. "But speaking with you and knowing the sedative I was to give you would put you in a comatose state appalls me. The first lesson I learned was to do no harm. Is that what I've been doing the past nine months? Sedating my patients into unconsciousness night after night, falsely maintaining a state of calm?"

What is she saying? That she's questioning her orders? Is she my godsend? My route out of here? Please, let that be true.

"This is a dementia ward," said Magda, "so I've taken it for granted that my patients are a danger to themselves and require extensive treatment. But maybe I've been deceived."

"Magda, the memory care unit has a problem that is bigger than both of us. The question is what can be done about it?"

Magda's chins shook. "I could take my suspicions to the chief executive officer of New Dawn, or I could go to the police."

"No. No, don't do that. You have no proof of wrongdoing. All that will happen is you'll be fired and I'll be confined to the ward forever." Milli sat back in the wheelchair. "What do you know about Katia Bridges?"

Nurse Magda shook her head. "Strange woman. Sometimes she's lucid. Other times, she's on a different planet. I never know which Katia will greet me."

"When she's making sense, does she tell you anything about herself?"

Magda's eyebrows furrowed. "Funny you should ask. Just last week she told me a story about her late husband, how he came to her in a dream. She said she missed him and had no one left who cares about her."

That didn't sound delusional to Milli. The patients in the ward all seemed afloat on their own islands with no rescue in sight. "And what's the story with the two patients who are tied to their beds?"

"They wander into each other's room at night. Ms. Fagan decided to restrain them."

"Would they have harmed each other?"

"I don't know," said Nurse Magda. "For several nights, they cried out for each other, so I reported it. This was the solution."

"I noticed that patients have more equipment in their rooms than is warranted? Don't you think that's odd?"

"It seems to be the protocol around here. I've been advised not to question policy."

Milli, treading carefully, needed to convince this virtuous woman that she was the answer to fixing the ward by revealing its secrets. Milli leaned into the nurse as if she were sharing a confidence. "Tell me, Magda, did you get your tea from Madame Sheeya?"

The woman's eyes widened. "How did you know that?"

"When I was on the lam, I lived in the walk-in apartment downstairs from her. Madame Sheeya took an interest in my health and prescribed the same tea that you're drinking."

Magda patted her bosom like she was fanning her heart.

"On the first floor at the front of the building is Lila's Florist Shop, which is owned by the Peabody family. Mr. Peabody is an attorney. Perhaps he can help us. And here's where I am putting my belief and trust in you, Magda. Please call the shop and explain to the young woman who runs it—her name is Victoria—who you are, where I am, and how we need her father's help immediately."

"And you're sure she'll listen?"

"I can't be sure of anything," said Milli. "But if we do nothing, I'm a goner." *And it will be on my birthday, no less.*

Magda pointed to the time: 5:45. "The day shift will begin arriving soon. You'd better return to your room."

"I don't want you to get into trouble. In the morning, I'll pretend that you sedated me. And if I may be so bold, I suggest you leave like you usually do, having made your regular report, and be sure to include the time you administered my shot."

"So I'll lie? I've never done that before."

"Think of it as admitting the truth to yourself."

Milli wasn't sure Magda would follow through; nevertheless, she clung to the belief that the nurse in her would do what was morally right.

Exhausted, Milli made her way to her private prison. She lay down on her bed and before she knew it the day shift came around with her breakfast and her morning pills, which she pretended to take.

"That's a good girl," said Nurse Hildebrand. "Ms. Fagan will be so proud of you."

Chapter Thirty-Two

Milli propped herself up in bed with Rachel Rousso's book of poetry and read a few lines of a poem titled *Dawn*.

The world awakens under the brilliance of sun
as night sheds its blanket of darkness.
It is in your power
to become prisms of light and the blaze of lilies
or reduced to layers of compost and brambles of thorns.

Milli loved the hopefulness of the morning, but she wondered if it was in her nature to carry darkness. She experienced the blazing lilies, but understood thorns better. She decided that life would go on without her, so she might as well be thankful that she'd lived to turn eighty-five.

The book settled open on her chest and her eyes closed.

Poetry Joe laughed out loud when he saw her pose. She heard him and opened her eyes. "Just absorbing a bit of optimism," said Milli. "It's nice to see you. I have a few questions, if you don't mind sitting with me for a few minutes."

"Always glad to be in your company," he said.

"Why did you choose New Dawn for Rosalie?"

Poetry Joe opened the chair across from Milli. He set both feet on the floor and placed his hands on his knees. "Rosalie was having trouble with her balance. She decided it was an inner ear infection, but then she started stumbling and bumping into furniture. She dismissed it as clumsiness, but I insisted we see a doctor. She had made an appointment, but just before we went, she broke her wrist. At the hospital, we learned she had Lou Gehrig's Disease, which had affected her mobility and began wreaking havoc on other parts of her body."

"I'm so sorry," said Milli. "How old was she when she was diagnosed?"

"Sixty-four," he said. "I was five years her junior and her dearest companion."

"So you weren't married?"

"Rosalie and I were content to have a common law union. When she fell, we had been together for twenty-five years, but she never took my name. We never gave it a thought until the hospital bill came and we couldn't pay it."

"How awful," said Milli. "What did you do?"

"She was able to apply for Medicare because of her disease. But even that didn't cover all her expenses. The social worker at the hospital filled out the paperwork for Medicaid and suggested she reside in a facility that would help her convalesce."

"The social worker didn't happen to be Ms. Fagan, by any chance?" asked Milli.

"No, but our social worker knew Ms. Fagan and that's how Rosalie ended up at New Dawn."

Milli gave this a great deal of thought and had one essential question. "Did your Rosalie have any other living relatives?"

"No. Just me, and we weren't legally related. Now that I've answered all these questions, why are you asking?"

"I have a theory about this place, but I can't prove it. You said that the residents rarely have visitors. You called it the ward of the forgotten. Why do you think that?"

"I figured they were old folks who had deteriorated to a point beyond recognition, so their relatives had given up on them. That seemed so unfair to me, which is why I still read to the residents even after Rosalie passed."

Poetry Joe stretched his long legs and paced the small room. His face was bowed and his lips pursed. Milli swore she could see his thoughts whir, pushing the air out in rippling eddies.

A knock came at the door and Ms. Fagan entered without waiting. "I thought I heard talking in here. Joe, I must ask you to leave us alone. Mrs. Tarnover and I have much to discuss."

"Of course," he said.

Milli extended the Rachel Rousso book toward Poetry Joe. "Please return this to Victoria Peabody. Maybe you can tell her how much I've learned from it, and you."

Poetry Joe nodded and accepted the book. After he left, Ms. Fagan sat on the edge of the chair, her legs and arms crossed. "I trust you are feeling better today? We cannot have a repeat of yesterday's behavior."

"And what if we did?" sing-songed Milli.

"We have strict rules for our patients to follow. Without them, the ward would be chaotic and we cannot have that. Now can we, Dear?"

Milli invoked the specter of her friend Anne Marie. What would she say when confronted with a self-righteous phony like Alexis Fagan? "I keep thinking about aging," said Milli. "Would you rather age from the neck up or from the neck down? I'd like to hear your opinion."

Her tongue-in-cheek friend Anne Marie had loved impossible questions. They put people at such a disadvantage.

Ms. Fagan stammered. "I have no opinion."

"That's what I thought," said Milli. *Oh how Anne Marie would applaud.*

"You know what I've been wondering, Ms. Fagan, do fish get thirsty?"

"Water is part of their atmosphere," began the woman, before realizing she was being played.

"And, pray tell, why do we call it lipstick if you can still move your lips?"

Ms. Fagan stood up. "I can see I'm getting nowhere. But I've got your number, Millicent Tarnover." Ms. Fagan went for the door.

"And oh, here's a good one for you, what happens when you swallow your pride?" asked Milli.

Before the woman slammed the door, she glared at Milli. "These boxes are a health hazard. Start cleaning them out, Dear. I have no problem erasing your past."

Somehow Milli felt she had lost that battle.

Chapter Thirty-Three

L ater in the day, Milli received a note from Ms. Fagan.

> *Mrs. Tarnover,*
>
> *On Monday, June 5 at 10:00 a.m., you will meet with*
> *Dr. Boothbury to hear the results of your evaluation.*
>
> *Sincerely,*
> *Alexis Fagan, MSA*

Milli used the day to pore through her belongings in the boxes. She didn't stop to study them, just to sort chaff from substance. Pile one: Leo. Pile two: Lionel. Pile three: keepsakes. Pile four: necessities. If she was going to be stuck here, she would make it her own. She hung clothes and filled drawers and organized other belongings in boxes marked SAVE. She threw what she no longer needed into boxes to be tossed and marked them TRASH. *So much of who I was I'm not anymore.*

If she remained at New Dawn, all her corporal needs would be met. And if her eighty-fifth birthday were her last, then who cared. And if by some miracle, she were able to ride on the back of a motorcycle with Kedrix and bake muffins with Apollo, she'd do it with less baggage.

Avoiding the sedative that evening was a feat of wills. The evening nurse who came to her room was a new hire, fresh-faced with a swinging ponytail and a bounce to her step. Milli feigned stomach cramps and hid in the bathroom until the nurse was forced to continue her rounds. When she came by again, Milli complimented her on her diligence.

"You're a tribute to the nursing profession. So proficient. I wonder if you can tell me the side effects of the shot you're about to administer?" said Milli.

"It's a mild sedative with very few side effects."

"Does it have anti-inflammatory ingredients? I am highly allergic. You wouldn't want to administer it to me and find me dead, now would you?"

"I will check the label," she said.

Milli at least stalled her for the moment. When the nurse returned, Milli again was in the bathroom. "Did you get affirmation about its contents?" asked Milli with as much officialese as she could muster.

"Yes, actually, it does have analgesics in it. I put in a call to the doctor. I'll be back later with his reply."

The young nurse on duty returned at eight p.m., way after the shot should have been administered. Right behind her was Nurse Magda.

"I came in early tonight," winked Magda. "Thanks, Stacey. I'll take care of Mrs. Tarnover's evening medications."

"But my instructions from the doctor were very clear," said the young nurse.

"Don't worry. I've been doing this for a long time. I'll square it with Dr. Boothbury. And as a bonus for you tonight, I'll cover the next few hours so you can get home early."

"Really? How can I thank you?" said the young nurse.

"One hand washes the other," said Magda.

After Magda made sure all patients were comfortable, she returned to Milli's room. "I met Victoria today. That's why I came in early. Her father, Alex Peabody, wants you to phone him at nine p.m. He needs you to answer some questions before he can help you."

"Magda, I am forever grateful. You're a life saver."

"That's always been my intention. It's why I went into this profession in the first place." She gave Milli her cellphone and showed her which buttons to press. "The phone connection is poor in the building, so I'm going to have to trust you. Get a sweater and come with me."

Magda unlocked the unit and led Milli outside to a bench in a small courtyard. "Sometimes I sit here if I arrive early. It's very peaceful. I'll come out to get you at ten o'clock. You'll be here, right?"

"You can count on me," said Milli, although there was a clear temptation to flee.

The phone read 8:45, so she had fifteen minutes to bathe in the evening. She recalled Rachel Rousso's words: *Let me enter that place knowing I have lived.* As she sat, she breathed in Leo and breathed out Lionel, and her body absorbed the night. She was on the bench in the Seaside Arboretum and the bench along the boardwalk. She sat in the patio on Porter Street and in the audience watching Leo make blueberry muffins. It wasn't enough to sit, she decided. If she had another chance, even at eighty-five, she would be like George H. W. Bush and jump out of a plane. She'd emulate Alice Munro and win a Nobel prize in her eighties. Or she'd be Dr. Ruth Westheimer's collaborator and administer sage advice about relationships. In her mind, she could be anyone; in her heart, she could feel anything; and going forward, in her body, she would live actively and with purpose.

At precisely 9:00 p.m., she unlocked the phone and pressed call.

"Mr. Peabody? This is Millicent Tarnover."

"Yes, Millicent. My daughter has implored me to help you, so tell me, what can I do?"

Milli began with the story of her escape from New Dawn and ended with the plan to meet with the doctor on Monday, her eighty-fifth birthday, to hear the results of the evaluation. "I am not incapacitated or incompetent. I am able to make my own decisions, but the powers that be have decided otherwise. My suspicion is they're defrauding Medicaid for their own personal gain."

"Those are very serious charges. What makes you think that?"

Milli didn't hesitate. "In every room, there's an abundance of devices that the patients can't possibly use, and from what I can tell, there are services on their charts that don't exist, and don't get me started on over-medicating us."

"Can you text me proof?" asked Mr. Peabody.

"I can try," said Milli, wondering how in the world she would do this. "Speaking for myself, I am out of time. Once my fate has been decreed, I'll never leave this place."

"I'm sure we can appeal the verdict," said Mr. Peabody.

"I doubt it. I have no idea why these people want to silence me, but there's definitely something sinister going on here. Maybe you can uncover it and save me at the same time."

Mr. Peabody wished Milli luck and they both hung up. Magda came out to get Milli and together they went into the ward.

"Magda, you agree that there's something underhanded happening?"

"I've felt an undercurrent of wrongdoing for a while," said Magda. "And I don't like that Mr. Grasin. He's a bully."

"Then will you help me expose these swindlers? If you scan my file and a few others like Hermione Zaccardi and Rodney Patrick, you can send them to Mr. Peabody. If there's evidence of fraud, I know he'll find it. I realize the position this puts you in, but Mr. Grasin and Ms. Fagan's scheme will continue without your help."

Magda's entire body trembled as if she were expelling demons. "Do no harm," she repeated as she retrieved the files. Together she and Milli sent dozens of pages to Mr. Peabody, hoping they would be proof of guilt.

"I have something special for you," said Magda, hours later. "I waited until our business together was finished to give it to you." She went behind the nurses' station for a small wrapped package. "This is a birthday present from Madame Sheeya. She said not to open it until the day of your birth has passed."

Chapter Thirty-Four

Milli woke on her eighty-fifth birthday feeling the weight of all her years. She sat at the end of the bed, dressed in her jeans and a t-shirt, and clutched her purse with Birdie's gift inside. She passed the minutes calculating her time on the planet: 8 decades, 960 months, 4,174 weeks, 29,220 days, 701,208 hours. *Take that, Dr. Boothbury!* Besides, she thought, she was celebrating being twenty four times, with a few extra years thrown in for luck. So what if a few of those decades had been squandered. She was here in the now and that was what counted.

At 9:45, Ms. Fagan escorted Milli out of the building to the same office where she had her evaluation. Dr. Boothbury was waiting for them.

"Good Morning, Mrs. Tarnover," said the doctor.

"Did you know it's my eighty-fifth birthday today?"

"Well, happy birthday, Little Lady," said the doctor.

"We'll get you a cupcake to celebrate," said Ms. Fagan.

"And some balloons," said Mr. Grasin.

"Have a seat, please. We have a serious matter to discuss," said the doctor. "I'd first like to share the results of your competency test. I'm sorry to say that you did not pass. In the third round of the alphabet, you missed the letter K. In the mathematical problem, you miscalculated. Furthermore, you did not intersect the polygons and you forgot the word bicycle in the list I gave you to memorize. I'm sorry, Mrs. Tarnover, but this indicates great lapses in your synapses and I suspect further deterioration is just a matter of time."

Milli knew she hadn't intersected the polygons, but it was the eraser's fault and he knew that. As far as missing the letter in the alphabet, she'd like to hear the doctor try it, fast, under pressure, three times.

"Furthermore, the testimony provided by both Mr. Grasin and Ms. Fagan is downright damning. It shows antisocial tendencies and aggressive behavior. Studies have shown that patients with Alzheimer's who exhibit these characteristics exacerbate these deficiencies with time.

"However, at present, I do not believe you need to be in a locked ward. Under strict supervision, you can return to the Downtown Crossing units and resume life in your own apartment. I have decided that you'll wear an ankle monitor so if you do wander, we'll be able to locate you. Moreover, we will equip your room with a video streaming device, so we can assess your medical progress, or lack thereof. Your medications will be prescribed by me and administered daily by a nurse practitioner whom we have on staff."

Milli understood this perfectly—house arrest, under the guise of living independently.

"I would say this is cause for a birthday celebration, Little Lady, don't you agree?" said the doctor.

"You get your cake and eat it too," said Ms. Fagan.

"And what about my social security check and my pension?" asked Milli.

"Just like before, New Dawn will take care of all your monetary needs. You won't have a care in the world," said Ms. Fagan. "You'll have full dining privileges, as well as the use of all the recreational facilities on our property."

Milli had the impression that Ms. Fagan knew exactly what the doctor was going to say and she was ready to follow it up with her own self-professed kindnesses.

"What if I want to go to the mall? Let's say I need new under-wear," asked Milli.

"There will be no need to leave the premises, Mrs. Tarnover. We will supply you with all you require. All you have to do is ask," said Ms. Fagan.

Dr. Boothbury fitted Milli with her leg monitor and patted her on the head. "This is all in your best interests, Little Lady."

Milli wanted to run, far and fast, but she knew it was no use. She would have to abide by the doctor's decree, and pray that Mr. Peabody will show up with the cavalry, like in the movies.

On their way out of the doctor's building, Ms. Fagan directed Milli to turn left.

"You won't be returning to the ward. We have your new accommodations prepared for you, Dear."

So Milli was right. This was all a sham. All pre-planned. The roles had been rehearsed and they played them smoothly. Milli was supposed to be thrilled to be out of the locked ward. She would be grateful, quiet, and subservient. That's what they thought. Milli would bide her time. Mr. Peabody was on this, she had to believe that.

Milli and Ms. Fagan walked toward a four-winged brick building flanked by parking lots. There were a few benches in front of the main entrance, and a good number of maples and oaks. Each unit had a large window, except on the lowest level, where the windows were wide and high.

"Your unit is similar to Downtown Crossing, which is in the west-ern section of New Dawn. Downtown Corners is in the east. It's more upscale," said Ms. Fagan, ushering Milli down a long brightly lit corridor. "We want you to be comfortable and feel safe. Ah, here we go. Apartment 101, Dear. It's a lovely unit with two windows."

Again Milli found herself in the bowels of the building. Milli's view were feet and cars' tires and puddles of rain; in the winter, there would be mounds of snow.

When they entered 101, two bouncy happy birthday balloons greeted her. There was a chocolate cupcake on a nightstand—no candle, of course. That would require a flame, which was forbidden.

"Happy Birthday, Dear. May you enjoy a long and prosperous life ahead."

Milli didn't doubt that Alexis Fagan would prosper from Milli's existence. She just hoped Alex Peabody would find proof of how she profited.

The air in the apartment was heavy with chlorine, as if it had just been cleaned. The surfaces of the bureau and nightstand shone. The bathroom was spotless with an abundance of fluffy towels. The bed was fully made and there were smiley faces on a rainbow quilt. Milli almost expected lollipops to grow out of the floor and bobbing apples to hang from the ceiling.

"Such a happy space," said Ms. Fagan. "I'm certain you'll never want to leave."

There was even a television, a radio, and a microwave. Looking around, Milli spotted a camera positioned near the ceiling and aimed at the bed, and there was an intercom on the wall.

"You're always within range of an aide to help you, Dear. See this string? Pull it and someone will come running. There's one in the lavatory as well."

A knock interrupted Ms. Fagan's lecture. "Come in," she said.

A burly man with New Dawn emblazoned on his shirt wheeled in Milli's boxes, even the ones labeled TRASH. In addition, there were two crates that held what had been in Milli's closet and on her shelves. Lock, stock, and barrel was what came to mind.

Behind the man, a woman, also in New Dawn duds, carried a tray with Milli's lunch: a grilled cheese sandwich, a salad, a milkshake, and the omnipresent green Jello.

"There's a cafeteria on the first floor, but if you want your meals delivered, just inform the morning nurse when she makes her rounds. And oh, yes, Millicent Dear, the door locks from the outside. So if someone inadvertently forgets and locks it, you'll need to call security."

More proof of prison life. "And the library? Is it available?"

"A lounge is open daily before and after meals. You'll be pleased at the selection of entertainment. Now relax, enjoy your birthday, and let us know if there's anything else we can do for you."

Milli bristled. "What about visitors?"

"Being on the grounds with other residents is clearly encouraged, but outside guests require permission and yours will be supervised. Schedule them with the front desk."

"Supervised?"

"Of course, Dear, we wouldn't want anyone else taking advantage of you, now would we? It's our responsibility to keep you safe."

"I wonder how I might go about making a personal phone call."

Ms. Fagan blinked. "For private phone calls, schedule them with the front desk too."

"Then they're not too private, are they?"

"Trust me, Dear, no one is listening."

Chapter Thirty-Five

Milli was too tired to die. Her eighty-fifth birthday should have been a big-bang day, one way or the other, but she no longer cared. When the nurse introduced herself that evening, Milli just nodded, accepted the injection, pulled the covers over her head and slept. A different nurse came around in the morning with the same routine. Someone brought a tray with breakfast, then lunch, and finally dinner. More injections. More sleep.

On the third morning, before the nurse administered the shot, she insisted Milli take a shower. Like a docile child, Milli allowed the nurse to clean her up and change her clothing. A team of New Dawn workers sanitized Milli's room, changed her sheets, and replaced her towels. Milli sat in a wheelchair in the hallway as they worked, clutching her purse to her chest. It was only then that she remembered Birdie's birthday gift.

She withdrew the small package and unwrapped it. She came face-to-face with a miniature rag doll with wild black hair and blunt limbs. Attached to its heart was a letter:

> You are in possession of a Protective Wanga Doll. She
> has the power to improve your circumstances. For her to

provide you with security and peace of mind, you must hold her to your heart, tell her how she can help you, then give her a name and say it three times.

Speak to her often, stroke her hair, offer her gifts and make her a safe bed to rest in, which you should place close to your own bed. Just make her aware that she is a welcome house guest, and she will reward you.

Crazy Birdie, thought Milli, but as she cradled the doll, she felt a vibration bubble up from her toes and electrify her fingers, like a transfer of power, immediate and shocking. Her legs shot out from under her; she leapt from the wheelchair, ran down the hallway to the exit and flung open the door. To her surprise, no alarms sounded. The June day was breezy; the sun winked between wispy clouds, saying hello to Milli for the first time since her birthday.

She made her way to a triangle of trees and an inviting wooden bench. A vision of the Seaside Arboretum catapulted her back to her first day of freedom from New Dawn, before she was captured and imprisoned. The closer she got to the bench, the stronger she felt, so that by the time she sat encircled by nature, she wept tears of joy.

She held the doll's arms out and marveled at its simplicity. Then she held it to her heart and remembered Birdie's instructions: explain the help you need, and give it a name. Milli spoke in a soft, smooth tone and invoked a poet's voice. "Please give me the power of the moment. Let no more days pass without my being totally present. Let me be the things I see. Let me enter into the small spaces between and experience the marrow within. You are my Beatrice. Beatrice. Beatrice. My beautiful Beatrice."

Milli kissed the rag doll, hugged it tight, and lay down on the bench in the island of green. She studied the sky, the feathery white in a sea of blue, her upside-down ocean. In the air, she saw bubbles of atoms floating and heard the flutter of butterfly wings and the hum of a bumblebee. The strawberry shampoo the nurse had used to wash her hair mixed with the earthy richness of the soil and she thanked

Birdie over and over again for the power of Beatrice. A tremor shuddered through the ground and when she looked toward the street, she saw the burly New Dawn guard who wheeled in her belongings on Monday thudding toward her.

She sat up. "Greetings, Sir. I'd like to be carried back to my quarters now."

The burly man lifted her over his shoulder like an infant. She half expected him to pat her back so she would burp, but she resisted the urge.

"You gave us a fright, Mrs. Tarnover," Burly-Man said, his voice thick like peanut butter stuck to the roof of his mouth. "That thing on your ankle told me where to find you."

"Well, lucky me," she replied. "I wonder. How many other fortunate folks have monitors?"

The man shrugged, his neck veins popping.

"Come on, now. That's not a difficult question. How many of us potential escapees are there in Downtown Corners?"

"Mrs. Tarnover, let's just say you're special."

"I knew it," she tsked. "I'm the lucky one." Milli could feel the bulk of his arms as he held her. Such a powerful body, but Milli suspected he was short on brains.

Burly-Man entered the building by the side entrance and set Milli down. "Mrs. T, don't be put out with me. I'm just doing my job."

Milli needed to understand what she was up against. "Don't you think it's kind of silly for a big man like you to come after a little old lady like me?"

Burly-Man's bottom lip jutted out and he clenched his fists into balls.

Milli winked. "I get it. Mine is not to reason why. Mine is just to do or die."

The man's eyes narrowed.

"Do you just work the Downtown Crossing unit?" asked Milli.

"I'm security for the special needs ward. You're my one and only resident in the Downtowns. Bailey Haley, at your service."

Milli examined Bailey from top to toe: his crewcut, his ski nose, his white teeth, and marveled at how small his head was in comparison to his body. Milli had an aha moment. He was a henchman for Ms. Fagan and Mr. Grasin. Intimidating. Forceful. Dumb and easily manipulated.

"Tell me, Mr. Haley, do you have another job? I mean, how much money can you make protecting the elderly from themselves?" Milli's voice edged with anger.

Burly-Man grunted. "I'm a bouncer for a bar at night."

Milli's interest was piqued. "Have you been to the D-Note in Oldham?"

"I work there sometimes when there's a big crowd expected."

"Do you know a bouncer named Kedrix?"

"My Man. Kedrix. He's a stand-up dawg."

"Well then. We have a friend in common."

Bailey looked at Milli as if seeing her for the first time.

"Bailey, I'd like to speak with Kedrix. Do you think you could call him for me?"

He shook his head, his thick neck barely moving.

"I'll make it worth your while." Milli dipped her hand into her purse and pulled out a wad of bills.

Bailey eyed the money. "What's the harm?" he said as he scrolled through his phone, dialed the number and handed Milli his mobile. "Be quick about it."

The voice on the other end was strong and real, no answering machine this time. "Kedrix? It's Milli Tarnover. . . No, I'm not fine. . . I need your help. Please see if Mr. Peabody, Virginia's father, has made any progress. . . Virginia. The girl in the florist shop above my apartment. . .Then get a message to me through your friend, Bailey Haley. . . Can you do that?. . ."

Milli handed the phone back to Bailey. He listened and nodded, signaling thumbs-up when he ended the call. Milli gave the man his reward as he left her at the entrance to Downtown Dungeon without escorting her into her room or locking her inside.

Chapter Thirty-Six

Milli approached her cave with a different attitude. She cradled Beatrice and stroked her hair. *Kedrix will help me. I just know he will.* She had won a round against Ms. Fagan, Dr. Boothbury, and Mr. Grasin by befriending Bailey, even if she did have to bribe him.

The smell of lavender knocked her flat immediately when she walked into her small space. She was amazed at how scrubbed clean the room was. The trash boxes had been removed and the cartons that remained were stored in the closet. Pillows were fluffed, towels were folded, windows were shiny.

"Look, Beatrice. We're brand new." She showed the doll around the room when their eyes landed on a stack of mail on her nightstand. She wondered if it had been there for the last few days, beyond her mental reach.

She read the return addresses: Madame Sheeya, Kedrix Forsythe, Pippa Passes, one unidentified envelope with big block letters—definitely from Apollo.

"Beatrice, my sweet doll, you've brought me luck. I should have met you days ago!"

Milli opened birthday card after birthday card. She lined them on her bureau and they sparkled just for her, each with its personal note of love. But there was no letter from Alexander Peabody. She wondered if Ms. Fagan had gone through her mail. The envelopes had seemed sealed, but that could have been manipulated. *I wouldn't put it past her.*

Milli looked through the cards again, searching for some sort of secret message, but there was nothing but happy birthday love.

The next morning, Milli awoke so early that the nurses had not yet made their rounds and the hallway lights were still dimmed. As she approached her door, she noticed an envelope at its edge with Kedrix's name in the upper corner and a red heart drawn with a sharpie. She tucked herself into a corner, away from the prying lens of the video camera, and opened the letter.

> *Dear Mrs. Tarnover (AKA Milli),*
>
> *I'm close to a big reveal about the principles in your case: Asa Grasin, Alexis Fagan, and Boris Boothbury. The documents you scanned have shown egregious crimes against residents at the New Dawn Retirement Village. The case requires further investigation and that takes time. I know you are in the difficult position of being isolated, but I urge you to have patience. I am working on your behalf and will be in touch soon.*
>
> *Sincerely,*
> *Alex Peabody (Victoria's doting Dad)*

Milli held Beatrice's stubby arms and twirled around the room. "We're going to get them. We're going to get them," she sang. She didn't care when. She would hang in there for as long as it took. She recited a new mantra: *I don't want to end up simply visiting this world. I need to live.*

Milli left her room, danced into the hallway and out the door into the fresh air. "Haha! I'm free!" She twirled and sang until Bailey Haley caught up with her.

"Mrs. Tarnover, Mrs. Tarnover, I can't allow you to run around like this, even if you are a friend of Kedrix."

Milli jumped into his arms. "I'm free! Don't you get it? The big wigs at New Dawn are being investigated. Which means I'm not stuck in this hellhole for the rest of my life."

Bailey's face crumpled. "Shhh, right now. Be quiet, Mrs. Tarnover. I did Kedrix a favor by putting that envelope under your door. You must keep mum. Can you do that?"

Milli wondered how much he knew about the underhanded practices that she discovered. Milli couldn't ask directly. "Bailey, do you report to Ms. Fagan and Mr. Grasin?"

"Neither of them. I'm the doctor's strong arm," he said, flexing his impressive biceps.

"Don't tell him I said this, but I don't think he's a good man."

Bailey grunted. "He's been mighty good to me."

"No matter. Justice will prevail, you'll see." Milli took a stab in the dark. "Tell me, Bailey, what do you do to make those muscles of yours so powerful?"

"They are pretty rad," Bailey said, posing like the Hulk. "Dr. Boothbury gives me these supplements. He said they're harmless but effective."

"Do you pay for them?"

"Hell, no. It's a bartering thing. I work security and he pays me in pills. I'm on track to take first prize in three body-building competitions. It's a win-win."

"Did you ever consider this to be illegal?"

Bailey grinned. "Nah. We all do it, but I do it smarter."

Milli gave that some thought. "So let me see if I understand this. You work for the doctor in exchange for supplements, but there are bodybuilders who have to pay for them."

"Oh, yeah. I refer them to the doctor. The more they buy, the more he gives me."

"Don't you think that's suspicious behavior?" asked Milli.

"Like I said, I'm smarter than the average bear."

"May I offer some advice?" Milli didn't wait for an answer. "If Dr. Boothbury is brought up on charges for mishandling supplements, you would be involved too. Even if everyone else does it, it doesn't make this legal."

"I'll give it a think," said Bailey. "No need to put the horse ahead of the cart."

Oh, God. This kid is doomed.

"Now let's get you back into the building before we both get in trouble."

"I'm on my way, Bailey. No need to accompany me. I can be trusted."

Instead of going to her room, Milli explored the cafeteria and the lounge. She saw several staff members in a side room at a large oval table. At the head was a man in a business suit taking notes. She inched closer to the door to hear what she could, but an aide took her by the arm.

"You have better things to do, Missy, than listen in on important business," she said. "Best be on your way."

When the night nurse came in to administer the evening injection of calm, Milli picked up Beatrice and waved her at the woman.

"The jig is up," said Milli. "I know you're just following instructions, but I refuse the shot tonight and from here on in. Take it up with your boss." Milli stood as tall as she could and began a physical lunge at the nurse, who backed away quickly.

"We'll see about this," she warned.

"Yes, we will," said Milli, dancing around the room again with Beatrice.

Chapter Thirty-Seven

Going to the cafeteria every night was too much work, so Milli ordered in and watched the news on television as she ate her meal. A knock interrupted.

"Mrs. T, are you in there?" asked a thick voice.

Milli recognized Bailey's heavy tongue, opened the door, and slipped into the hallway so the cameras would not pick up on their interaction.

"I got another message for you from Kedrix." He handed Milli a note and he stood there waiting.

Milli retrieved her purse and gave him a ten dollar bill. He didn't move. She added a fifty. *Ah, the price of freedom.*

"Thank you, Bailey, you're a good man for helping me and Kedrix."

"He's my main man. Brothers gotta stick together."

Alone, she read Kedrix's words:

> *Hey Ruby Tuesday,*
> *I checked in with that hottie Victoria to see if she had another envelope for me. She's even better looking than Phebes. Do you think she'd go for me? Anyway, she said her pops was on it and for you to be patient. Hope that*

helps. BTW, don't depend on Bailey. He's juiced and makes bad decisions. Got 'roid brain, if you catch my drift.
                                                        Take good care. Kedrix

Juiced? 'Roid brain? Milli figured the words described Bailey's dependence on the pills he got from Boothbury. *No matter.* Kedrix sent good news. She held her Wanga doll and stroked her hair. "Beatrice, my mother taught me that a handful of patience is worth a bucketful of brains. I never knew what it meant, but I'm getter smarter now that I'm eighty-five. I feel it in my bones. Anything worth having is worth waiting for, right?" Milli felt the doll's warmth heating her heart.

For a week, Milli cruised the lounge, the cafeteria, and the grounds outside of Downtown Corners without being hassled. Sing-alongs were held under a summertime canopy and Milli found a few books of poetry in the library that soothed her. She paid attention to personal hygiene and made sure she spiked her hair, even without red streaks. She needed to be youthful and vibrant and positive. She carried Beatrice in her purse wherever she went and had conversations with her out loud and proudly.

The following week on Monday, Milli sat in the cafeteria eating her three egg omelet, toast, and home fries when a trio of women joined her.

"May we sit with you?" asked a woman with orange hair.

Milli was surprised but pleased. "Of course."

"Are you new here?" asked a brunette.

Milli recalled a similar conversation in the Alzheimer's Unit and hoped these ladies had lasting memories. "Yes and no," said Milli. "I usually take my meals in my room."

"Oh, I used to do that, but not anymore. Eating with others is so much more enjoyable," said Brunette.

"Do you play canasta?" asked the third woman, a blonde.

"I used to when I lived in the high-rise units. But it's been a few years."

"How about joining us? We need a fourth," said Orange. "Meet us in the lounge at ten if you're interested."

Why the heck not! The ladies lingered and chatted about their kids and grandkids and discussed a novel they had all read for the Downtown Corners' Book Group.

Blonde asked Milli what kinds of books she enjoyed. "I love Rachel Rousso's poetry."

Blonde gushed. "Now there's a down-to-earth nature poet. Good choice."

"I'm an Edna St. Vincent Millay fan," said Orange.

"Did you know she was Rachel Rousso's favorite poet?" asked Brunette.

Milli studied the women. Why had she thought no one could compare to Anne Marie? Why hadn't she given anyone else a chance? These ladies seemed comfortable in their own skins, which they had inhabited for as long as Milli had lived in hers. She joined them in the card room for canasta and learned their names. Brunette was Hamida, Blonde was Connie, and Orange was Patrice. They had lost their husbands when they were in their seventies, sold their homes, and moved to New Dawn.

"We love it here," said Patrice.

"What's not to love," added Hamida.

"At first, I was so lonely, but once I gave the place a chance, I realized that we all have so much in common. And so much to learn about each other. You know, Milli, we're taking a ballroom dance class this evening. There'll even be a few men there." Connie winked.

"And cocktails," said Hamida.

"And a decent dessert, not that god-awful Jello," said Patrice.

"Give me a good muffin any day and I'll be in heaven," said Connie.

"That's breakfast," said Hamida. "Do you remember Jordan Marsh blueberry muffins. Now those I could eat any time of day."

"Do I? Toasted with a little butter. The best," said Connie.

"My husband Leo was the baker for Jordan Marsh," said Milli, who hadn't said Leo's name aloud for way too long.

"Wow! Lucky you! I'd be ten thousand pounds if my husband had been a baker. He was a plumber, and a darn good one. I called him Flush Gordon," laughed Hamida.

"My William was the best salesman ever. He could talk you out of your britches," laughed Patrice. "Got me out of mine all the time."

Milli loved how the women didn't dwell on how their husbands had died or their flaws or their own regrets. They shrugged and laughed off their grievances as if they had never permeated their lives. When she knew them better, perhaps, they'd reveal their secrets as she had with Anne Marie, but for now, they were upbeat and twinkled with life. It was their choice to be at New Dawn. They had found a home of warmth and friendship.

Isn't that what I want? Yes, but not with an ankle monitor. Not with Ms. Fagan, Dr. Boothbury and Mr. Grasin puppeteering my movements. Why am I their victim? What crime did I commit? All I wanted to do was relive a family memory? How could that land me so far afield from women like Hamida, Patrice, and Connie? Who's to blame? Bernard? Me?

At night, Milli stroked Beatrice's hair and thought about the people in the complex. Sure it was an assisted living unit, but the people were vibrant and friendly and active, at least a good number of them. It wasn't like she was still in the Special Care Unit. That was different. Those people had no control over their illness, and she never really gave anyone a chance to be her friend when she was in the basement dungeon.

Milli made a conscious decision to be open-minded and open-hearted and not dwell on the negative. No more Mad Milli.

A week later, Milli saw Ms. Fagan being led out of the cafeteria by two men in tailored suits. The woman's hair showed gray roots and her skirt was wrinkled. Milli breathed in confidence and inched close enough to the woman to pipe up, "Ms. Fagan, Dear, are you ill?"

The woman stared at Milli. "You! You!" she slurred. "People! Look at this witch. She's no good, I tell you. Stay away from her."

The whole room stopped its buzzing. Brows went up. Had Milli's new friends heard? Would they believe Ms. Fagan? That night, Milli ate dinner in her room. She didn't want to deal with any fallout from Ms. Fagan's outburst. She kept the TV on for company and watched the evening news.

A photo of the special care unit of New Dawn flashed across the screen. *Now they advertised?* But it wasn't an ad. It was a news bulletin that three employees had been charged with fraud, embezzlement, and drug trafficking. Head shots accompanied the story: Asa Grasin, Basil Boothbury, and Alexis Fagan.

Milli leaned into the television and turned up the volume:

> The case came to light when an unsuspecting octogenarian left the New Dawn Retirement Village without informing anyone of her intent. She had been eager to spend a day on her own at the Seaside Arboretum in Oldham and decided to stay in the town as a resident. Her disappearance turned into a nightmare for the Assistant Controller Asa Grasin, Social Worker Alexis Fagan, and Geriatric Physician Basil Boothbury.
>
> When the trio located Tarnover, they sequestered her in the New Dawn Special Care Unit, fearful that an investigation would unravel their scheme to defraud Medicaid, which extended beyond Mrs. Tarnover to other residents at New Dawn.
>
> When the law firm of Peabody and Peabody was employed to represent Tarnover's restraints, attorneys uncovered extensive evidence of illegal practices: submitting false diagnoses, performing unnecessary procedures, embezzlement, trafficking in the distribution of drugs and billing for medications and procedures not performed.

Milli didn't understand half of what was revealed, but the gist of it boiled her bones. Those people used her and others to cheat the system. *But why me?* She recalled her first private interaction with Ms. Fagan after Bernard died. The woman asked if she had any other relatives who could help her. *Was that suspect?* When Ms. Fagan filled out her applications for Medicaid, Milli thought she was being generous, but deep down, she knew something was suspicious, she just couldn't identify it.

No matter. Alex Peabody would get to the bottom of this. She hugged Beatrice and danced around the room. "Ain't no stoppin' us now, we're on the move! Ain't no stoppin' us now, we've got the groove!"

Later that evening, Milli listened to another news broadcast. This time she learned that nurses' aide Reshma Ramirez, who was fired for not cooperating with Ms. Fagan, would be a key witness for the prosecution. "I knew that girl was the real deal. Yessiree, Beatrice."

Milli felt as buoyant as a cloud until she heard a knock on her door and saw Nurse Magda Manowicz. Her face was shadowed and her eyes sagged. She was in street clothes, not her uniform, and she looked like a thundercloud surrounded her.

"We need to talk," she said. Milli welcomed her into her room. "I have something difficult to tell you."

"Did you lose your job? Am I to blame? That's the last thing I wanted to happen," said Milli.

"No. No, nothing like that. I feel like a hero, actually. But I've learned some information that affects you and since I'm responsible for much of this case being exposed, I thought I should tell you in person before you hear it on the news."

Milli couldn't imagine what was coming, but she picked up Beatrice from her cozy bed and clutched her to her chest.

"When Dr. Boothbury was charged along with Ms. Fagan and Mr. Grasin, I was reminded of a time when I saw the doctor one night in the courtyard. You know the place where you made your phone call?"

"Yes, the bench where you like to sit?"

"Exactly. Well, he had met a young man there. A tall, thin dark-haired man. They were discussing money and pills and I remember hearing them say oxycodone and Ativan and a few other potent drugs. I figured the man was also a doctor and they were talking about a patient, but when I looked at your folder again, and studied the photo ID of Bernard Monk, I realized he had been the man with Dr. Boothbury."

Milli wanted to close her ears, but she held on to Beatrice for courage and opened herself to more bad news.

Magda swallowed. "Millicent, one of the charges against Dr. Boothbury is trafficking in illicit drugs. Your nephew was also involved in illegal activity."

Blocks fell into place. *Bernard had sold drugs for Boothbury, but he hadn't figure on Bernard dying.* Milli knew how secretive her nephew was about his addiction. He had fooled his mother for years and when he went into rehab, he stayed clean just long enough for Linda Mae to die. Then it was no holds barred. *Why didn't I pay better attention?*

When she first moved to New Dawn, Bernard fawned over her and paid close attention. As the years passed, he grew distant and his visits perfunctory. His appearance had changed from business-like to careless. Milli thought he was going through another one of his phases. He'd been like that since he was a child. A few years happy-go-lucky, the next few down-in-the-dumps. Sometimes warm and affectionate, other times irritable and brusque. Then he'd flip and be sweet and doting. There was no predicting which Bernard would arrive. Had he fooled Boothbury into believing he was stable? Shouldn't a doctor recognize Bernard's bipolar behavior? Milli had carried guilt since Bernard's death, believing she failed him. Now she blistered with the knowledge that Boothbury exploited his pain.

"Magda, my nephew had a long history of drug abuse, but I thought he was handling his addiction. I still don't understand why

Ms. Fagan and Mr. Grasin stuffed me in the Memory Care Ward? To shut me up? About what?"

Magda hugged Milli. "I expect this will all be revealed soon enough."

After Magda left, Milli searched for a recent photo of Bernard, one that might reveal his secrets, but all she found were cherub cheeks and milestone moments. Frustrated and confused, Milli needed answers.

In the morning, Milli went to the front desk. "I need to speak with someone in charge of New Dawn, like a senior officer?"

The man looked closely at Milli. "You're the woman Ms. Fagan was yelling at, aren't you? The one who created all the chaos."

"I didn't create anything. Those three vile people used me for their own nefarious purposes, I tell you. But more than that, they used my poor nephew Bernard and I aim to find out more about his role in their business."

The man stood up, held out his right hand, and reached across the desk. "Let me first congratulate you on your accomplishment. My team here has lived under Ms. Fagan's iron rule for too long. To find out she was swindling the village the whole time just skinnies my minny."

Milli had to laugh. She'd never heard that expression, but she liked it. *Skinnies my minny, Minnie Yanover. Minnie Hah Hah! That would be me.* "I have so many questions."

The man brought out a directory and scanned the names. "Ah, you could try talking to the Chief Executive Officer of New Dawn. Here's her name and number."

"I don't have a private phone," said Milli.

"Hmmm. You could send her an email."

"I don't have a computer."

"Why don't I call her office and set up a meeting for you. Would you like that?"

"Absolutely. You know, there are so many nice people around here. Sometimes it's easy to overlook that."

"There are plenty of us, but we keep our opinions to ourselves because of internal repercussions. Sometimes it only takes one tear in the cloth to unravel the whole garment."

"I have to remember that," said Milli. She waited near the desk while the man made a few phone calls.

"All set. Hazel Gormley will see you on Friday at one o'clock in her office."

"And how do you think I'm going to get there, wherever her office is?"

"I'll take you personally. Meet me here at noon."

"That's more than nice of you, ah, Mr.," Milli looked for his name tag but it must have been under his lapel.

"Huxley Zacks the third. Call me Huck."

"Call me Milli. I wonder, Huck, if my lawyer could meet us there?"

Huck grinned. "The more the merrier."

Milli gave Huck the name of the law firm and information about Alexander Peabody. Huck promised he'd call.

Milli returned to her room and tucked Beatrice into her comfy nest. "We're going to do this right. No one should be held without her consent and kept in the dark about why. That skinnies my minnie!"

Chapter Thirty-Eight

The complex stopped buzzing and everything seemed quiet for two days. Milli played canasta with her ladies and joined them for a current events class where articles in the daily newspaper were discussed. Not the Fagan, Grasin, and Boothbury case, but civil rights and climate change.

When Friday rolled around, she went to the front desk at eleven o'clock and waited for Huck. At noon, he still hadn't arrived and Milli approached the receptionist.

"Might you know if Huxley Zacks is coming in today?"

"Nobody by that name works here," she said.

"But he was here the other day. Tall, thin man with a starched white collar and a blue suit jacket. Very polite."

"Oh, you mean Huck?"

Milli sighed with relief. "Yes, Huck."

The woman laughed. "He doesn't work here. He's a resident."

"Then what was he doing behind the desk?"

"Oh that man. Such a prankster. He must've seen a chance to be someone he wasn't. What a card."

"But he set up a meeting with me and Hazel Gormley, the CEO of New Dawn. We're meeting today at her office at one o'clock."

"Huck pulled a fast one on you. Ms. Gormley is on the custodial staff."

Milli withdrew Beatrice from her purse and stroked her hair. "Now what?"

Days melted together with no further news, either on the television or from her outside-friends. She refused to pout and went about her daily doings with her head high and Beatrice by her side. She joined a morning walking group, attended a paint night, and even won at bingo. She made a point of speaking with men and women on her floor, playing canasta, and sitting with her ladies at meals. She would not devolve or disappear. Every day, she lived for each moment.

When she felt overwhelmed, she breathed in Leo and breathed out Lionel, stroked Beatrice's hair, and sang, "*Qué será será, whatever will be will be, the future's not ours to see, qué será será.*" Even though Ms. Fagan was no longer in charge—the terrible trio had been led off the property by policemen to the cheers of residents—Milli still had the leg monitor on and she was still a prisoner of New Dawn.

The complex was preparing for its July Fourth celebration. The grounds were decorated with flags, balloons and banners, floors were buffed, and the rooms were tidied. A special meal was planned after an afternoon concert in the Gardens. It would be the first time Milli would see the high-rise section of New Dawn again. She was not looking forward to it, although she'd be with her friends, and of course, Beatrice. The day was bittersweet since independence was not in the cards yet for Milli. She knew Alex Peabody was responsible for the arrests, but maybe he was too busy to see to Milli's needs until all was settled. She had requested an audience with the new social worker but had not heard back about a date to meet. And court cases took months. *Can I wait?* Milli felt she had no options.

On Thursday, July 4, Milli awoke to horns beeping outside her building. And kazoos. And those noisy air blasters, megaphones, and cow bells.

"The celebration is beginning early!" Milli peered out her windows, but she could only see shrubs close by and automobile tires in the distance. But the noise permeated the air and she had to check it out.

She dressed quickly, grabbed her purse and Beatrice, and made her way to the back entrance. The first person Milli saw was Bailey Haley walking toward her building, his bulk on display. *Wow, my monitor is on alert this morning!*

Milli had no plans to surrender to him, and as he approached, she stood her ground, ready to do battle, even if he was a bodybuilder. But Bailey wasn't in uniform. Instead he wore jeans and a tank top with a capital M on his chest.

Behind him was Kedrix, also wearing a tank top sporting an M. Magda and Birdie were next up, the two of them like twin hippos in their M tops and black tights. And then Victoria, Pippa, and Apollo—who wore Lionel's sunshine hat—skipped hand-in-hand right up to Milli and embraced her. Suddenly Milli realized the parade of vehicles was for HER.

"We're coming to take you away, ha ha, ho ho, he he. We're coming to take you away," sang the whole group, who surrounded Milli and danced in a circle around her.

Bailey swept Milli up in his arms, and brought her to Kedrix's motorcycle which was decorated with cans and streamers.

"Now you wait right here, Your Highness," he said, and entered Milli's building with Kedrix, Virginia, Apollo, and Pippa.

Milli's heart thudded out of her chest, and her hair spiked on its own. Beatrice shimmied in her grip. All she managed to squeal was thank you, thank you, thank you.

Birdie cooed as Magda cut the monitor off Milli's ankle. Within thirty minutes, all Milli's possessions were loaded into Bailey's truck as Milli left New Dawn on the back of Kedrix's motorcycle at the head of a caravan of her friends.

In the crowd of residents that had gathered, Milli saw her canasta ladies: Hamida, Patrice, and Connie.

"Stop, please," she told Kedrix. She waved and called them to her. "I want to tell you how much your friendship has meant to me."

"But why are you leaving? You seemed happy here," said Connie.

"I have to listen to my inner voice and it's telling me to be on my own. New Dawn has some great advantages, but I have a chance to create a different future for myself."

"Well, there's always a place for you at our table," said Hamida.

"When I figure out where I'll be living, I'll let you know," said Milli, who was so overwhelmed by her rescue that she couldn't think beyond the moment.

"We'll miss you," said Patrice. "Keep in touch."

"I will," said Milli to her ladies. As she waved good bye to them, she knew she'd see them again. She remembered an old saying from her childhood: *Make new friends and keep the old, one is silver and the other gold.* These gals were her silver pals during her silver years. Precious and permanent.

"Okay. Kedrix. I'm ready. Let's move on out!"

When the entourage arrived at Lila's Florist Shop, Rashida, Keysi, and Bianca stood under a Welcome Home Milli sign, each holding a glorious bouquet of yellow and purple lilies. A handsome middle-aged couple approached the motorcycle.

"It's so nice to finally meet you. I'm Alex Peabody and this is my wife Gloria," said a well-built man with a full head of salt and pepper hair, a George Clooney look-alike. He held out both his hands and gently enfolded Milli's in a soft embrace. "Before we begin our celebration, let's talk together in the back room."

Milli followed the man and sat on a lounging bench that seemed newly purchased. *Victoria sure did invest in the store, and did it up right*, thought Milli.

"How are you doing?" asked Alex.

"I've stayed positive even when I wanted to give up," she said. "I have you to thank."

"Not just me. There's a throng of people out there who adore you."

Milli considered this. "What I don't understand is why you all care."

"In my daughter's case, you remind her of her granny. For Kedrix, you're a straight-up gal who tells it like it is, and for Apollo, you're a rock star. But that's not what I need to discuss with you."

"It's about Bernard, my nephew, right?"

Alex stood and paced the room, which took about three strides. "I'm not sure how to explain this, but . . ."

"I know he was a junkie and he died from an overdose of opioids," said Milli.

"Yes, but there's so much more to say. Over the last few weeks, I've delved into Bernard's background and his relationship with Basil Boothbury. It seems they had quite a business together, and it was based out of your former house."

Milli puckered her lips. "But he sold my house. I signed the papers. I gave him access to my bank account. I gave him Power of Attorney."

"I'm so sorry, Milli. Bernard tricked you into thinking the house had been sold. It seems the cartel used your house as a safe zone for distributing product. Its location is near a highway and on a main street, but set so far back and bordered by trees that no one noticed the daily traffic in and out of the long driveway. Bernard's unexpected death put the kibosh on Ms. Fagan and Dr. Boothbury's long-range plans. When you disappeared, they had no idea how much you knew or didn't know. Ms. Fagan realized you had no other surviving relatives, so when they found you, they decided to squelch your voice with medication and isolation. That way they could keep the house, carry on their lucrative drug trade, and no one would be the wiser."

Milli had listened to each word, but she wasn't sure it was sinking in. "And that awful Grasin man? How was he involved?"

Alex sat beside Milli and put his hand over hers. "Asa Grasin was a sloppy newcomer to the scheme. He kept two sets of records which the accountants at New Dawn have uncovered and shared. He was more the Medicare and Medicaid conman. Our investigation is on-going and it might take a while to unravel all the misdeeds of the trio. I still don't have all the answers."

"So New Dawn was not to blame, just the no-good threesome?"

"The New Dawn Corporation has asked my firm to represent them against Boothbury, Fagan, and Grasin. At some point in the future, you and I need to discuss how to proceed with your nephew's involvement. A wrongful death suit is one option. And we have to figure out the details about your house."

So much information to process, thought Milli. *Is my home still my home? Are the papers I signed valid? Had Bernard died because Booth-bury coerced him to sell opioids? Did Ms. Fagan select residents who had no advocates so she could scam Medicare and Medicaid? Will I ever know the truth? Does it matter?*

"Have other families been affected by that gang's dealings?" asked Milli.

"So it seems. Your friend Louis Jefferson provided testimony about his common-law wife Rosalie's experience. And nurses' aide Reshma Ramirez and Nurse Magda Manowicz corroborated the practice of overmedicating residents in the Memory Care Unit. We have months of discovery ahead of us. Because of you, the New Dawn Retirement Village will move forward more thoughtfully and with better purpose. They'll probably have to compensate for the loss of loved ones to mismanaged medication, but that's yet to be proven."

"So I got the ball rolling?"

"Not only rolling, Milli, the day you snuck out of New Dawn, you triggered an avalanche."

"So now what?"

"Ah, I was getting to that. Come out to the front of the shop. We have a few surprises in store for you." Alex took Milli by the arm and side-by-side, they stepped into a celebration.

Everyone raised a glass in honor of Milli—champagne for the adults, grape juice for Apollo and Pippa. An enormous sheet cake blazed with eighty-six tiny flames.

"To Millicent Tarnover, the voice of senior citizens everywhere who deserve to be treated with respect," said Alex. "When any one of us becomes a pawn to be moved around on a spreadsheet, bad things happen. I am proud to represent Millicent and my firm is prepared to bring justice to New Dawn."

Milli stood in the center of the room surrounded by her friends. "Thank you one and all, all and one. Now help me blow out my candles."

Victoria distributed pieces of cake and then brought a chair to the center of the room. Like a bride-to-be at her shower, Milli beamed.

Apollo brought Milli his gift first. Blushing, he handed her a large thin package. She unwrapped it to find a mirror with a wooden frame. The handwritten words along the edges said: *Books are more than words. They're filled with places to visit and people to meet.*

"Victoria helped me make it. Do you like it?" said Apollo, holding it high to show it to all in the room.

"I'm so proud of you," said Milli, putting an arm around Apollo.

"Me too," said Victoria, beaming ear to ear.

Apollo shrugged and smiled as the room broke into applause. He leaned the mirror against the wall and brought another package to Milli. "This is from my mom."

Surprised that the woman who testified against her would give her a gift, Milli opened it to find a coffee mug. On it was the saying, *You're never too old to learn.*

"You know how you taught me to enjoy reading? My mom told me she dropped out of school in the tenth grade and was never a good student. When my daddy made her teach me at home, she tried, but she was bad at it. After you showed me I could learn and she told me her secret, we decided we would read books together. We're both getting real good at it," said Apollo. "She's working today and couldn't be here, but she's happy you're not at that place anymore."

With tears in her eyes, Milli gave Apollo a hug. "You're a special young man and you have a mom who wants you to succeed."

Kedrix stepped forward. "Geez, we're all gonna cry. I got something for you just for fun." From behind his back, he revealed a Lady Pink Flower motorcycle helmet. "We're gonna ride!"

"Tonight?" asked Milli.

"Any time you want, you're my biker chick."

Victoria placed a hand-woven crown with forget-me-nots on Milli's head. Birdie gave Milli a pair of amethyst earrings and Pippa created a necklace out of sea glass and shells. Magda presented Milli with a golden key inscribed with the words *Your Kindness and Concern Unlocks the Hearts of Others.*

As Milli soaked in the love, the door opened to two new visitors: Reshma Ramirez and Poetry Joe. Milli jumped up to embrace them.

Alex clinked his glass. "More heroes! These two people provided essential information to help Milli. Bravo!"

"I am overwhelmed and grateful," said Milli, tears streaming. She did a soft jig around the room. "So what have I learned? Life begins at eighty-five. Remember, you heard it here. I'm just getting warmed up! I'm just getting the hang of this curious journey called life. Magic is all around me and I bask in the elder bliss of knowing each day is precious. I vow never to waste a moment on regret, but to drink my birchbark tea, walk the beach, smell the proverbial daffodils and lilacs, and rejoice in love. Let's do this again when I'm one hundred! In the meantime, party on."

There wasn't a dry eye to be seen. Gloria Peabody, an older version of her daughter, stepped forward. "We'd like to invite you all to follow us."

The group paraded out the door and onto Porter Street where they gathered in the small patio outside Milli's former apartment. Milli first noticed a brand new fountain and in it were three ceramic figures: a frog, a fish, and a turtle. Milli knew who had placed them there, her sweet young women. She hugged each of them, promising to create more stories with them at the L Street Pizza shop.

"And here are the keys to the palace," said Alex. "We decided, if you agree, that you deserve your own place. But there's one condition."

Milli was too stunned to talk. "But what happened to the tenant who Grenadine said rented the apartment?"

Alex stepped forward. "Grenadine had no right to rent the apartment, neither to you nor to any other tenant, if there actually was one."

Milli felt a pang of guilt. Even though Grenadine had exposed her to Ms. Fagan and Mr. Grasin, she harbored no ill. What was the sense in that? "What will happen to her? Is she all right?"

Victoria's mother spoke up. "We've arranged for Grenadine to stay with my mother in Maine. They both will benefit from being together."

Milli felt relief as she approached the door to the apartment, recalling that there was a condition involved. "As long as the condition is that I can come and go as I please."

"Yes and no," said Victoria. "I need you to help me in the floral shop during the summer and keep an eye on the store in the off months. What do you think?"

"I think we have a deal." Milli took the keys and opened the door. What she saw brought on more tears. The apartment had been painted lavender and yellow. There was a flowery quilt on the bed and new fluffy pillows. A television with one of those wide modern screens hung from a corner wall, and the kitchen was updated with a new table, chairs and microwave. Lilies were distributed in vases throughout the room. Milli was so beyond words that she just twirled and fluttered through the space like an uncaged budgie.

Lined along the windowsill was a trio of Wanga dolls, all with wild hair and blunt limbs, each with a tiny sign. Birdie introduced them. "Meet Love Wanga, Wisdom Wanga, and Luck Wanga. They're here to join you on your new journey."

Milli reached into her purse and brought out Beatrice, her Protection Wanga. She nuzzled her into the other dolls. "My power girls," she said.

As she looked around her loving home, she saw how everyone

had pitched in to unpack her boxes and put her possessions in logical places. Beside her bed, on the nightstand she saw her book of poetry.

That night, as Milli lay in bed, with inspiration from Rachel Rousso, she opened the book to a blank page at the end of the book and wrote:

> *Let the unknown arrive.*
> *Let the lilacs dance*
> *And the daffodils flourish*
> *Let the sky shimmer and the ocean roll*
> *... and may Millicent Milli Minnie Ruby Tuesday Alice*
> *Yanover-Tarnover enjoy it all.*

The End

Made in United States
Orlando, FL
14 March 2024

44783672R00150